MW00892793

WALKING BETWEEN TREES

A JOURNEY TO KINDNESS

a story

JAMES OWEN

The author gratefully acknowledges use of extracts from the story The Lily *taken from* My Uncle Silas *by* H. E. Bates. *Published by Jonathan Cape (1950) Reproduced by permission of* Pollinger Ltd. And The Estate of H. E. Bates.

James Owen

Copyright © 2010 James Owen
All rights reserved.

ISBN: 1450548938
ISBN-13: 9781450548939

CONTENTS

The Beginning   *v*
What's This!   *vii*

The Story

The First Walk   *1*
Walk Again   *123*
Epilogue   *213*

The Practice

Reflection   *215*
First Practice – The Life Tapestry   *216*
Second Practice – Where intention abides   *217*
The Third Practice – Sitting Meditation   *218*
The fourth Practice – Walking Meditation   *219*
Fifth Practice – Integration   *220*

Walking Between Trees

Reflection   *221*
Practice One   *221*
Practice Two   *222*

Beyond Self

Reflections on Divine Metta   *225*
Post Script   *227*
Appendix: The Metta Sutta   *229*

THE BEGINNING

The diary lay on the
bare board floor,
he lay beside it.
He treated it with great
Respect.
It told him things.

There was no time here,
only truth. He liked
The Truth.
The truth was he was in
love with it,
yet it lay just
beyond him.

A siren calling from out
Of its own oblivion…

A temptress, disrobed of
opinion and form,
bare essentials,
(you might say).

The nature of being,
who could resist it
he thought
and started writing…

WHAT'S THIS!

January 1st

Today I began a diary of thoughts, reflections and observations. At the same time I wrote the first line of a story – a story of imperfections, of distractions and of mysteries, a tale of birth and death, love and loss, anger and kindness. Seeming to begin on the front page and end on the back page, yet having no beginning and no end, a thread woven into the story of life, making therefore of itself a tale to be told.

Yes, it's true, these events happened, yet only one thing shall you find in all this to satisfy your curiosity as to its truth. The old farmhouse still stands.

January 4th

We live in a grey world of lies, just as if one put a spot of black paint in a can of pure white, it will be forever a shade of grey. I'm not sure I can find the truth under such circumstances – not easy, in fact I may never find it, but I have to search, I feel compelled. Yet I fear the truth will see me coming and run.

Sunny for the time of year. I walked today.

January 5th

Last night I had a dream. I hid, disguised as someone else, James Owen. I realized in the dream, he would not be seen as I would, he would not be known and stopped by his ego from the certain revelations that truth would demand. Yet I could whisper to him this and that, observations on his story, asides on real life, life as I know it to be in all its joy and sorrow, real and imagined.

I awoke excited by the sheer idea of at last being able to tell the truth that lay beyond reach in this confused and suffering world.

Me? Well I am not to be found, but James Owen, in telling this tale, is revealing mine, perhaps it is yours also.

> *What is this life is full of care,*
> *We have no time to stand and stare.*
> *No time to stand beneath the boughs*
> *And stare as long as sheep or cows.*

These lines are from Leisure by W. H. Davis. I always thought Wordsworth wrote them, funny thing memory.

January 6th
The wind is up today, scuttling leaves around my feet on the walk. I got to thinking afterwards…

What is it that makes us lie, what in the beginning set us on such a path? I suspect, should we become conscious of the truth within us, our fear would make us truly crazy.

Well, I'll risk the craziness of my own nature for Nature, for it is unto itself an honest state. Our history of lying is now bringing down upon us changes that threaten our very existence as a species, and that may be how it shall go. It is only our arrogance that suggests to us we are immortal, indestructible and something special in Nature.

We kill each other on a vast scale, watch as many of us go hungry while others have a glut. We are destroying the very fabric of the world along with many of its creatures. We are strangers to true compassion, for such requires the courage we do not have. While there have been and remain some individuals who break through this ignorance, the evidence of our species' behavior reveals that although we have certainly become smarter and skilled, we have hardly grown in true understanding.

It has become urgent that we overcome the denial of death and fear of life. How we let slip life such that even its transitory time is cut to a half-life, a shallow skim across its surface. How deeply can we live while we keep our thoughts on an illusion beyond life? If we cannot be with nature, the integral flow of existence, we lose ourselves, for it is nature that births us and eventually takes us back when we are done.

January 7th
Well, I just had to get that stuff off my chest yesterday! Now I'm about as ready as I'll ever be to leave you to journey with James. I'll drop in now and then with a diary entry. You may just find what I have to say gives you pause for thought.

THE STORY

THE FIRST WALK

*How did it grow so late,
have we learned anything?
Are we more mature, wiser,
more perceptive, kinder?*

John Steinbeck

ONE

I was walking slowly from tree to tree, back and forth. The year was 1984. It was winter and I found myself living in a Buddhist monastery. I say found myself for I had been walking the English countryside on a sabbatical from, well, everything: my work, my marriage, my life as it had been. It was a time for reflection.

The English winter brought cold nights and rains that January so I sought refuge. At first it was a country pub, The Coal Barge, and it was there I met a man, as sometimes happens, who told me that over in the hills above the next village some Buddhist monks had moved into an old army barracks and were working on its repair. In the course of our conversation I had informed him of my many years in construction. He recommended I visit and see if they perhaps wanted help. At least the structures were wood, a better baffle against the night airs than my tent walls.

I rose early next morning. The village I was headed for was some twelve miles away and the barracks were a stretch beyond it up in the hills. The day broke bright, a pale blue sky stretching over downs the night frost had covered, leaving the grass stiff white blades, and the just ploughed earth like broken sea-ice. The road led out west of the village,

1

so after about an hour the sun began to warm my back and head, obliging me to remove my wool hat and feel its touch directly; it felt good. I picked up my stride with a sense of anticipation. From where this came I don't know, for all I sought was a warmer shelter, yet there was something about my destination that caught me up.

I began to think who these monks were, what they were doing in the English countryside. But as happens my mind drifted away on to this and that. I thought of my wife at home. Things had been imperceptibly changing between us. There was no antagonism, you understand; it was not anger or even frustration, just a sort of unexpected change in one or both of us that shifted our orbits, so to speak, to different paths. I still loved her, yet I was not unhappy being away doing this, whatever it was I was doing. I fingered my wool hat, remembering how we came to learn spinning and dyeing together from an old friend; how we would make a trip each year into the countryside to a farm. I think it had an odd name, something like Stickleback farm. I thought stickleback was a fish. I discovered after we stopped making our annual visit that there was a river running through the place. It was just another piece of jigsaw, an enlightenment of sorts.

On the farm the general smells of farm life hid the pungent aroma coming from the unwashed sheep fleeces, but going home in the car we would joke about who hadn't bathed that day. It was an easy-going relationship, it should have lasted, but then life has a mystery about it, something that weaves a path unseen until met with.

January 10th

I guess none of us know just what will come into our lives, we know only one thing for sure after we're born – that we will die. I'm going to bed.

The crunch of my boots on the gravel road brought me back to the walk I was on. The road was beginning to incline; I had to change gear, taking longer, slower strides. I removed my old parka and stuffed it in the backpack along with my hat. The frost had gone. The air had grown still and warm for January. I felt good; no, more than that, elated. It could almost have been spring. Walking has always done that for me.

I've always known a walk to straighten things out. As a boy I would leave the house early and head out, never quite sure where I was going. I was happy to let the weather, particularly the placing of the sun, determine which way I would turn out of our front door. Some days I would spend in the garden lying in the long grass or climbing trees.

∽

Our garden was a great long stretch of grass and paths that was surrounded by tall waving poplars, the London Plane tree. They reach up like tall green candles, branches held close to their sides as if they had a secret they were keeping from me. One time, a sapling, no more than three feet high, waved to me. There was this particular leaf that a finger of wind caught and made it wave back and forth catching my eye. A heart-shaped pallet of light and dark green, changing in the breeze. I was eight years old. I was mesmerized, and knew from that moment trees would be forever talking to me. Climbing up in their branches, the wind would sway me into a reverie of excitement. I would dream of the future; I would leave home and travel far.

From the familiar poplars stretching to the sky I learned to stretch my imagination. Once I tried to climb to the very top. My feet sliding into the tightness of branch to trunk had to be pulled out each step up. It was as though the tree was trying to hold me back, warning me, perhaps. She (I thought of the poplars as tall elegant ladies) was so determined to keep me safe that I never made the top. But that may have been because of Andrew.

Andrew was about nine-and-a-half when he fell out of the poplar tree. It was my first hard lesson in life. Andrew and I had been friends since as long as I could remember. I stood looking at him, crying his name; he looked very strange, his legs didn't look right and he was totally silent. That was unusual.

At the funeral I kept thinking about the trees and how they tried to warn us, but Andy was bolder than me and older. It feels strange and unexplainable that I am here and he is not. I look at the sky, trying to find Andrew, perhaps. I do that when I'm thinking, searching; I think I'm looking for answers. There are a lot of unanswered questions in my life, that's why I walk.

∽

The road is behind me now and I'm on a path along the side of a farmer's field, heading up into the noon sun. The sky is bright deep-winter blue. The birds call and dance in the trees lining my walk. These are big English oaks. Bare of leaves they sit against the sky, sculpturing the air with heavy branches as thick as the poplars' trunks. The plowed field flows away across the hill in waves of good earth. I shall stop here a while and lunch.

Leaning against its body, I let an old oak hold me while I rest. My eyes take in the land, field upon field ringed with hedge-rows of hawthorn, cut and layered into thickets the sparrows and robins will soon begin nesting in once again. I think, 'season upon season measures this place, silently counting the years away in peaceful solitude from the cares of man's world'. It wasn't long, of course, before I was remembering again; half asleep, I let my mind wander to a time when I was eleven years old, laying in the long grass at the end of the back garden, looking at the gentian blue sky. The sun is diamond bright beyond the tips of the trees that weave their way into my peripheral vision, waving again for my attention. I think sometimes of Andrew and where is dead? What does it mean – to be born? The question, never quite forming into words, is always there. It seems I was not going to be allowed forgetfulness, at least not in respect of life and death.

Perhaps it started when I was two years old. I nearly died. It may have been that I did die and was fished back from that unknown place. In any case, the facts were history. I contracted a serious lung infection; the devil was in my breath where air should have been. I was sliding down into the twilight of life. My mother prayed, the doctors operated, meanwhile the bombs dropped; humanity was at war, a war of which I was to learn much later in life I fell victim to.

My first real memory was convalescing by the sea, where I was encouraged to get the unsightly wound into the salt sea-water. I still have what I describe as a hole in my back. Many a time I've been asked what happened to my back. I couldn't resist the reply, "I had a knife in it." Strictly true but, well, what kid doesn't capitalize on what he's got. I tried not to take the story to the heights of imagination. I was basically an honest boy. Perhaps that's why I have to face the question that dwells behind all of us, why I want to know the truth.

❧

The elm tree, forty or so yards in front of me, stood silent; its straight trunk, rippled bark, dark yet peaceful, drawing me to it. It was a find. The elms had been struck down with a fearful blight two years ago; they were swept off England's soil, falling like soldiers in a futile battle. I think some unfortunate beetle took the blame. I'm sure he or she was only doing what came naturally, eating the bark away, they said. I believe the beetle innocent of all charges. It's a bit late once one has been sentenced.

January 14th
Why are we so quick to condemn, what is it in us seeks revenge faster than forgiveness.

The reprieved elm towers before me, majestic, quiet, seeming to my mind to understand, to know better than we the nature of things, perhaps even our own nature. I feel small, yet not belittled. This has something to do with my familiarity with trees. I'm the same with big dogs, and zoo animals whose ancestors probably ate mine.

I recall on a visit to Regent's Park zoo in London, standing in a timeless space just looking into the eyes of a giant Silverback gorilla. I don't know exactly why. I'd like to offer a clever observation, something about man and his cousin stuff, but I'd be making it up. Truth was I was searching, as usual, for answers. I'd look anywhere. I didn't like the two inch round bars set just far enough apart for his arm to reach through and give the watchers a scary moment. I didn't like the hard concrete he had to sit on, or the cell-like home he inhabited as our guest. I think I tried to stay looking at him long enough so that he would get that I didn't do this to him, that I would never do this to anyone. There were no trees.

The tree story that fascinated us kids was of course Robin Hood. To be living in Sherwood Forest was the perfect paradise of a boy's imagination. When older and smarter, though I'm not sure any wiser, I went to Sherwood. It was less than I expected, smaller, like a park. But of course we have been chopping away trees since we came down from them. It could be said with much truth that Sherwood built the British Empire, its trees becoming the warships and merchant galleons that roamed the world for plunder. With our trees we robbed the poor to pay the rich, but for us kids there was Robin Hood, robbing the rich to give to the poor; what a contradictory can of worms that opened in history lessons. Was this children's politics or just the primitive urge to fight and win the prize?

The prize for me at seven and eight was Mary Peters, the school May queen two years running; that's enough to tell you I didn't stand a chance. Anyway I kind of avoided girls back then. Oh, I liked them well enough, I thought them all beautiful, so much so that I hesitated like I would when handed tea in a delicate bone china cup; I could see calamity coming. I would need something solid to hold on to; I chose the trees. The May-tree Mary sat under, after her crowning, was a big old English oak; it's trunk had been doing yoga for at least a hundred years and had perfected the spine twist. It wound its way up, leaning over and throwing its arms out in a profusion of bright new green leaves that the sun halted at, and allowed the shade to protect our queen-for-a-day. That day was many years ago, but I still see it as yesterday through loving eyes, and I ask the question yet again, what is it, this life, so beautiful and so grim in its parts?

∽

I arrived at the elm and took my watch out of my pocket. I had about two hours of good light left, not enough to linger. I gave the tree a hug, though it always feels as though it's the tree hugging me, and stepped back onto the path. A few yards on, I noticed gravel had been laid, and the sides of the path were hemmed in with a wood lapboard fence. Within a hundred yards, I was standing back on a road lined with houses I guessed had been there at least a hundred years or more. I was in the village. I needed directions, but the place was silent and bare of persons. Which way to turn? I relaxed, what was the hurry, isn't this like life? Who knows which way to turn, it's all a guess. My feet, now used to walking, continued on; my thoughts went their own way too.

'Perhaps I should have stayed at the elm tree, after all I'm still carrying my camping gear, and the day stayed clear. It would be a dry night, cold for sure, but I can stand cold.' I pull myself up short and look around. I'm literally at a crossroads. The signpost points out the next village, Nettleden, and the one I left, Bourne End, and the church, Saint Barnaby's. I head for the church. The sign reads St. Barnaby's Finedon. So at least I know where I am. I recall my father telling me as a boy, "It's many a man knows not where he is going, but it's a fool doesn't know where he's been." I must admit I felt a little foolish until now, which I think is okay, my father wouldn't. My father didn't tolerate fools gladly, in fact he didn't tolerate them at all. Growing up with such fierce criticalism I protected myself with its adoption. It has taken many years to break its shackles. He would wonder, too, why I headed for the church.

I walk under the carved wood arch with its angels and cherubims, up the path to the heavy door, probably another bit of Sherwood. Touching the wrought-iron handle, I find the door unlocked, a most unusual thing. Entering, there is that aroma, not definitive but always the same. What is it? Sometimes I think it the smell of peace, certainly of quiet, which to me is synonymous. The granite pillars reach up and hold arching timbers ending in a roof I recognize as of Norman origin. Not old. The Normans came in AD1066, a date every English schoolchild has imprinted somewhere, often on the hand with 'six-of-the-best' if it doesn't get into the brain.

January 17th
Where I live, the church was built in AD500. Now, that's old. It was built by the Saxons, but the Normans thrashed the Saxons and in the usual manner of the day, (have we changed I ask myself) they destroyed all the evidence they found of what was Saxon.

I wandered through the knave and up to the alter rail, every brush of my clothes and backpack echoing like a friendly ghost around me. I thought of Malcolm; I thought of lighting a candle, conveniently provided, as were matches, but then I wouldn't want to neglect anyone, and the fire would be too much. I have known enough death for a young man. I should explain Malcolm. Not easy, he was my son.

As I was leaving the church, the sun was slanting through the gravestones. I had been longer than I realized; it had lowered its beams and was soon to set. I hitched my pack higher and headed back for the elm tree; Nature and my drifting mind had decided my night's residency for me. Life, if we truly accept it, has a way of doing that. But a turn in the road was yet to come before my head laid itself to rest.

I retraced my steps of the afternoon, finding, this time, some cars parked and the village peopled here and there; some strolling with their dogs. One such animal, a Great Dane I believe, sought to reach my shoulders with his front paws. The horrified owner, was on the point of apology when he saw I was not the least concerned, but, in fact, welcomed the contact after a day alone. He did, nevertheless, apologize, and we got to talking. To keep it short – not that there's any particular reason for doing so – he invited me to spend the night with him and his family.

The dog, Bowser, I learned, was perhaps the most pleased, lacking the anxiousness of first acquaintance. He insisted on rubbing against my legs every so often to tell me of his delight; something different was afoot and it was being brought home. His owner, Richard, was a tall thin man, but he didn't stoop as often happens with tall folk. He seemed relaxed in his body, and as far as I could tell as we walked and talked, bright-minded. I was a practicing therapist when I took this sabbatical, so it was my habit to listen carefully, and without wishing it, some perception would naturally form in my mind of the speaker. Yet, quite apart from my professional ear, I liked the man. It's not often I don't like a person. Sometimes the liking is instant and goes deep; that's how it was with Richard. Talking came easy, so much so I suddenly found we were at his home and I had no idea of the route we had taken. Going through the front door was a confusion of inquiry, interest, greeting, and a general muddle of conviviality.

I dropped my pack in the hall, and my coat was taken from me by Richard's wife who secured it in a cupboard under the stairs whilst turning over her shoulder to welcome me. While I was passively receiving these kindnesses, their children, two girls, were making the most of my arrival by running with questions to Richard and returning to gaze at me and giggle.

It wasn't long before we were all at the dining table, and Rosalyn, Richard's wife, was setting down a hot winter bake and a pot of soup. She sat, and Richard said, "All ready?" At that they lifted their hands out to each other and me, closed their eyes, and bowed heads. I waited, expecting someone to say grace. All remained silent. In my right hand was the small hand of one of the girls, Amy. My left hand was held in the firm grip of Richard's hand. In spite of his grip, our newfound friendship, and the pleasant situation I found myself in, my hands twitched. I counted fervently; sometimes it works. In new places it's hard to still the insistence of my nervous system, it mostly gets its own way. After what seemed an eternity of movement, my hands were released.

Richard again, "Let's eat." Rosalyn asked for the girls' bowls and ladled the soup into each in turn. While Joan, Amy's sister, was intent on retrieving her full bowl, Amy, whilst politely trying not to, looked at me. I knew why, and knew it would have to enter the conversation at some point. After the girls, Rosalyn asked for my bowl. Handing it to her I said, "Just half full would be good, thanks."

"Oh, are you sure? There's plenty, please let me fill it up for you."

"I'd be happy to have the other half for seconds; I'm afraid a full bowl might spill." This is where, I was thinking, they begin to worry, "Is this fellow a bit weak in the head? Who have we brought into our home." But Richard had been holding my left hand, the worse shaker of the pair, and began to realize, or guessed, the basis of my request.

"Two halves make a whole, or is it two halves make a bowl?" The girls giggled and Rosalyn took his little joke as a flag of acceptance. If Richard understood, she would soon learn why. She graciously handed me half a bowl of soup.

Amy was still curious, so, for everyone's sake, I told the story of my birth and the war. I tried to keep it short, but the questions would come, they always do, and so it went on past the girls' bedtime. When they were in their pajamas and their mother told them to say goodnight to me, Amy rushed into me and gave me a hug; Joan, not to be bettered, hugged my back. Between these two innocents I felt blessed; which, I suppose, is exactly what they were doing.

Of course, they were blessing the little baby who had reluctantly struggled into this world with bombs dropping and fearful sounds blasting his ears. Slow to come, I was pulled with forceps in a hurried attempt to secure my birth before death by war took us all. Discovery of the damage done was to wait for five years, until school.

After Amy and Joan had gone to bed, Richard thanked me for explaining, and added, "You must get tired, though, feeling you have to explain yourself," which I thought was insightful and kind of him. I told him, "Confession, they say, is good for the soul." That turned the conversation to religion so I asked them about the silent grace, why no words? Rosalyn answered, "We're Quakers; we are content to sit in God's presence in silence, and be thankful for what we have."

It struck me then that the furnishings of the house were plain. The living room we were in could almost have been a Quakers' meeting room out of the eighteenth century. Its windows, small and square, divided into further squares with leaded spars. The glass of some panes had the look of running water, making the trees outside wave as one moved around the room. The timber lintels were exposed and cleaned, left without adornments, set into white painted walls and ceiling. It had a feel of peace and homeliness. As we talked, I could feel their strong commitment to the peace their home reflected. They had as much compassion for the futility of that war, as they saw it, as for the plight of my birth. They admitted their own lives had been blessed to the full; tragedy of any significance was a stranger to them. Yet they understood it well enough.

‧ ‧ ‧

The next day found me deep in the English countryside. The hospitality and peacefulness of Richard and Rosalyn had filled my heart and mind with many reflections to take on my journey. The day though, was grey, with heavy rain clouds testing the balance between freedom of the road and thoughts of a darn good soaking. It quickened my steps and kept my head down.

The Dawkins invited me to stay longer, but I knew myself well enough that to linger was to be lost. They insisted I pass by on my return, wanting to hear of my adventure with the Buddhists. It would be April, and a wiser me, before I saw them again.

The dim light could not dampen the thrushes' song nor keep the cheerfulness from the robins' twittering in the hawthorn bushes. A slight breeze brushed my face like a warm feather. Thank you wind, I thought to myself, for I could see that the clouds were rolling fast across the sky; there must be a good wind up there. I knew as long as the wind stayed, the rain would not fall. "Thank you, God," I said to the sky, then wondered at my foolishness, for certainly if he was anywhere, it wasn't up there. Up there, beyond the atmosphere, was space. I'd lain many a night in the long grass of our garden and stared into the cosmos.

Once, when I was six years old, the rain was coming down like a sheet, a waterfall. I sat on my windowsill and wondered, where did all this water come from? I had to go out in it and find out, so I did. Standing in a deep puddle that had formed in a dip in the lawn, almost to the top of my Wellington boots, I looked up right into the falling water. What I saw was each drop hurtling to the ground, balls of light that splashed into a hundred tiny lights that stung my eyes and face. I didn't care, I kept my eyes open. I was busy finding out where the rain came from.

I was never admonished, arriving home wet and sometimes dirty from a river or lake. The routine was always the same, accepting, almost pleased, that I had forged out to make my own discoveries. It seems that habit has stuck, for here I am once again on the search. Catherine, my wife, and I, often got ourselves soaked exploring together; she, I think, for the same reason as me. The root was to get out of the house when we were children. Not all homes are like the Dawkin's. Sometimes nature is more amenable than nurture. Nature being so kind in its acceptance of me, attracted my attention. It was trees and grasses I noticed first. I'd lay in the long grass and it would frame my vision like thick hair blown from behind. I'd pick a stalk, long and round, peel the outer green and chew its end. I could sometimes lay for an hour just looking up, so, of course, the trees also attracted my attention. I suppose I may have been called lazy, except I wasn't. Lazy people don't go on walks.

❧

I'd had left the village late, around ten-o-clock, having been breakfasted with almost as much food as the evening's dinner. It being Saturday, the family enjoyed their slow morning. And I had no hurry, I thought, as Richard had said the place I sought was known hereabouts since the monks moved in, and wasn't far to go. Now it was nearing noon; the wind was up and running across the fields to batter my old parka into a flap. Seen from a distance, bent into the wind, I must have looked all of the ploughman plodding his way home. (I thought of the line from Houseman's poem, which as kids, we were asked to turn around and around in an effort to teach us subject and predicate, nouns and adjectives). But the wind soon blew all thought away.

The trees along the field edge I was walking were speaking loudly now. The few grasses on the path, along with me, were bent to Nature's will. The birds had gone silent, in fact, they had gone altogether. I feared that when the wind suddenly dropped, as it surely would, the sky would open. It was growing darker by the minute. One could understand, in such circumstances, how the primitive mind experienced fear. I was getting a little anxious myself. As a boy I had a ducks-back for rain, but age makes one porous to the bone. The wind dropped, and with the expectancy of a deluge, I found a big oak to protect me. As luck would have it, it had been fired at some point and was hollow in its trunk. Removing my pack, I climbed into the blackened nest. There was just room to stand with the pack at my feet. I leaned back, thankful for the refuge it offered.

The rain fell so straight it looked like strings of lead flux, heavy and shiny against the dark sky. This was one of Nature's powerful times, a time of reminding us just how vulnerable we are, how much we take her for granted. I wondered to myself, do I take Catherine for granted? It's such an easy thing to do; familiarity, they say, breeds contempt. That may be a bit strong, but it may cause us to neglect. I think back to when we met; we were both so in love that neglect just couldn't happen, forgetfulness some times, and then heart-pained apologies and beautiful making up. We were besotted. Strange word that, sounds a bit like the soaking I'd be getting if I was out there. I suppose it actually is like that, soaking and blinding one, obliterating all blemishes. Not that I think of her now as having blemishes. Our shifting marriage is not because of unseen sands of reality we missed seeing, it's just, I don't know, it's just...

I let the cloud inside burst, the tears feel right, as though the storm invited them. I sink down in spite of the cramping, and succumb to the invitation.

> *We're the best of friends,*
> *have been for a long time,*
> *she leads her busy life*
> *and I follow mine.*
>
> *A gentle house full of peace,*
> *noisy with the sound of dogs and cats.*
> *Our bond is looser now, easy*
> *no strings, no holding*
> *one another back.*

If, as may happen, we part
it will not be a tear, a break,
just changing orbits
to a different path,
opening awareness, a give and take.

But still, I wonder if it comes to it
to separate. Who's going to unscrew
the pressure cooker.

When I awoke it was evening and the sky was a rose-colored bowl of peacefulness, clear and quiet. My body felt cramped, as it surely was, like old socks pushed into a shoe. Extricating myself from the womb of the oak, I stood amazed at the evening. The last clouds resting on the horizon, pink, and soft as children, brought tears once again. But these were tears of joy, or would that be salvation from the storm? For it seemed a storm had been blowing through my veins, a resistance to an inevitable break with Catherine. I wondered at the manner of its happening. Was there a hand somewhere in such serendipity; the Jungians would call it synchronicity, a meeting of self and archetype, the outer storm and my tears revealing the shadow thrown by love? I was to learn the Buddhists would frame it quite differently. Contrary to their religious vocation, they would be less mystical and more pragmatic.

Thus, with such thoughts I set out to find the old barracks the Buddhists had inherited. They were not so far from where I had taken shelter, for as my legs brought me to the top of the field the oak stood by, I could see a long, low structure painted now with the last flaming of the setting sun. There was no sign, no flags or ornaments that told me it was anything but a collection of wooden huts set in a field.

There were trees I recognized as flowering cherry trees, for in the garden of my childhood there stood such trees...

෴

...Looking out of the living room window, three stories up, on a summer's day, I could see the flowering cherries growing in between the three wings of our apartment block, reaching with outstretched arms, trying to touch the confining walls of the building. The trunks, strong and slender with red shiny bark, are split with age into bracelets. At the end of April the deep pink of the coming flowers push to be born. By mid-May there it is in all its profusion, lighting the courtyard with bright blossoms. From the living room window I can almost touch the branches. On the ground, playing, I look now at it from below, climb it, hug myself to its shiny red bark. I'm the tree; the tree is me. I'm absorbed into the rising sap of summer, a boy soon to know the joys and frustrations of manhood. The cherry tree is my senior; it has been around since before I was born. Every year its leaves and blossoms return after winter. When at the end of summer the blossoms drop in bunches, I play with friends on a carpet of red, wet and squishy with the rain. In the deepest winter the skeleton branches shine in the morning with a coat of ice basted in the night air, onto which with warm breath and fingers I make patterns to compliment the tree rings. Each winter it seems to die, yet does not.

◌◌

These winter trees were a welcome sight, and once again I wonder about the blessing of an unseen hand oblivious of my agreement. As I walk under the branches in their winter rest towards the buildings, I feel the silence, I know instinctively this is the place I sought. But it is deserted, not a person or sound of such appears to be around. As my steps slowly progress forward, I see a larger central building beside which is a children's playground, laid out just like the one in my first school! My chest and stomach begin to flutter at the incredible convolution of past and present. All thought seems to have stopped.

January 21st

The Buddhists say we all experience suffering; it may be the single common bond amongst the species. Buddhists concern themselves with the resolution of this affliction to human existence. It seems before such concerns can be manifested in practice, one must first understand suffering. This is not as easy as one may think. As I see it, we all know of certain forms of suffering, physical and mental suffering; what we are mostly unaware of is the inevitable suffering that comes with being born.

In middle of the playground was a small roof of red tiles supported on stout wooden posts and beams. It was just high enough to step under. Hanging from its central apex by a plaited rope was a large ornate bell. Now I knew for sure this was a Buddhist monastery. At that thought there appeared from the building a figure robed in deep orange attire; a monk, his head clean of hair, slightly bowed, was making his way towards me.

13

The fluttering stopped, everything had stopped. I stood motionless, just waiting. When he was but three feet from me, his head came up with a broad smile and he said, "Welcome to Indriya, would you like some tea?"

Untangling the prepared profundity that had silently built up in me, the expectations and assumptions, the 'now I enter a new world of wisdom and insight' with answers to long sought after questions, the decision was 'Tea!'

"Yes, yes, please, tea would be just the ticket." What did I say, did I really say "just the ticket" to a Buddhist monk? Great!

The monk, meanwhile, had turned without a further word, yet a definite beckoning in his movements.

I raised my rucksack on one shoulder and followed as he returned to the big building. Actually, it wasn't so much big as more square than long, unlike the other huts that were the old barracks. We were heading for the kitchen.

Bare of all but essential bright steel cooking items, the kitchen surrounded a large black, double-oven wood stove. I knew these old stoves. I had put one, smaller of course, in our house and cooked on it. In winter it was heating, cooking, and hearth of the home. Catherine flashed into my vision; she would be sitting with our dogs Tess and Bryn laid out before the stove on the rag rug we had recycled our old clothes into.

Two men in white robes were finishing cleaning down. Two hot mugs of tea sat on the prep table. At the appearance of the monk, they placed their hands before them in a greeting, the eldest one spoke, "Welcome, bunte, can I offer you some tea?" The monk had come prepared, for he withdrew from beneath his robe a similar mug and placed it beside the others. "Thank you, and perhaps for our visitor," he said, opening the palm of his hand towards me. The older 'white' turned to me and said, "Welcome, I'm anagarika John, this is anagarika Richard." A picture of Richard Dawkin in white passed through my vision. I said, "Thank you, that would be most welcome. I've come quite some distance; I was hoping I may stay for a while." I turned to the monk, "Do you think that would be possible, sir?"

He said, "You're welcome to stay, but I should warn you we are a little primitive; we've only just moved in and there's lots to be done."

I said, a little hastily perhaps, "Oh, good, I mean, I've worked in the building industry and I'd like to help, if you can use me."

"It sounds as though you have been sent to us. Yes, we could do with someone who knows a thing or two about buildings."

The tea having been poured, the monk left us, cup in hand. As he did so he turned and added, "We'll fill you in at the work meeting in the morning."

The two anagarikas again closed their palms together and bowed slightly.

Left alone, we got to talking; I learned that John had been here seventeen months and Richard just five months. As the months seemed significant, I asked what it was. John explained that to become a monk here, one had to first spend about two years as an anagarika. That, I learned, is something like a postulate in the Christian tradition. When the monks decide, you would be invited to join them and be fully ordained. Such ordinations are eagerly awaited by most anagarikas, though some leave. That's the whole purpose, to weed out the wheat from the chaff (interesting Christian metaphor to lay on Buddhists). That was as much as I learned that evening, besides being told meditation was at five the next morning. I was to feel free to attend or not, as it was just my arrival day. Anagarika John left Richard to show me where I might sleep.

We walked out of the kitchen building into a cold night. Over us the sky was black and more full of stars than I had ever seen. Of course, there was no ambient light to cloud my vision. Neither was there any way to see where we were going! By the light of a very small flashlight Richard led me on, across the playground, under the trees, turning occasionally left or right. We came to a stop in front of three steps leading to a door that filled the wall of what looked like the end of a wooden hut. "In here," Richard said, pushing open the unlocked door to reveal an even greater darkness than outside.

As we stepped inside, the echo of our conversation told me it was a large empty space. As my eyes adjusted, I could see from the spacing of windows down each side, it was a long building, almost as cold inside as out. He said, "I would try the corner there, slightly less of a draft, I'd say," pointing into an abyss at floor level. "I'd better go, I'm on breakfast duty tomorrow; I'll feel like crap if I stay up any longer. Good to have you here. Sleep well, James." And with that he left, closing the door behind him, which did nothing for the temperature and even less for my thoughts about the religious life. He'll 'feel like crap', I said to myself, but then felt somewhat better about 'just the ticket'. What strangers language makes of us all.

Falling into a restless sleep I dream...

◦◦

A small boy with a big spade digs, falling over with the effort to reach the handle, lift and turn sod. I dig deep dens into it, slide in on a piece of old linoleum and pull a 'roof' over my head. I am alone; it's dark and cold and smells of earth. I am the earth, the earth is me.

∾

Next door to the home I grew up in was an old farmhouse, Fallowfield farm, built in 1576 when the land was country, and the city of London was a distant two day's travel away. The oldest tree I know was the farm-house oak. It stood in my path on the way to school each day, a greeting from the past, yet here it was in the present, full and luscious with each spring. It leaned under its aged weight and fell towards the farmhouse wall, hanging over passers-by like the greeting of an old friend. I'd reach for a branch and pull off a handful of leaves.

like the greeting of an old friend

The leaves like hands look back at me and curl their fingers around mine. Passing by the place on my way to school, I would read the date on a plaque and wonder what it was like back then.

At home under the bed-covers I read old tales cloaked in mystery, as were most of the ways of past times. Superstition and suspicion followed a traveler in those times. Even to inquire into things was considered a dangerous manner of thinking. The order of the day was acceptance, acceptance of the decrees made by the church. To take my present journey into the thoughts and ways of an alien culture was to invite a sure and unpleasant reprimand. The cathedrals, churches and quaint parish meeting halls such that Richard and Rosalyn attended, surviving out of that grim past, give no hint of their bloody history.

୰

Waking in the night, sweating and freezing at one and the same time, I found my own mind to be a confusion of past and present, of uncertainty and desire, longing and loss. The night was still, cold, but not quite soundless. Somewhere in the black vastness of the building I presently inhabited, there was the sound of tiny feet scratching on wood.

I had never actually seen a rat. Some ancient instinct told me I was prey being sought for supper – or would it better be called a midnight feast. I had no idea of the time, but I did have a flashlight and watch, which I quickly put together to discover the hour. My sudden activity seemed to deter the unseen predator from further venture, and shine my light as I may, we never came eye to eye. I was not displeased. There was no more sleeping to be done this night. The rat and the time-seeking had fully woken me from the tortures of restlessness.

> *Awake again at four a.m.*
> *The past pumping*
> *in the veins colliding*
> *with tomorrow.*
>
> *Not knowing who I am.*
> *Breathing hard*
> *at the night*
> *and waiting for tomorrow.*
>
> *Tomorrow, they say, is another day.*
> *(I don't hold with old clichés).*
> *Each day, like apples*
> *keeps death away.*

While scrabbling in my pack, I discovered the sandwich Rosalyn packed that I had completely forgotten about; my stomach cried for its instant ingestion. Sitting on my bedroll, my back against the hut wall, I ate. I had retrieved my parka and hat from the pack and wrapped my scarf around me. My head had gone dead again, so I just chewed slowly, not out of any good eating habits, I have to confess. I just wanted this stillness – and the sandwich – to last on.

Morning came slowly into that old barrack hut, easing dim light in patches across the dusty wood floor, picking out my night visitor's tracks. I watched, as fascinated as I was when a child and car lights crossed my bedroom wall as the neighbors went out for the night. Checking my watch, I saw that morning meditation would be soon over. I decided to find the kitchen.

The morning air hit my lungs and grabbed my arms and legs. Walking was a slow operation for a while, which was just as well, for I needed to get my bearings. Turn left, turn right, I had no real idea, but I reasoned the whole place couldn't be big enough to lose oneself in, so I proceeded. After a while, I found in front of me the field I had come up the day before; I'd clearly taken a wrong turn. Yet I stopped, for now the sun was part up, the long shadows of the trees thrown over the field of still-frosted grass held me there, just looking for sheer joy.

I became aware of something I had been working over in my mind for some time. Just the fact of being here, I thought, what a miracle that is. The number of possible threads, of evolution, genetics, and biology, that creates the weave that brings us forth, is infinite. They are quite literally uncountable. We are a miracle of nature. Whilst you and I are miracles, and I wouldn't want to detract from that, to nature we are just every-day miracles. 'All that we survey in nature has arrived in the same way', I thought, through evolutionary time-threads that make up the grand Tapestry we are a part of. I realized each form, each life, has its place in the weave. Beside each of us woven into the Tapestry are all those who we know or have known: family, friends, lovers, associates, strangers, foreigners. There are trees, plants, grasses, and flowers; there are animals, insects, fish and fowl. The list is infinite, as infinite as nature itself.

I stood at the edge of the field remembering the night, the rat, the unsaid thoughts, the feelings, and the dream. I thought, 'what curious seekers we are'.

January 26th

Our seeking has a fearful shadow to it, wanting to know and at the same time shunning what is most obvious. We fear to know death, thus we fear life, is that our neurosis? Are we trapped in the claws of a paradox that by definition seems unsolvable? Well, I certainly hope not forever!

I cannot answer these thoughts today, I am too taken with the miracle, I want to continue to search it out and live it out. To live one must eat; now, where is the kitchen?

෧෨

The gathered monks, and some nuns, I was surprised to see, along with John and Richard and two other anagarikas, numbered about twenty, I guessed. It felt somehow impolite to look too hard, as an actual counting would require. The room we sat in was next to the kitchen; I was to learn later to call it the sala, a place of gathering.

We sat on the carpeted floor in a circle. There was an aroma about, musk that mixed with the porridge and tea smells. The Buddha statue at one end of the room nearly touched the ceiling, about seven feet of gold sitting cross-legged with a look of satisfaction on him. Around 'him' were an abundance of flowers. In winter! I thought, they look real enough. In answer to my curious head turnings, a young monk sitting to my left told me they were using this room for morning meditation. "Oh, right," I said, not having a clue what that might entail. But I guessed it had incense involved in it somewhere.

Breakfast was a quiet affair consisting of passing round, without a word, bowls of gruel and mugs of tea. Sugar in plentiful supply in a large bowl continually made the rounds, as it was liberally added to both the tea and the gruel. It was Richard, I noted, sitting to one side, who was generating this fare from two identical urns until all had their mug and bowl before them; he himself being the last to eat. I was glad of something hot, and even sought the sugar bowl as an added fillip to my appetite.

After, when bowls and mugs were gathered up and transported to the kitchen, a meeting to decide the day's work began. But first, all eyes turned to me, as the monk I had met the previous evening greeted me once again and invited me to share what brought me here. I was a little flummoxed, not being prepared for such a direct invite. I hesitated for a moment trying to think of something profound and religious, then I said, "It was the storm." I was about to go on, try and explain or at least repair the damage, when the laughter stopped me, mouth open. It seems monks and nuns arise out of all sorts of circumstances and coincidences, and that sheltering from the rain was as good a reason for being in a monastery as any, at least this monastery.

I decided to keep a diary, something I had often enough thought of but never quite had the willpower to carry through, at least not past January, for it was always a new-year resolution sort of decision. But this I felt was different. I had a feeling I had stumbled upon a world unknown to me before, people who had dared to look beyond the everyday experience. I was sure I would want to remember this time, stay or leave, whatever came of it.

୭ଚ

My feelings did not deceive, for in fact Indriya was to change my life, but I leap ahead. Better I just offer you something of what I wrote. Perhaps, if you don't mind, I'll begin with something I penned shortly after my arrival here.

> ### January 31st
>
> *This afternoon I went for walk. I can see for miles up here. The distant hills like swelling seas flow away, down to the place of people, cars, cares and...*
>
> *The wind is firm and gentle today. So many thoughts, so many feelings. By now I have practiced 2 meditation sessions (pujas) and they, like yeast to dough, are working their effect on me, bringing me into the life here.*
>
> *I have been awake 12 hrs today, and spent most of it outdoors. Feelings of the immediate (fields, sky, beauty, air, freedom) are punctuated with longings – for Catherine, the familiar, Tess and Bryn. Here I am alone very much with who I am.*

The two pujas I managed to attend were both in the evening; I still haven't managed to rise in time for a morning session.

I decided to pitch my tent inside the barracks and made myself a refuge of sorts; I'm at least sleeping okay now. The sangha[1] have left me alone, as Richard says, to let me settle any way I find best for me. I get the feeling they are glad of the potential help I may be and don't want to scare me off. Truth is I don't really have anywhere else to be right now. This 'sabbatical' was, by mutual agreement, Catherine's and my way of loosening our bonds; we had agreed it would need at least two or three months apart to keep us civilized.

---

1 Sangha. The monastic community.

February 4th

The company of the monks and nuns is open, straight, simple and unattached company. I like them. They come in all sorts, but I find myself reluctant to judge them for what they have chosen to do with their lives, or their reasons for doing it. The pace of life here, the place and its nature give rise to asking questions of myself, not of others.

Up on the roof of the sala building, I'm nailing slipped slates into place. The sky is such a bright blue it's almost white, and the air has a Jack Frost feel to it. I think to myself, snow. The monk I'm working with is Venerable Kusalo. Venerable is the normal manner of addressing a Theravadin monk. I think it means something like wise, though sometimes hard to believe when I look at Kusalo, he's about twenty-three. If I think back to when I was of such an age, wisdom was not one of my strong suites. He told me he's been a monk for under a year; January through March the monastics are in rains-retreat, his first. Strictly speaking he shouldn't be talking much, and certainly not idle chatting. It's supposed to be a time of reflection and learning.

So I get on with my work. The storm that (partly) drove me here has lifted part of the roof and thrown it down onto the playground. John's head appears over the eves and he plants two more fresh slates on the roof. "How's it going, James, are we nearly there?" I answer that I think mealtime should see it done. I turn to Kusalo for his assessment. He's happy to concur and chat a while. Hidden from stray ears, he confesses his uncertainty about staying in the order. My mind jumps with excitement, feeling privileged and sad at one and the same time. Is he asking something of me, or just off- loading a bit of anxiety? I ask him why he is unsure. "Well, it's not that I doubt the practice, I think the Buddha got it right; I think, especially here, that our practice is straight and true, leading to deathlessness and the end of suffering." It sounded a bit textbook to me, like something I had read in the library a day or so ago.

The cold breeze had got to my bladder, in short time I was seriously going to need a pee. I waited. He went on, "It's not the practice, or this place; the abbot is great, a great teacher. It's me." Surprise, surprise, I thought; my bladder was making a smart-alec out of me, I was getting close to just wanting off the roof and into a bathroom, the one I could see just across the playground. I think it was something about my posture, or maybe his instinct cut in. He slowed to a stop and said, "We'd better get down for mealtime. Thanks for listening, I didn't mean to bend your ear like that, it's just…" I interrupted him as I made for the ladder. "That's okay, better out than in, I reckon. Let me know how you get on," I said as my head disappeared below the eves, following my bladder that was already halfway across the playground.

∾

The playground in my pre-school nursery was a plain concrete slab, not that we played on it, we slept on it. In the July sun, when England had summers that could be called such, army cots were laid out in rows and we kids, small enough to sleep one each end, would be commanded to take our afternoon nap. I was four years old. I would lay on my back under a thin grey blanket, look into the sky, follow the flight of birds, and planes that made proper airplane sounds – that inviting low growl of propellers. They gave us a third of a pint of milk in the morning. It would be just about through my small body and seeking a return to the outside world when we had been laying down for about ten minutes. But rest period was forty minutes. Between fifteen and thirty minutes, hands would begin to rise straight up into the warm summer air, usually accompanied with a chorus of 'please, miss, please, miss.' The regimentation of rest succumbed to the chaos of nature. She always gets her way in the end.

February 7ᵗʰ

I believe my time here will be long. It is only a few days I've been here yet it feels like months. In fact I'm losing a sense of the past even as at the same time I remember it.

On a walk through some woods today, I thought of the nature of attachment, (a constant theme of the talks the abbot gives), especially of my attachment to Catherine. Is attachment a good thing, a bad thing? Is real love an attachment or is attachment a denial of true love? I do not pine the setting of the sun, accepting the night with ease. Yet I have loved the sun since a small child and it reciprocates that love every day with brightness, warmth – life itself. But I know for certain I will experience these things many times, unending. Even in the depth of night I know it.

Thus I can love (the sun) and not seek to possess it because of uncertainty. I don't have to be attached to or please or achieve anything for its presence and gifts to be a part of my life. So it seems attachment arises from uncertainty.

Love – free, real, open love – is the child of certainty.

It is surely the nature of love and attachment that defines life. Just as they are the immediate question between a mother and her child, so they must in some form identify us within nature. It was nature that alerted me to a strange change in myself, one I could not even today explain.

You may recall my thinking, when on the sala roof, that snow was in the air. That night it fell, laying two feet thick by morning. I thought nothing more of my 'prediction', particularly as we were all busy finding anything big and flat to shovel pathways between the huts and sala. It was the snow-fall, perhaps more than anything up to that point, that drew me in to the sangha. Monks and nuns that had seemed distant figures I dared not approach, proved to be as human as I in their openness to having fun with this task. It was a silly reticence on my part to have thought they were otherwise.

It was some days later, when once again we were working outside on the buildings, that I ventured it would rain in a couple of days. Sure enough it did. When my unconscious predictions of weather continued to prove such a few more times, others began to notice. One of the ana-garikas, Peter, told me there had been some discussion among them and a couple of junior monks that would include Kusalo, about how such instincts arise and show themselves in monastic life.

"But," I said, "I'm not a monk or anything close to being one."

"You're closer than you think."

"How's that," I asked.

"I hear the abbot has asked you in for a chat."

"Yes, that's so, but is that significant?"

"I'd say so. He likes you, you know, I suspect he thinks you may want to stay here, and you can't stay indefinitely without joining us. That's the rule." I was somewhat stopped in my tracks by this news. It hadn't occurred to me that my time would run out, that I would have to leave. I asked Peter, "So how long could one stay before having to join up." Peter laughed, "It's not the army, mate, even if these are barracks, or were. No one's going to force you in; relax, you've got about three months before you *may* be asked to leave. But I doubt you will be even then, we need the help, and your skills are rare in a place like this." Well, that was a reliev-ing complement, and in about three months I figured on going home to Catherine anyway. Or maybe I will stay. I didn't want to think about it, I didn't want to think about anything, except profound questions. The day to day stuff out there had become a tangle of change and pain.

"So," I said, "Have I been dubbed a psychic or something because of my weather prediction, because don't ask me, I don't know how it happens."

"No, nothing like that, we just notice – you're not the first – living this detached life seems to open us up to awareness that gets locked up in regular society. After all, that's the whole point of being here when you think of it."

The truth is I'd never thought much about *why* one would become a monk, but from here on I was to think on it a lot, not least because two days later I was asked if I was intending to ordain.

Of the five nuns, Sister Khema was the senior. It was in the playground, under a clear blue sky that gave one a feeling of expansion, that she approached me. Always direct and to the point, she said, "So, James, are you going to join us or leave us?"

ᙣ

When I was a boy the day to day stuff was profound. For a while there was a question I couldn't get straight and it wouldn't go away. I would ask my mother almost daily, 'Do you love me?' I was seven-years-and-nine-months old. 'Of course I do.' 'How much?' I would press. 'Lots,' she would answer. I kept it coming like sticky tape you can't shake off your finger, 'How many lots?' Sighing, she'd say, 'Lots and lots, dear me, James.' 'But how many lots, Mum?' 'Hundreds,' she'd say in exasperation. 'But how many hundreds, Mum?' 'Oh, goodness me, James, I'm busy, I've got work to do, son. Go on with you.' 'Yes, but just tell me,' I'd plead. 'Millions of hundreds, now go on and play.'

> **February 11th**
> *Many things happen to one who walks in this place. The sun splashes its light across the countryside and a single human mind starts to open. My ears pick up the crows cawing in the surprise warmth. Smaller birds filling the tree tops bathe in the unexpected 'spring'. The fields fall away before me as I follow the footpath down to Nettleden. Coming up, I see the familiar simple brown attire of a nun and the white of her postulate sister. As we are on a path, I reflect: These women have chosen their way, that alone, I think, makes them stronger than those (of us all) who follow a path of comfortable imposed familiarity. Catherine must have gone through a similar choosing in going to Greenham[2], and her subsequent decision to be who she wants.*

---

2 A reference to the women's peace camp at Greenham Common US military base.

The nuns' quarters were, of course, set apart from the monks, in a corner of the monastery amidst gardens they had judiciously laid out and dug in spite of the winter weather. Their plan was to have them ready for the opening ceremony in the spring. The monks and nuns here now were the advanced party. It seems Indriya is to be more open to the public than the other monasteries in the order, thus there will be many more monks and nuns arriving after the opening. I wondered what that would be like, not too sure I would like it. It played on my mind after Sister Khema's question. I liked being in the middle of the countryside with a handful of companions and lots of spare room, and I had the feeling that though rules were kept, it was with more ease than in the closed monasteries.

I recalled a conversation with John. He was nearing full ordination time and had been sent to the other monasteries for several of his months of anagarika trial time. "It's pretty tough," he was saying. "It's not just the rules, the schedule and so on. It's the stuff that comes up in your mind. Each week we all meet and discuss what is happening with us, including confessing to failures of rule keeping."

"Sounds a bit Catholic," I said. "I didn't know you had confession. Who's your confessor, the abbot?"

"It's not really like that," John said. "I grew up in a Catholic family, this is quite different. For one thing, we're all in this together, including the old man. That makes all the difference. You don't feel overburdened with authority like I did in the church."

I said, "But he's still the boss, right?"

"In a manner of speaking, but he earned his place by going through for many years what we're all going through each day of practice. The only element of boss, as you put it, is that he passes on his experience to help us on the path."

"To liberation," I said.

"Well, yes, that's the idea."

My recollection of our conversation came, as thoughts will, out of nowhere. I was in the garden tool shed busy with a task I had volunteered to do, I think, out of a love of gardening, but maybe for the love of Uncle Silas. I was cleaning the spades, forks and hoes and refurbishing the handles, sanding and oiling them to a pristine condition. I loved the work. I suppose the things John had told me on the sala roof contrasted with this ideal I was living.

The shed, set as it was at the edge of the nuns' gardens, reminded me of Silas's garden. Uncle Silas is a fictitious character created by H. E. Bates. I was given a book of his when a small lad that I read so often Silas became and remains real to me.

There was a small chair where I was working, and sitting in it with the door open, looking down the garden, I was for all the world sitting with Silas, to whom I would casually remark, *'you shall live to be a thousand,'* to which he always replied in a broad Bedfordshire brogue, *'I shall, I shall.'*

I took a drink of water, imagining it wine that Silas had had brought up from the cellar by his housekeeper, a frosty woman with whom Silas loved to argue and curse in a manner we have no mind of now. For then it was simple ribald humor, as earthy as the soil I was cleaning off the spades. But there I go drifting into the past, when so often the abbot has said, 'the past is a memory, the future unknown, now is the knowing.' Yet that past had a future to it; present times seem lost in nihilism, for we are destroying this grand beauty that is nature and possibly ourselves along with it. This knowledge drives me to find an answer to our dilemma. Perhaps that is why I came here.

I received a lot of thanks over the spadework. Well, there are some things that just come naturally. I love Silas because I love the garden. When I was growing up, at weekends I would go to the allotment, land set aside for families to grow food during the war. In the company of my father I learned many things, digging, planting, making compost. I would stop work and watch the pond at the garden's edge. In summer, teeming with life, frogs, fish, dragonflies, butterflies, birds who came to drink, and ducks that splash down, look at me, and take their leave. In winter frozen over and ringed with brown grasses at rest, its stillness infects me. And I learn to wait. I learn what gardening is, what the earth I live on feels like. I walk the streets on quiet Sunday mornings with a bucket and shovel, picking up the gift of the milkman's horse. The allotment and the park are my countryside, where I learn of nature, and of nurture. This is where I hear the cooing of pigeons, the singing of birds, and the singing of the trees.

February 21st

Such long days, so full of peace and beauty. I'm writing this, sitting by the bell I encountered on arrival. Last time I came out here, one of the three monastery cats requisitioned my lap. I just let it sit and took my lesson from its ease as I watched the sun slip down out of the sky.

Today is another passage of glorious moments, the still silence being measured by the wind chimes above me, and the population of birds playing out the midday.

My eyes are greeted by the green of the monastery's back field and the sun reflected in the brass bell. The soft old wood of the bell house is painted in the brilliance of light. Everywhere there is sky. And the borders of earth and sky are woven with trees in their winter stillness. Occasionally the figures of deep orange, brown or white cross the playground, make for the field to walk or move along a path to their room. Peace!

The peace of this place is grounded in meditation practice. There's a cartoon pinned to the notice board in the kitchen. It shows two monks sitting cross-legged side by side; one is turning to the other, the caption is "nothing happens next." Outside the monastery, the humor is that meditation is nothing happening; in here it's the opposite! There's another little handwritten quip on the board, "meditation is not what you think!" Yet I cannot stop thinking no matter how much meditation I sit.

I've been here now for over a month, even getting up at four-thirty for morning puja. It's just like Kusalo said; it's not the hard time-routine or the one meal a day or the work, I guess it's not even the rules, though I don't have those to keep. It's the mind, my mind. The endless stream of thought that won't release me from the past, from Catherine, from Malcolm, back and back it goes, Andrew, my pet cat, a dead bird found on the path when I was four years old. Yet I'm certain that somewhere here is an answer to the eternal dilemma that drives my thinking into those dark places. Often I think to live here and *not meditate* would be best, for in the light of day, in the round of peaceful work, a simple meal and friendship I find peace. In the easy movement of the countryside, of the farms surrounding this place, of the seasons that will assuredly arise in a pattern both familiar and nourishing, I find peace. Yet when evening comes and before me I witness the patient walk of the monks, the stream of robed figures moving once again to the sala, I am persuaded by the deep companionship and wisdom of the elders to join them.

I sit on a floor cushion at the back, before me the monks on the right side in neat rows, the nuns, likewise, on the left, are separated by a four feet wide carpet that ends at the Buddha's feet. In the falling light of evening I once again witness the soft shuffling of the kneeling figures bowing as they settle themselves on their cushions. I don't bow, why would I? It's not that I have any particular aversion to statues, it's just, well, I don't.

Once settled on their cushions, the abbot lights the candles and three incense sticks, at which point everyone bows in unison three times, except me. I just watch, fascinated by the bobbing bald heads all going down and up, down and up, down and up. The first couple of times I watched this ritual I had to stifle an urge to laugh, but now I wait in anticipation of the chanting that will follow the bowing.

Something happens when humans voice in unison. Some deep swirling in the gut pulls under and drowns the critic sitting in the seat of cleverness. I may laugh at bowing, but I am silenced of all judgment when the sangha sings. Though it is not truly singing, it reaches my ear as song. It is said that all religious practices arose out of the ancient singer of songs, that shaman of remembered verse who would travel the country with stories and spells to dispel our fears and give form to our hopes. For somewhere deep in our past, perhaps as far back as our descent from the trees, we knew fear and needed succor to abate its grip on us.

As the chanting ends, all is silence, robes are wrapped around bodies as once more the whisper of movement settles into meditation. The hall is now almost dark save the flickering candlelight splashing the Buddha. The air has become full now with musk and my breathing slows as I wrap a blanket around me, close my eyes, and sit still.

For just a moment of immeasurable time there is nothing. Then, as though by a will of their own, thoughts push and shove like rush hour passengers on the underground crowding into my head. This they think is their job, to keep me alive, constantly cognizant and on guard. What is it they serve, what darkness do they work so unceasingly to hide from me? Is it any relation to the mite in the ant's brain?

I read one time that when ants climb up grass stalks they know not what they do. Lying in the grass, I would watch the little creatures labor their way up the waving stalks, weaving like drunks on a tightrope, to reach the top. Having achieved this senseless climb they would wave their bodies in the air. What, I thought, is the air fresher up there? Do they do it, as we climb a mountain, just because it's there? Well, it seems it is not the ant that seeks the grass mountain top, but a mite in the ant's brain, making of the ant a servant of its own desires. For the top of the stalk may, if the mite is lucky, be chewed off by a cow, and thus make its way with mite (and a sorry ant) into the cows innards where the mite wants to be.[3]

> **February 25th**
> *It's highly possible we have a mite or several mites in our brain, but whatever seeks to make servants of us is far less tangible, hidden from view, certainly hidden from the guard that fills the brain with uninvited thoughts. Yet there remains still that moment while the guard sleeps, lulled by the chanting. Is it possible that with courage and perseverance I may yet pry open that dark cave?*

I was walking slowly from one tree to its opposite neighbor and back again, a path of about thirty meters. This practice had been done for over two thousand years, each foot on the path bearing witness to the search for clarity, and resolution of the human problem. Some had indeed found freedom from suffering; many had overcome their striving individualism and lived wholesome community lives. All had to finally come to terms with death.

The band of light brown ribbon invited me also to tread this path of awareness, to stand composed at one end of 'the path', to walk mindfully to the other end, stop, turn, and walk yet again, back and forth. As I walked I was trying to 'stay in the moment'. Yet surely, I thought, the moment is but the threads of the past being viewed as one would a tapestry or painting. Even that which passed before my eyes wherever I chose to look, the tree ahead, the ground, the grass around me, becomes the past as soon as viewed. I didn't get it, this being-in-the-now business. But I loved the trees and walking, so I just walk slowly back and forth.

It was when I wasn't really trying (to be in the now) that something happened. It was as though the moment of nothing that occurred between the chanting and rush-hour during sitting meditation flooded my being. The sudden drowning of thought left me dislocated and without

---

3 I'm indebted for this piece of science to the evolutionary biologist Richard Dawkins.

borders to my body. The moment was fleeting, yet strong enough to see me folded to my knees and rolling to the ground. I lay, looking up into the trees, fully conscious now, covered with a feeling of total peace. The trees were more beautiful than I had ever seen them, the grass greener, and the sky a million miles high. A pigeon cooed close by, and on the breeze came a reply from the fields just beyond the monastery's boundary.

To this day the cooing of pigeons will send a ripple through my body, a gossamer of physical remembrance, and I will know that peace, fleeting yet strong. It wasn't that I was a stranger to feelings of peace, for when I was a boy...

෧◡๑

...In summer the air was hot, the sky deep blue, everywhere full of brightness. At certain times the light was to me an intense brilliance that bounced off leaves and flowers, even the brick walls. In the back garden, laying in the long grass, I let time go, feeling only the quietness and dustiness that summer brings. Airplane's propellers buzz gently across the sky, carry thoughts and questions to a place that spells peace.

෧◡๑

...In the early morning quiet when alone in the garden, the coolness of the night breathes on me; I find myself a separate independent being from the family of my parents still sleeping upstairs.

෧◡๑

...In the Park, the rose garden, closed in by its seven foot high walls of old soft dark-red brick, traps the air that is a burst of perfume rising in the July heat. Roses form floating plates of color that pull my eyes this way and that, while the yellow roses on the climbers wave to attract my attention to some secret corner of the garden's maze of pathways and hidden seats. I stop running to count how many different colors can be seen from where I stand: white, deep yellow, pink, light red, plain old red, scarlet, and a deepest dark color that my eye cannot name draws me to its perfume. The smell is as deep and overwhelming as its color is hypnotizing.

෧◡๑

30

It was decided to plant a Buddha grove. Theravadin Buddhists originate from Thailand and Burma. Like the Buddha they live in forests and their practice is very much connected to trees. Beautiful though the downs and moors of the English countryside are, they are not forested. The Buddha grove would be the start of trees within the monastery, at least. The first I heard of the project was when I was asked to go down to the village.

"We need someone to handle the money." Monks are banned from handling money or any dealing at all. Strictly speaking, John could carry money, but as he was nearing ordination, the abbot decided it better if he let go of that worldly activity.

After three months in the monastery, the village seemed crowded, hectic and disturbing. I hadn't appreciated how the gentle rhythm of life at Indriya had unwoven the natural tension of 'normal' life. Now I was feeling it in all its force and wondered what a town or a city would be like. It was beyond contemplating. After picking up the young trees, I was glad to be returning to my new home.

The trees would be planted in the back field around a stupa, a round monument that usually holds relics of a past Buddhist master. It is said that to walk around one several times brings good karma into one's life. This stupa drew me to contemplate once again on purpose and meaning in this life.

My beloved spades were brought from the garden shed. Peter and I laid our lines and plotted the spots for the trees. Two long lines we laid in a cross formation intersecting at the stupa. Along each line we marked ten trees seven feet apart, five each side of the intersection. Taking a row each, we began to dig. Though the earth resisted we persisted. I thought about that resistance; we were intruding, breaking what was once whole. Monks are not allowed to do this, it is considered defiling to risk killing the creatures whose home is the soil. For someone who had been gardening since the war ended, this took some accepting. I thought again about the earth's resistance, and how the poplar tree's resistance had possibly saved my life. I thought of the hidden hand of nature trying her best to take care of us.

It took us two days to plant twenty trees. It was a beginning. I felt complete somehow after the trees were up and swaying gently in the breeze. I wrote to Catherine that evening.

> *Dear Cathy,*
> *I'm still here at the monastery, I've been here since I phoned you in January. I'm not sure if we agreed to write or not write, but anyway I seem to have been closed in here and thinking little of the outside*

world. Though I hasten to add you are very much a part of my closed world. I think I understand why you wanted to spend so much time at Greenham, how close one gets to those who are following the same path. I have become very much a part of the community here. I think it helps. On the way here I wasn't at all sure I was doing the right thing, but I think I have found something important to me, even precious perhaps. I still love you. I can't see that changing, I know you want to change things – I can't say leave – but I can feel a bit more ground under me now; I'm sure we can talk it through.

I've just spent two days planting trees; it feels so good to have done. You know how we always said we should plant a tree a year. Well I just made up for ten years. I shall leave here soon. I'll call you. I'm not sure, but I think I shall be coming back here. It's hard for me to think of it, but the reasons are not all to do with solving us. I feel positive about the possibility of becoming a monk. This must sound a bit sudden and maybe confused, but it's not. I see it as a crossroads, a bit of a sharp turn maybe, but right.

Lots of Love XX

The day I left, everyone turned out to say goodbye. I was a bit shaky; I hadn't thought to be so missed. I'd planned to make my way to the back field and out onto the farmer's field and head for Nettleden. But after morning gruel, the abbot announced my departure and that was that. I had to grasp hands or make anjali[4], being watched and watching through tears I had not expected. Several of the sangha walked with me to the back field. There Ajahn Panno, the first monk who met me on arrival said, "Goodbye, James, it's been a good start. We'll see you again soon, eh?" I made anjali and mumbled something about returning. The last three, Richard, John and Kusalo, saw me to the perimeter fence. John and Richard gave me a hug and backed away leaving me to Kusalo. He made anjali and then unexpectedly hugged me. I looked at him, surprised. He said, "It's okay, I'm going to disrobe this week. I'm not strong enough for this life. I'm going back to the States. I guess that means we won't meet again, at least in this life. It's been really good to know you, James; I wish you all the best. Take care." Then he turned and joined Peter and John walking back to the sala.

---

4 Anjali. The practice of placing ones hand together in front of the heart.

Two

After immersing myself in the storm, searching where the rain came from, my mother insisted I get in a hot bath. To go from that wild, stinging cold rain into the safety and warmth of the bath was, of course, to come home to the known, the comfort of a controlled life. Without realizing it, half my bravado in the rain rested on my knowing there was a warm home to go to, a place familiar – of family. Yet, so too was nature my family, and the rain was a familiar. I was just not yet strong enough to turn to it alone, but I would be.

∽

As I walked down the field, retracing my steps of three months earlier, I found myself counting, just as I had at Richard's house. I had been counting since before I was five and started school, for there I had tasks to do that revealed the shadow of war in my nervous system. I discovered my trembling hands. I don't recall how the counting started, only that it was a kind of refuge, a place where, whatever happens, the numbers are unshaken, two always follows one, three follows two, four follows three. It was a kind of miracle, my miracle. Like all miracles it was an illusion: it didn't work, but inside me when I was small I didn't know that. I do now. I know now if I'm counting I'm escaping, just not looking at what is rising in me.

I stopped my walking, stopped counting, collapsed to the ground and listened. It was like a death. If you've known a death you will recognize that feeling of 'how can the world just go on like nothing happened – don't they know, don't they see?' And so it was. The breeze was a slow free-flowing breath. The trees opened their arms in greeting, showing the first signs of bright green buds on their fingers. The earth had softened under the furrowing plough, becoming a quilt of light and dark browns. Birds sang their strong calls of spring. The world was going on, while a dark grey creature crawled around in my stomach, sorrowful, crying out alone, and reaching up to my throat to pull on my breath. Of course, I wanted to count.

I could not afford the seduction of numbers anymore to save me from this suffering. It was a short stop, an aspirin of momentary relief.

I unhitch my pack, walk out a few yards and lie on the earth. On my back, the sky looks back at me with indifference. But the good earth holds me. Down my spine it presses, my legs fall between its furrows, touched along their length, and my head has a pillow that wraps around to my ears. Sound becomes muffled; the breeze stays high and leaves me alone.

I am the earth, the earth is me. The dream comes to me again and from there the remembering...

⚬

...Lying on the army cot in the nursery; Wendy, a young assistant, comes around and tucks us in; her hand, silk on my forehead, as she strokes with the touch of a butterfly, encouraging sleep. As her fingers float back and forth over me, the creature awakens, alerted by sheer pleasure running through my small body. Somewhere inside I am screaming, 'Don't stop! Don't ever stop!' For I know the dark sorrow that will grab at my breath when she does. "Have a nice sleep now, James," she gently whispers as she moves on to the next child. The unbearable pain forces blackness as I pull the blanket over my head, turn on my side, curl up as tight as I can, and start counting. With the safety of the earth behind me I let the creature have its way...

> **April 6th**
> *A sound at once human and unrecognizable fills the space between earth and sky. It is a voice, yet a voice that is forbidden in our civilized conventional lives. Never bring that up, never utter such depths into the shallow waters of lives running from an ancient fear.*
>
> *And so it has no name, it must remain buried even from linguistic labels, from words that might squeeze recognition into our awareness. I must learn to live with it as everyone else does, yet something in it aches to be known, to be accepted.*

The day before I left Indriya I made a final entry in my diary...

> **April 4th**
> *The first Noble truth of Buddhism is 'Life contains suffering.' Thus we should practice letting-go. To let-go of life, I fear, may be to negate this amazing and beautiful miracle. Yet to embrace life with a grasping hand is to try to hold a moving force. Pain happens, it cannot be put aside yet who would embrace it?*

Rosalyn met me in Nettleden. I climbed in the front seat having deposited my pack in the car boot. She turned to look at me as I sat and buckled up, "How was it, James, I hope you're going to tell us all about it." I looked at her and took in the delight that shone from her. My breath caught, Wendy flashed, the silk and the sorrow, I heard that distant sound of myself. My eyes watered up.

"James, dear, what is it, you're..."

"I'm fine, Ros, I'm okay. It was hard to leave. Nothing a cup of tea wouldn't put right." "Well, if you're sure. You know what? We could stop on the way, there's a nice tea shop in Bourn-End. It might be fun."

I didn't know what to do. There were too many loose ends of life's tapestry flapping around in my head, Catherine, Kusalo, the first Noble truth, Malcolm, all braiding themselves into tangles of feeling, and holding them all together right now, Rosalyn, beautiful, peaceful, bright, real, and physical. I clasped my hands behind my head, bent back and looked straight ahead. "That would be good," I said. "Tea and toast, I haven't had a piece of toast for months."

As we sat in the near empty tea shop drinking tea and crunching toast, I had to keep diverting my eyes from Rosalyn; I felt my desire for her blazing like Silas's Lily.

> *Sitting by the door, sipping the sweet, cold wine, I looked at the Lily. Its strange, scarlet blossoms had just begun to uncurl in the July heat. Rare, exotic, strangely lovely, the Lily had blossomed there, untouched, for as long as I could remember...*
>
> *Silas drank, and as I watched him, I said, 'where did you get her in the first place?'*
>
> *He looked at the almost empty glass. 'I pinched her,' he said.*[5]

When we picked Amy and Joan up from school, they were so excited to see me I had to move into the back seat between them, blessed again by the innocence of children. They started to fire me with questions until Rosalyn turned her head and said, "Hang on girls, we all want to hear the adventure, let's wait until Daddy gets home, alright?" I was relieved, wondering how was I going to tell of an 'adventure' that was inside my head. Would anyone understand, especially the girls. I felt I wanted to share something with them all; they had been so kind and open with me.

Rosalyn said, "Well, anyway, you managed to keep your nice hair on."

Please don't say nice, I thought, as my heart jumped at her gentle flirtation. "Yes," I said, "It's not a simple hair cut in there, it's the whole way, so to speak."

"Do you think you could, you know, commit to living the single life?" "Not how I feel right now," I said. Rosalyn looked in the rear view mirror, our eyes met for an instant only, and there was the Lily.

---

5 My Uncle Silas by H. E. Bates.

Back at their plain, peaceful house I leveled out, the intenseness of feelings receding behind the business of getting into the house with the girls hanging on to each arm. I took my backpack up to 'my' room, as Amy loved to call it, and hung about there unpacking, a quite unnecessary task as I had hardly any clothes, but I sought time to reflect and, as one might say, come to my senses.

I was relieved on going downstairs to hear Richard's voice. I went through the hall into the kitchen where the whole family was gathered. It was a large kitchen, almost as large as the living room, with an oak table in the middle where we ate. The ceiling was low with beams crossing it. Richard was standing very straight, the top of his head just touching the beams. He was saying to the girls, "Look how I'm holding up the house with my head. I must be the head of the household." Amy and Joan giggle at his little joke, even as Amy said, "No you're not, Daddy, everyone knows its Mummy." Rosalyn was standing at the sink preparing vegetables, smiling.

"Oh, hi James," Richard turned to me, "So how was your sojourn up the hill. I see you kept your hair on."

"Yes, well, I'm not so sure I did, metaphorically speaking. I may have kept my appearance alright, but a place like that can change a fellow."

Amy said, "I think you're just the same Uncle James, isn't he Daddy?" To which Joan added, "Of course he is, he's only been up the hill, not to Africa or something."

"All right, darlings, can we leave James to settle in before we quiz him." It was Rosalyn, "Now, who's going to help me with the dinner?"

"Homework, Mummy," Amy said, over her disappearing shoulder.

"Joan, I expect you've got some to do too, right?" Richard said, "Off you go. Uncle James and I will help Mummy." Joan rushed over, gave me a hug and waltzed out of the kitchen, with a smile on her, the image of her mother's.

In the event, Rosalyn sent us both packing to the living room. A case of too-many-cooks, she said. On the way through the house Richard suggested we walk in the garden.

"The girls are very fond of you, you know, James. They came up with the Uncle tag, I hope you don't mind."

"No, not at all, it's a sort of refuge, just knowing you're all here right now." The evening breeze brought a sweet aroma to the air. I stopped walking in its midst and took a deep breath.

"I just wondered," Richard was saying, "I know your own family life is, well, under strain and, you know, I didn't want it to..."

"Force comparisons?" I said, "Don't worry, I'm not about to do that. It's just that I've been through this age with my children; they're all growing big now, getting independent. It's nice to remember, through Amy and Joan, how sweet that age is. No, the strain, as you put it, is between Catherine and myself."

"Have you been married long?"

"To Catherine, nine years, but my children are all from my first marriage." Richard's slow steady footfalls faltered, almost imperceptibly, but real enough for me to begin explanations that felt like excuses. "It was a hasty mistake, the first marriage. We were far too young, but Stella was on the way and I suppose I thought it the right thing to do."

"That must have been hard, marrying young with the responsibility of a baby right off."

The night had begun to move over the sky, the light was going; we turned back from the bottom of the long garden towards the house. I felt my incompetence beside this young man who had patterned his life with care, marrying at the right time, securing his family with forethought and planning. My life was a patchwork of threads woven in the wind, tangled and knotted with feelings and urges coming from I knew not where. It spoke the war that infected my nervous system, shaking with some unfathomed fear.

I said, "It was a challenge, but you know, when the baby came I found the delight in her impelled me to action. It took me just over two years to secure our first house. I was twenty-three."

"Good heavens, James, I was thirty and in a good job before I even thought of buying a house. What did you do?"

"I worked for a structural engineering consultancy. But when Stella was born I sought work abroad; I took my wife and baby with me to Holland. Allan, our second child, was born there. I could earn over twice my UK salary and save for a deposit." I began to feel a bit better, Richard was clearly impressed. But the knowing I held within wasn't moved by my heroic life actions, impressive or not; it still demanded answers to the unformed fear that questioned my life.

We had reached the back door of the house that opened to a small jumble-room off the kitchen. The smell of Rosalyn's cooking told us we were ready to eat. As we removed our shoes, Richard said, "I'd say that was potato pie if I'm not mistaken. Come on James, sustenance."

∽

When I was a boy, Sunday lunch was a strange affair. If I was around the house at all, I'd be in the kitchen with my mother, where she would show me how to cook. When I was small I'd climb on a chair and 'help', which usually amounted to stirring the cake mix, sending flour in all directions, prompting my mum to hold my hand and move it for me. It was these little moments of contact that I waited on. When older, I was usually at the sink peeling spuds and carrots and turnips, a lot of which I'd just pulled from our allotment garden in the back. By the time I was eight – that's just about the same as Amy and Joan – I could cook a pretty good Sunday lunch on my own.

Between my dad showing me how to grow food and my mum showing how to cook it, you could say I had a good upbringing. But they were out of love, and that made it entirely different.

When the lunch was close to being ready, my mum would send me to the pub to fetch dad. Dad didn't cook, not in those days. He worked, he dug, and sometimes he drank. On Sunday mornings he drank. Just past the Fallowfield farmhouse and the old oak tree was The Fallowfield, our local pub. I would approach the double swing doors of the public bar and open them slowly, like I did the church doors when I went exploring. Only I wasn't expecting to find ghosts or Jesus, just my dad hidden in the fog of cigarette smoke and the pungent aroma of fermented hops, ale and Guinness, and the voices of men putting the world to right, or betting on horses.

Eventually my head would be seen around the door and someone would shout, 'Ah Jimmy, your lad's here!' and my dad would turn his back to me, put some money on the counter, and call the barman. I'd let close the door and sit on the pub steps waiting.

"There you go, Laddie." It was my dad with lemonade and a packet of potato chips, "I'll be just a wee while. You all right then?" I would nod my head. He would ruffle my hair, as once again our hidden conspiracy of maleness let the dinner go cold. Of course Mum was mad at us both when we eventually showed up. She never believed I liked the lunch just as fine cold as hot. And my dad was too far gone to care either way. Only later did I know the hurt she kept hidden behind her mock anger. What choice did she have?

That evening, after the girls were in bed – insisting I read them the story of the Black Tulip – Richard mentioned my past skills, and asked me if I would be prepared to make a survey of their house.

"Do you need a survey, or is there something amiss with the house?" I asked.

"Well, as you probably know, it's very old, and while it looks alright, I reckon it's moving."

"Moving, as serious as that?" I said. "What have you noticed then?"

Rosalyn said, "A little dramatic there, dear, don't you think. The house makes sounds, you know, creaks and groans. But then don't all old houses do that, isn't that where they get their reputations for ghosts?"

there was this very old farmhouse

I said, "When I was growing up there was this very old farmhouse right next door to our apartments, built 1500 something, and still there as far as I know. Well, we kids used to run past it, sure that the old woman living there was a witch.

"Before I trained as a therapist, my last post in the industry was working for a local authority. One of the jobs I had was to go and check on old historical properties in the borough, and the old farmhouse was on my list.

"I was quite exited as I went out from the office that morning. It was a bit foreboding; I mean, that's a lot of age to have over your head. The old woman who let me in looked at me closely and then said, 'You. Well, I didn't expect... You'd better just go wherever you want, but mind the top floor. One death's enough,' and left me to it."

"That's all she said?" Richard asked, "Just 'mind the top floor. One death is enough.' And what did she mean, you! Did you know her?"

"Yes, that was all she said, then she went into the kitchen. No, I didn't know her, not straight away anyway. I wondered about the 'you' but I thought it was a reference to my job, you know, some people don't like the intrusion."

"So what happened? Do tell, James," Rosalyn pleaded, "Did you go to the top floor?"

"I had to. The top floor is where any survey has to start. If you think about it, you'll see one has to follow the weight down the building and see what is happening to it."

"Oh, James, we don't want a survey lesson. What did you find?"

"Ros, give the man a chance. I don't think I've ever seen you so keen on a piece of bad news. I suppose it was bad news, James. What did you find?"

"Well, it was a dark, windy attic floor. The loose roof tiles whistled and moaned in the blackness. The place was full of cobwebs." That got a shiver from Rosalyn. "Nearly all the floor boards – you could hardly call those rough planks boards, they had gaps between them you could put a child down." Now Richard was wide eyed and had become very still. "With my flashlight and trusty tape measure I scoured the whole floor, room to room. I found…"

In unison, Richard and Rosalyn spoke one word, "YES!"

"Nothing, nothing except cracks, slipped bricks, fallen tiles, and a load of rubbish."

"What, that's it?" Richard said, "What did the old woman say?"

"Ah, well, that was the thing. While I was working my way down the house doing the survey, I could hear two women's voices rising and falling as though in some sort of argument, but I couldn't make out any words and didn't think any more of it. I heard the front door shut and then the place was silent. But when I got down to the ground floor, the old woman was gone, and another younger woman came out of the back of the house and invited me into the kitchen for a cup of tea. Well, in a manor of speaking, I was already there, it being the last room on the ground floor. As we sat drinking I said nothing. She was looking at me with a sly twinkle in her eye. I kept looking at her, thinking there was something to be said but not sure who would say it.

Then she said, 'You remember, don't you?'

I said, 'I think so, but I was so much younger; things look different when you grow up.' She rose from her chair and said, 'Come with me.' I followed her out to the back of the house. The very last room on the back was a single stone-built place with a thatched roof still intact, though dusty and sagging with age. She opened the back door, and just outside on some flat stones there were two chairs. 'Now sit,' she commanded. 'And look down there,' she said, pointing down the long garden, walled in with factories on one side and a twelve foot thicket hedge on the other. At the very end of the garden was an old Nissen hut bomb shelter, but before that, two thirds of the way down the garden, was an oak tree beneath which was blooming a red and scarlet Lily, flaming and bright against the confines of the garden walls.

Then I remembered everything..."

∾

The clock on the mantle over the fireplace softly dinged its hour. "Good heavens," I said, "No wonder I'm feeling tired, I've got used to an eight-thirty, nine-o'clock bedtime, and here it is chiming eleven."

"Oh dear, but what did you remember?" It was Rosalyn pleading. I nearly continued, but I really was drained. "Can I tell you tomorrow, please, I'm pretty whacked out," I said.

"Only if you promise," Rosalyn said. "Cross your heart."

"And hope..." Our eyes met and this time held for a moment. "To tell," I said.

Richard stretched and readily agreed to go straight upstairs, "Work in the morning, 'night, sleep well, James." "Thanks, Richard, for everything," I said, "Goodnight."

Rosalyn followed Richard upstairs.

...Yes, I remembered alright.

It was one early summer's day when I was on my way home from high school.

The day had been very warm and still. In class, the wall that faced onto the playing fields had its windows open, I say windows, but really it was the whole wall above three feet. The 'window' was a set of concertina-like frames that could be rolled back against the side. So the air, the sound of bees, and occasional bird song, floated unhindered into the classroom. We sat in our rows, heads down, scratching a nib across workbooks.

I was overcome; there's no other explanation, overcome with a sense of ridiculousness. I lifted my head and listened to the silence. What was I doing? I should be out there. I opened my desk, put in my work and pen, and closed the lid very slowly and quietly. At the tiny squeak of the closing lid, Mr. Andrews, our teacher, raised his head from the book he was reading and looked straight at me. He said nothing. I smiled at him, stood up and flashed a look out the window. Moving as though walking on eggs, I started for the door. He just nodded his head and bent back to his book. The strange part of my exit was that nobody else seemed to even know it was going on. Not one other kid raised his head or stopped scratching pen on paper. It was like those scenes in a movie when everything stops while a couple dances down the street between people and cars frozen in time.

I got out into the field, laid under a tree with my hands behind my head and closed my eyes. I dreamed the strangest dream...

෧୬

I was standing in the back garden of our apartment building. The sun shone bright and hard into my eyes, yet across the grass I could see a spot of color blazing, red and scarlet. I put my hand over my eyes to shade them and better see what it was. I thought it a flower, but then I realized it was moving towards me. It was a flower and yet could not be. I watched, fascinated, as it became a young girl, small, and moving in an ungainly way. She tried to imitate my arms, which, I found, were open in invitation, but hers just flailed around her body like loose streamers left behind from a grand parade long gone, her legs seeming at any moment to fold up with the same streaming, flapping gait.

As she came closer, I became aware she was heading towards me with great intent. Now, I don't know if I was a man or boy in the dream, but I was much taller than her, and as we came together I gathered her up to me while thin delicate arms now tied themselves around my neck like a soft silk scarf; her legs held my body just above the waist. She buried her face into my cheek and I felt its roughness. She squeezed hold of me. My arms, holding her small frame, felt over-sized, too powerful. I made the touch light, not wanting to crush this precious gift.

The flood that overwhelmed us was love, love like nothing else I had known or could describe. It seeped deep into my being, soaking my bones, and making me weak with joy.

I thought my heart would burst. Then I held her gently away from me and looked into her face, beautiful to my eyes. It was round like the full moon. Small dark eyes squeezed their sight out from between the dough-like form of her cheeks and flattened nose. The girl's mouth, open like a lost O floating in the white flesh of her face, was surrounded by curled back red lips. Her hair, black and straight, lay flat against her large head, hiding small ears. She laughed and reached again for my neck. As I hugged her to me, a tear of joy forming in one eye was lost in the next wave of love. Tears poured from my eyes, diamonds that fell at our feet. The feeling was so intense I woke up.

Going home from school that day, I was a mixture of puzzlement, happiness, sorrow, and plain tired. I was dragging my school bag over my shoulder, thinking of all that had happened and not thinking at the same time, when suddenly the farmhouse door opened, just as I was about to pass it.

"Not running past today, then?" the woman standing there said. "Don't you think I'll get you, then?" I stood staring at her. For one thing, none of us had actually *seen* the witch before, and here she was. She was a thin woman, but she didn't have a hooked nose or warts, neither was she old like we all said. She was plain, or maybe not, about thirty or so, but not frightening. "Lost your tongue then, young man?"

I said, "Sorry, I mean, No, I mean, I was thinking."

"And what was it you were thinking so hard about, then, that you couldn't say hello?" She was backing away from the doorway and said, "Why don't you come in and tell me about the girl." I didn't know what to say. I just stared at her. She waited, then I said, "How did you... how..?"

"Are you coming in or aren't you? C'mon, lad, I want to close the door." Her softer tone eased my confusion and I stepped over the threshold. "Leave your bag there on the back of the door. Come with me." I followed her into the back of the house to the kitchen, but she carried on through saying, "We'll have some tea later, I've something to show you first." We went into the garden, overgrown with weeds and wild flowers that had gone to seed many times. It reached up to my shoulders as we walked down a rough stone path for about a hundred yards or so where an oak tree stood. Much the younger of the old oak out front, but with the same broad leaves like hands stretched out to touch. I said, "Beautiful," and touched the tree, turning to look at the woman. She was looking at me in a way my young brain could not comprehend, but I knew it was for something she saw. "Like that tree, don't you?" she said.

"Yes, it's still young and perfect," adding hastily, "I like old trees too." She said, "Oh, I know that; I've seen you grab the leaves out front on your way past." I was about to try and apologize when she cut me off, "You're a tree person, it's all right. I know you don't mean harm, just saying hello, I expect."

We just stood there for a while. I didn't know what to say and she said nothing. The traffic in the street was muffled back here, just a soft sea lapping a shore somewhere. The birds, sparrows mostly, chattered in the oak. The sun was still filling the enclosed garden with warmth. It all seemed very still. Then she said, "Tell me about the girl, the one in your dream. Come back to the house, we'll sit a while; you've got time, this is your mother's late night, right?" She looked at me for my reaction; she was not disappointed. Now I thought, 'perhaps she is a witch or a gypsy or something.'

"I'm not quite the witch you thought, then?" she said, as she invited me to take one of the two chairs outside the back of the house.

"I... No, no you're not, but how did you know? I mean about the dream?"

"I'll come to that; there's more to it than you know or perhaps ever will know." She sat down on the other chair. "I've got something I want to ask you. I know you can dig, and I know you're out early mornings often 'till dark on weekends. How would you care to come over here and dig me a garden?"

So many things were going around in my head, I hardly heard the question; it being so ordinary a thing to ask, but she was patient. She just watched me settle my thoughts for a while, then said, "Well?"

"Yes, okay, yes I think I'd like that. I think I could do that."

"Good," she said, "Wait here." She rose and went into the kitchen. I sat and surveyed what I had taken on. It was pretty thick with any number of grasses and wild plants. I thought, 'It will take forever.' She returned with a brown paper bag containing what looked like a potato. "The first thing I want you to do is plant this. I'll show you where. Take your jacket off; you'll find spade and fork just inside the door there," she said, pointing into the shadows of a shed built onto the back of the kitchen. Then off she strode down the path. I found the tools, shouldered them, and followed her. She stopped just short of the oak and handed me the bag. I dropped the spade and fork and took the bag from her. "Be careful with it, like you were with the girl." She looked straight into my eyes, and in a softened voice added, "Just like you were with my daughter."

Then she knelt down, pulled some grass out of a patch about two feet round. I went to help her, but she turned fast to me, "You hold her. Your turn will come." I waited until she stood and asked me to hand her the bag. "Now, you dig; make it deep, mind, two feet and plenty of room."

"Right," I said, "Deep." As I rolled my sleeves up and got started, she laid the packet under the oak and said she would be back for the planting. I dug and turned, as the evening crept in. The light turned soft and a breeze rustled the oak leaves. I finished and stood a while wondering what next. I looked at the bag sitting under the tree and remembered the woman calling it 'she' and something about her daughter. But I was well and truly tired now, and couldn't think clearly. Then she was there, with a wheelbarrow half full of what I recognized as compost. "We'll bury her in this. Put some in the hole will you?"

I did as asked, dropping a couple of spade fulls in the bottom and smoothing it out. She picked up the brown paper bag, reached in, and handed the contents to me.

I could see now it wasn't a potato, but a very large bulb, deep purple with brown stripes. "You do it, it's yours to do," she said. I was too tired to ask questions. I put the bulb in the hole as gently as I could. Then I stood and began to shovel the compost softly around it until it was entirely covered and the ground level.

It was dark now. We were two shadowy figures, a wheelbarrow, and a spade and fork standing against an oak tree. She put her hand on my bare forearm and said, "Thank you." She turned towards the house, "Leave the tools; c'mon, let's get some tea." I followed her, feeling strange yet not uncomfortable, confused yet all right.

...the feeling left in my arm... I knew it

I found I had a feeling inside me for the woman that I couldn't name, a feeling I had never known before, except... the feeling left in my arm. I couldn't quite find the words. I knew it... but where?

∽

I'd arrived at the Dawkin's on the Tuesday before Easter, thinking I'd stay a couple of days and make it back home for the weekend, but life had other plans. I phoned Catherine next day to be told that sure, come home, but the house would be empty. She had arranged to go away for a few days with a friend, and I was left in no doubt as to the nature of the friendship. I hadn't reckoned on things moving so fast.

As I held the receiver, taking in the certainty it conveyed, I didn't know what to say. Catherine was saying, "Hello, James, hello, are you there?"

"Yes, yes, I'm here, it's... just, well?"

"I thought we'd agreed. I thought when you agreed to go for a while... That was the whole point, wasn't it? To give each other some space? You know."

"Yes, yes, of course, you're right, that was the reasoning. I suppose I just... I don't know. I suppose... I thought maybe with time apart we..."

I felt weak, insubstantial. I found myself leaning against the hall wall and sliding to the floor. I knew there was nothing more to say, but I didn't want to put the phone down. I didn't want the finality.

From the now limp receiver in my hand, Catherine's voice sounded distant, "I'm truly sorry, James, but what can we do? It's been coming, and, well, it's just that Iris got a hold of this cottage for the weekend... I thought you might stay at the monastery, in your letter you sounded very positive. I was happy for you, James. James, are you there?"

"Oh, yes, yes I'm here. Yes, it's right, you should get away for a bit yourself, right. Iris is very nice. Look, I'd better go. I'll call next week some time, bye, Catherine, bye."

"Goodbye, James, take care; I still love you, you know."

"Yes, yes I know. I Lo... I do too; bye, goodbye."

Rosalyn found me sitting on the hall floor, "James, dear, I'm not going to ask if you're all right; you clearly are not. But I am going to the kitchen to make some tea. Why don't you join me; I'll need someone to help finish the pot."

We sat at the big table, utilizing just the one corner nearest the stove with the pot on it. Tea, for very different reasons, is nearly as good as a long walk for sorting one out. A warm cup is something to hold on to; it relaxes the mind and loosens the tongue. It was especially so when Rosalyn said, "Would you like to talk about it, James?"

I looked across at her, avoiding her eyes, but seeing her just the same. It eased things in a way having her, I mean a woman, to share something with. The cup she had given me was a large mug; I wasn't sure if that was to get plenty of tea in me or a consideration of my shaking hands; big mugs are easier to keep steady, you see. Anyway, I was feeling more contained now. I said, "Thanks for the tea; it helps, always does." She waited. "I, er, I don't know about the weekend, Easter. I was going home, leave you folks to celebrate or whatever Quakers do for Easter. I, er. What do Quakers do?"

"We sit, as always, only it's more intense, I suppose; I'm not sure. We don't go in for ceremony. Usually there's a little more discussion at this time." Then she said, "But that's not why we're sitting here. But if it's the weekend you're concerned about, you know you can stay. You don't have to go; use your room as much as you need."

"My room? I know Amy looks on it that way; I wasn't sure you and Richard had planned on an 'uncle' moving in."

"We hadn't, but it's alright. As it turns out, you're an easy person to live with, and, anyway," she said, looking away. "I expect you will form some plan and then be gone. Then we may never see you again." She swiftly put her cup to her mouth and drained it, "Have some more, James, we can't waste it; we'll have to empty the pot."

Her sudden action cut me off from protestation. I didn't want to think I would never see them, or Rosalyn, again. I gathered my thoughts as she poured, "If there is any plan to my life, I certainly don't hold the blueprints. When I was young I fantasized, what else can I call it, about getting married to *the one,* as my mother put it, the girl out there specially for me. We would live on a smallholding and have two beautiful children and... well, you get the idea. But life has a way of taking some of us by the neck from the start and tossing us on the wind."

Rosalyn just stared at me, her eyes watery, "I'm so sorry, James, I didn't mean, I mean I thought the monastery..."

"Sod the bloody monastery! I can't think about it right now. I mean, it's... I've just got too much to deal with. I need to walk." I started to rise, "Rosalyn, I had no right to speak like that, especially to you, you've all been so kind and..."

"Oh, James, stop it, stop with the kindness. You're not a charity case. Don't you think it's a thrill for us. We get something out of this too. It's not just the girls who look forward to your being here. Richard and I... it was getting..."

I picked up the tea pot and cups, trying to appear calm and practical. My heart was beating like a hummingbird. "Look, why don't we go for a good walk," I said, trying to keep the anticipation out of my voice. "The girls aren't due out of school for hours. It's a bit windy, but we could stand a good gale through us both."

With the same air of common sensibleness, Rosalyn said, "Yes, right, you're right. Let's go up on the downs." The phrase tickled both of us into a smile and Amy's giggle was on Rosalyn's lips.

> We were banging in hard a-carrying hay and I was on top o' the cart and could see her just over the wall. Not just one – scores, common as poppies. I nipped over the wall that night about twelve o'clock and ran straight into her.'
> 'Into the Lily?'
> 'Tah! Into a gal. See?[6]

A gale was up. The wind wrapped around us and pulled us hard along. I always thought 'scudding' perfectly descriptive of clouds running across a storm driven sky. Now I knew how scudding felt, for that is what our bodies would have looked like to a distant viewer. We had to shout to be heard. "I think we should find shelter, Ros," I said, "If this wind drops I fear we're in for a drenching."

---

6 My Uncle Silas by H.E. Bates.

"Oh, come on, James, this is so bracing. Let's get to the top there," she said, pointing to the crest of the field we were walking. "We can look back and see the village from there."

As she spoke she put her hand out, I took hold of it. "Okay," I said, feeling the excitement the wind had got up in us both. As we climbed, in silence now, against the rise and the wind, all my awareness was on the softness of her hand in mine. We got to the top. I pulled her the last yard up to me and wrapped my arms around her. The intimate space between us was filled with catching our breath. Even through the coats and jumpers we had on, I could feel the rise and fall of her body against mine. For a while the rhythm held us. She spoke, the words blowing around me almost inaudible in the high wind, "James, what's this; what's happening?"

"I'm not sure," I said, "but I'm not counting."

"Counting?"

"I'm not counting on anything, Ros. I mean, it's just what it is right now, holding together in the wind. Wouldn't you say?"

"James," she moved her head ever so slightly to one side. Our breath had settled.

The kiss defied the gale, but woke the dark greyness that slept in my gut. As we parted, tears swelled in my eyes. Rosalyn looked there and pulled me to her, placing a hand on the back of my neck. I cried until there was just emptiness, and peace.

May 16th
Buddhists have a phrase, part of their daily chanting: Beautiful in the beginning, beautiful in the middle, beautiful in the end. It voices the nature of truth; it is in fact the truth of nature. I think beauty is potentially within all of us, for we are a species of nature. We cannot, neither should we wish to, return to the trees or the cave. Let's face it, we're not going to turn back time.

When we live straightforwardly, we live courageously. For it is when we accept what comes along without faltering towards illusion that we experience life. If what comes is unpleasant by common measure of such, the beauty of it is hard to see. Most of us want to turn away from the unpleasant, to have it taken from us. We cleave to desires and spurn suffering. Yet, to be born is to risk the experience of suffering, which will not yield to reason, but only acceptance.

While Rosalyn went to fetch the girls from school, I busied myself with preparing vegetables for dinner. It didn't allow for too much thought.

I sank into the familiar movements of peeling potatoes and carrots, chopping onions and mixing herbs.

I had been preparing vegetables forever, it seemed. It's as good a way as any of preparing for life, for the expected and the unexpected; for who knows how it will turn out, each meal as unplanned as life, at least my life, without a recipe. It's a manner of living that some cannot stand, having to have a place for everything, and everything in its place. Well, I tried; it just was never going to be like that.

From the beginning, it could have been a tale told by a gypsy, or the curse of a witch, or just plain luck. But it was none of those things; it was the ways of man. It was a man's war and a woman's suffering that birthed me. It was 1942...

∾

...The amniotic fluid stroked every arriving nerve-ending in my skin; the warmth and wet encouraging growth. The movement that held me awoke my newly formed senses into the excitation of life. When my eyes formed, the light of life, a rose-pink hue, entered my being and said: "Come." Yet the invitation was marred.

The anger in her breast sent sudden waves of tightness through her body, barbed-wire pain that squeezed her womb and raised pressure. Through my skin, along the nerve pathways into the cerebral cortex, came the shock. While half-formed ears vibrated to the sounds of war.

The invitation, crushed and burnt, was more like a sentencing. I refused, turned my back, curled up, and remained.

After ten hours, I was pulled with force, exhausted, out of an exhausted mother. We were parted, 'to recover' it was said. It was a recovery that would take over half a century.

∾

Rosalyn returned with Amy and Joan, both of whom, smelling dinner, ran into the kitchen. "Uncle James," it was Joan, for once, who got in the first word, "What *are* you cooking? It smells delicious."

"Super, what have you made?" Amy asked, as she wrapped her arms around my waist.

Rosalyn followed the girls in, "Come on, you two, I'm sure you have homework to do, upstairs with you."

"Oh, but Mummy, it smells so yummy, it's making my tummy grumble," said Amy, hanging on to my arm now. "Couldn't we just have a taste?"

I started to say something – about it getting better if she waited, but I was cut off by Rosalyn with a harshness I'd not seen in her before. "Amy! Let go of James and go upstairs. Please do it now." Joan, having got the message telegraphed by Rosalyn's mood, had already disappeared. Amy released her hold on my arm, imperceptibly stomped her foot, and ran out of the kitchen.

As we stood across the big oak table, Rosalyn let drop the tightness in her body and almost fell into a chair at the table. I turned and picked up the kettle, filled it at the kitchen tap, and placed it on the stove, took the matches from the window shelf, turned back to the stove and lit it. I took two mugs from the high cupboard over the preparation counter, and from the back of the counter picked up the tea caddy, a square tin with Chinese pictures around its sides and a gold dragon embossed in the lid, opened it and put two teaspoons full of tea in the large brown teapot.

As the kettle began its soft, familiar, wind-through-a-hole sound, I turned, pulled a chair out on my side of the table and sat opposite Rosalyn.

"You didn't warm the pot," she said, "The tea will be tepid."

"Well," I said, "A little cooler brew may be a good idea just now."

Her eyes shot to mine, not hard, but guarded, opaque, holding in her light. "James, I... I don't know what to think. You're confusing me; I mean, your being here is confusing me. You're cooking, you're fitting in too well. I don't..."

"That's easily remedied," I said, "Tomorrow I'll go. It's not as if I have nowhere *to* go. I still have a home, a hearth, and two dogs that will be glad to see me. So you see..."

"Oh, stop it, James. Stop being so bloody okay. You forget, it was you who cried."

"I'd hardly forget."

"Oh, I'm sorry, I'm sorry, James, that was horrid of me. I don't pretend to know how it is for you, with your wife and all. And, well, it seems deeper than that. I've never felt anyone cry so deeply as that. I was a little frightened for you."

I stood up. "How about that tepid tea, then?" I said, turning to the fridge for milk. "This should really keep things cooled down," I said, holding up the bottle.

"Alright, alright, you're right. I'm judging and assuming things I know nothing about. But you did kiss me – and it was the sweetest kiss. There was happiness there; I know that, even if it left us in confusion."

I handed a full mug across the table and sat down with mine. "Yes, there was happiness; more than that, there was a completeness, especially out there with wind and trees moving us. It was a moment of completeness."

"So, the tears, James, the sadness? It was so... so deep."

Her question was unanswerable. Usually people don't ask; it's the fear, I suppose, a fear that the answer will speak of them, reveal what should remain hidden, for that is what is in me when it arises. Bidden by, I was about to say love, but, no, something greater than that: tenderness, kindness, a wisdom born of perception.

I remained in the hospital, swaddled tight, like a parcel not meant to be opened, weak and unmoving for six weeks. If there was thought, and later indications are that it was so, they were of suffering and only suffering. I did not know it then, but that first affliction, aided by subsequent events, would impel me on a journey that would end walking between trees.

THREE

The dogs, Tess and Bryn, were, of course, pleased to see me. I had raised them from puppies; we knew each other intimately and easily, just as my marriage to Catherine had been. I awoke Good Friday morning early, and lay feeling the two of them beside me in the big bed.

It's funny how animals know. I didn't move – not withstanding the little tremors that always woke with me – didn't open my eyes, yet within a second, tongues are licking my face clean for the morning walk. "Hey! C'mon girls, can't a chap get some breakfast around here first." I would not discount the dogs, but I was alone.

I reflected on how certain times of the calendar are set aside for the lonely: Separating hours into minutes, minutes into seconds. Separating weeks into days, years into weeks, separating life into unfitting parts, un-fitting people, making strangers of ourselves, and strangers with nature. Easter was one of those times.

But it wasn't loneliness I had to deal with, it was the knowing of finality between Catherine and me. I looked out of the kitchen window, not seeing beyond the glass, a mirror of memories reaching back to our first meeting, to an instant knowing we were going to be together. And, as rapidly as the kettle took to boil, I had seen them all. Now they were past, and balanced by a morning cup of tea, drank alone. After, I took the dogs for a long walk.

In amongst the conifers, deciduous maples, and occasional oak, we ran. Ferns, chickweed, crabby ancient crab-grass grab at our ankles. Late snow-drops and early bluebells waved in the moving air as we passed. I jumped puddles left by the night's rain and missed most, getting a soak-ing the girl's loved. At each stop for breath they were excitedly around my legs, sniffing and urging more running. Coming out of the woods and reaching the car, we were a bedraggled breathless fusion of dogs and man, the stamp of evolution hardly visible between one and the other. 'I' did not exist. For a timeless passage of being, there was just animals and nature, and even those could not be separated. I sat in the car listening to the dogs panting, and hearing my own breath as it slowed, and separate-ness arose. I closed the car door, turned on the ignition, and accepted the protection we have constructed so well to keep us safe from nature.

May 18TH
It is not easy to own up, is it? Truth is a light we learn early on in life to put a shade over. In fact, we are handed down a shade, parent

to child, generation to generation, from deep in our past. It's part of our enculturation into the species. It may be that we cannot deal with bright lights, that this inquiry is asking too much of us, that we have lived in the half light for so long that the ultimate truth will be unbearable to us. When I try to bring this inquiry to my friends' attention, I notice they divert the conversation to safer ground.

By the time Catherine returned after Easter, my backpack was ready against the hall wall. She arrived late in the evening of Easter Monday, flushed and tired, like one gets after open air physical work. The dogs were all over her in the living room. "Tea?" I said.

"Tea would be lovely. Tess! Get down, dear, sit now, sit. Yes, tea would be great."

The kitchen was tiny compared to the Dawkin's place, just a small scullery off the living room. I called from the stove, "I've made a nut roast and some veggies, okay?"

"Oh, James, that's... you didn't have to... thanks. I thought... How are you?"

"I'll bring the tea first; you look as though you've been energetic. I'm okay." I carried two mugs of tea in and sat opposite Catherine by the wood-stove, "Bit chilly out; I stacked the fire a bit." I put the mugs on the stove top.

"Thanks," she said taking her mug, "I wasn't sure you'd be here, thought you might have stayed with those people you phoned from."

"Richard and Rosalyn, Dawkin and two sweet daughters. No, it being Easter, I wanted to leave them to their own; they're Quakers."

"Oh. No relation to the biologist then, you know, Richard Dawkins, Oxford. He's an atheist isn't he?"

"I believe so; no, no relation. So, where was this cottage then? How was it, Catherine, okay or better than okay?"

"James, please, you don't really want to know... It was in the Lake District. It..."

"You're right, of course, I don't really want to know. What I really want to know is why, how? I mean, what happened? It was after Greenham all this started! We were fine until you decided to join the women-only gang."

"We were not fine, as you put it. *It* was never fine and you know it. It was never fine for you either. It was adequate, it kept us sane, that was all."

"But everything else was more than fine, Catherine. We were a match, we could have worked that side out."

"We've had years to work it out. It's never going to work. We're not the same flesh, we don't move in the same orbit, we're..."

"Alright, alright, please don't spell it out." We both fell into silence, deep, painful, without a boundary to hold us. Our eyes met. We reached out our hands and pulled down onto the rug in front of the stove. The softness of her long hair folded over my face, her smell filled my senses, her body easy against mine moving to a place of comfort. We just lay holding each other. I said, "I know what you say is right. Just tell me it was good for you with Iris."

"Oh, James."

"I need to know; it will make letting you go possible. I love you, Catherine; I want you to be happy. Will that be so with Iris?"

With her head turned into my neck I hardly caught her reply, "Yes, it was good. I think I will be happy." That night we loved each other and held each other for the last time.

The next morning I moved around quietly; it was six-o-clock. I closed the door behind me while the house slept on. I was on the road again.

May 19th

An end comes to everything, as the Buddhists put it. All that comes together, parts; all that arises, ceases; nothing born continues forever. For plants and creatures that have no means of reflection, the end arrives quite naturally as a part of life. But for us humans, who seek answers in life, endings pose a paradox. The very fact of our birth invites, so to speak, our demise. While parents are busily engaged in the arms of procreation, that they are inviting the death of their offspring never occurs to them, for nature has fashioned it so. There are reasons why we may decide not to give birth, but the inevitable death of our children is not one of them. So it is that we have separated birth and death. What is it we fear? Is it death? – or could it be life?

&c.

1970, I was twenty-eight. That summer was cool, not like my own childhood. The sun shone out of a paler sky than I had known as a boy, and occasional rains splashed the dust into a Jackson Pollack painting of browns and of greys in the back yard. It was Sunday. Nothing special was planned, yet all our plans would go wrong that Sunday.

55

My eldest, Stella, had just returned from walking the pram with Malcolm, our new baby, just three month old. She left the pram in the front of the house, told her mother and me, and went off to play. She was seven years old. The baby was asleep. I didn't know where the other two were, the boys, Allan and Noel. It was Sunday; Sunday had no rules, just have fun. Tomorrow the gears turn, and we all fall into the machinery of school and work.

There never was a 'must do' on Sundays, sometimes there was an occasional 'shall we' or 'do you fancy', not exactly plans – that could be spoiled – just something to do with the children. That Sunday was free, open for anything. But not that, no. No one is ever ready for that.

After Sunday lunch, the rains dried up and the sun had become friendly like you wanted to go out. It was a shall-we sort of decision, to go for a stroll with the children. That meant finding the children. Stella was easy; she'll be with her best friend across the way. I'd have to resort to calling, shouting, really, to find the boys. Meantime, while I set to searching, Malcolm will need changing. His mother went out front to the pram.

You can't forget a thing like that.

The sounds and shapes and colors fix on the canvas of your mind. The scream came first, then his mother running through the house, the tiny body stiff and cold was thrust into my hands as she ran past and out the French windows. Then utter silence as she fled the house.

The questions don't come straight away, only after, on reflection. But there's nothing to reflect on, it's too final. There's nothing to grasp hold of. The empty space is like a thing, yet there is no thing. Sounds of voices are echoes bouncing off the harsh canvas of a Sunday afternoon, when nothing happens and there are no plans to upset. That canvas? Oh it's here somewhere. The colors are a bit faded. *I'm told it's worth quite a bit in the market place of experience, but then you'd have to know your canvases to judge that.*

∽

I didn't go far that first day out of what had been home for just over ten years. I took a long-distance bus north to the next city, to stay with a friend. Paul and I had met up during the days of active peace demonstrations in the '70s. Our roots were very different, but we had arrived at a common view of life. I started out a working-class communist. Paul came from a middle-class artistic family and had embraced anarchism at art college. We discussed Trotsky, Kropotkin and the whole gang of what we saw as exciting revolutionaries trying to bring in a better world. As we

56

grew older and together, maturity taught us the subtlety of debate over youthful action. But as we watched the French change things from street level, we wondered why we, as a people, were so frightened to say what we wanted and thought. But that summer, Indriya, Buddhism, and subtlety would take a back seat. There were plans afoot to disrupt the city of London's financial district.

As I knocked on his door I wasn't sure what sort of reception I would get. I was sure he'd heard about my time in the world of monasticism. I wondered how a convinced atheist would take it.

"James, come in, brother," he said, embracing me and kissing both cheeks French style, as he always had. "It's been a while. Drop your pack and take a seat. I heard you were 'monkying' now. What brings you here?"

"Well, I never quite got to the haircut bit. I just stayed a while, while Catherine and I worked out things. Which we have done, so... we're not together."

"Oh, right," he put his hand on my shoulder, "So, are you out? You looking for a place?"

"Well, yes and no. She's okay with me staying, but I thought, 'If I stay, what chance does her new relationship have?' If it's what she wants, it will have a better chance without me hanging around."

"But... you two got on so well. How did it..."

"It's just life, Paul. You know that. How many times have we said marriage is just a capitalist device, nothing to do with real comradeship?"

"Yes, a device of greed, but I thought you and Catherine were beyond that; I'm not even sure I know you're married. But you had better than that."

"Well, that's true, and maybe that will survive, but her lovers from here on are of a different gender, and there's not much I can do about that."

"Oh, right, right." He stood, "How about tea, or would something stronger..."

"Make the tea; I'll put the whiskey in myself. I'll sit in the kitchen." I like kitchens, always did.

⁂

When I was eight years old we got a television. It changed *everything*.

For my parents it meant a referee had come into the house, something they both had to pay attention and listen to, something not to be argued with. In fact, something dead that would render them dead. I reacted. I'd lost my parents. I grew to detest TV.

Our apartment consisted of a medium living room, medium bedroom, a very small bedroom, mine, and a small kitchen off a small hall. It was not cat swinging space. I chose the kitchen because it was furthest from the sound of the TV, and I could eat while doing homework. But many nights I didn't have homework. In the winter when cold and raining I would put on the stove, maybe bake a potato or two, and sit in the kitchen. Now, you may think this a strange thing for an eight year old going-on-nine to do, but I felt a lot better doing it than sitting glaring into a flickering screen with two other human beings and no one talking. Now, *that* I thought a strange thing for anyone to do. Sometimes I still think it so.

∽

On the way to the workshop, Paul was saying, "You'll like her, I guarantee it. She's intelligent."

"Oh, right! Intelligence is just what I need right now."

"She's more than intelligent, I mean she's. Just wait, trust me." We reached the workshop and Paul started through to the back. "She's a bit hidden away," he said beckoning me to follow, "Back here."

As we reached the office, behind the half dismantled motorbikes I could see her. She was sitting behind a counter that was covered in papers and small stacks of files, drinking a hot cup of something that smelt like cocoa or chocolate. "Hi Paul," she said, "how's things?" Her eyes were looking over the cup at me. Paul went around the counter, and in his usual effusive way, gave her a kiss on each cheek. Releasing her, he said, "This is an old friend, James. James, Kate." She offered her hand over the counter. I took it in my right hand and covered it with my left. It was slightly rougher than Rosalyn's, smoother than Catherine's. She works hard, I thought, doesn't garden though. "Hi, Kate, good to meet you. Is this your hiding place?"

"Kind of," she said. "A retreat, well, it would be nice if it was, but I just work here."

Paul said, "Yes, but nobody bothers you, and the boss, I mean, does he ever come round? I thought he was always busy biking. You pretty much have the office to yourself, right?"

"Something like that. So, James, what brings you here?"

Paul had diplomatically disappeared into the workshop. She leaned with her forearms on the counter. Her blouse was not low, not high either, of white silk that had been carefully ironed. Her skin was a slightly darker shade of white, more cream and still smooth. I reckoned her age perhaps a little older than mine, all together attractive. I could see she was, as Paul had said, intelligent. Seductive only if you were seeking seduction.

"Well, you might say I'm on a sort of sabbatical, between this and that. So I thought I would look Paul up." Her intelligence, her intuition, or just plain being a woman computed the situation faster than I could think up excuses.

"So you're on your own," she said in a voice decisive but friendly. "You staying at Paul's place?"

"For the meantime, yes, till I decide what next."

"Well, I hope you like bikes." She came around the counter carrying a handful of files and put them on an empty low shelf near the desk. Seeing all of her moving slow and relaxed was like hearing a secret being told in whispers. It sent a conspiratorial answer through my brain.

"I love bikes... I'm a bike lover." 'Who the hell said that! I *never* talk like that, get a grip, James.'

Paul had appeared back at the counter with a box, "I'll take this, Kate, can you bill me, okay? I'll leave the tag on the counter. Come on, old boy, let's get going. Terrie will be back with the kids soon. Thanks, Kate."

"Okay, Paul, see you." She turned to me, "Well then, I expect you'll be back soon then." She had laid all the files on the shelf. She held out her hand and I took it in mine. Its feel had changed; it was charged. She squeezed a little. "Bye."

"Bye, Kate," I said, "See you again."

May 26th

I wonder, what do we know of love? For it has been prostituted in the service of so much distraction, even of hate. What do we know of the heart, that has been lionized in trivia and trivialized in what is meaningful. Out of such falsity has poured so many words. I'm still hopeful that one thread is surely true and in the silence it may just be found, by the still waters, under the blossoming tree, in the long grass, in the earth, even in sickness and death, perhaps walking between trees. I know to find it requires strength, patience, digging, recognizing and embracing such that it finally embraces us.

She rarely left her den, she said, even for her breaks, which she was free to take as she wished. So it was with some sense of anticipation that I picked her up as agreed, to take her for lunch. When I arrived, she met me with a small backpack in her hand. "Hi, James, hold on to this," she said, handing me the pack and going back, saying over her shoulder, "I'll get my scarf; it's a bit breezy don't you think?"

"Yes, but we'll be inside..."

She was out the door and saying, "I thought a walk in the park, it's only a street away. I've made sandwiches and coffee, okay?" She took the pack and shouldered it and started walking.

"Sure," I said, "sure, why not, you must get a bit claustrophobic shut in there all day."

"Oh no, I love it. I don't know what I'd do without this job. It's my little empire, my den, from which I command my life."

I was feeling a bit overwhelmed, out of my depth. I had watched Catherine change from a quiet, devoted wife to a feminist, to a strong, independent lesbian. Kate was no lesbian, but had the same air of self-determination, like no one was going to tell her what to do, even where to go on a date. If that's what it was; I thought it was, now I wasn't so sure.

She took my hand, that was something at least, talking in sound bites as we made our way through the lunch-time crowd and entered Gladstone park through its ornate gates. "Shall we sit by the pond, then if the sandwiches aren't suitable, we can feed them to the ducks?"

"Okay," I said, "but I'm sure they will be fine."

"How do you know?" she said, "You're just being polite. I might make rubbish sandwiches, better wait and see."

"I was brought up to eat whatever I was given, so I can't claim politeness, only habit. The fact is I'll eat almost anything."

We arrived at the pond to find the place populated with lunch-timers. Kate went on, stepping among them, and turned and called, "James, over here." I followed her, around couples and occasional loners, and we sat. While she opened her bag and started taking out packages, a flask and cups, I looked over the pond. The trees on the other side, closed off to the public, were new plantings, saplings of oak, as though the city council had agreed to put back Sherwood, which in its day would have been covering where we sat.

I thought of the trees I had so recently helped to plant at Indriya. My mind was running over my time there and at the Dawkin's home. "Penny for your thoughts," Kate's soft voice eased me back to the patch we sat on.

I was a little taken back by the softness. "Oh, er, thoughts, you know, just stuff, just thinking."

"Who is she, or was she? You don't have to say, James, only if you want to. I mean, it's really none of my business," she said, looking, or trying to look into my eyes that were studiously avoiding contact. Too much sympathetic talk always brought up the problem of longing, a longing that had nothing to do with the present and everything to do with the past. I didn't want us to get off on *that* kind of footing.

I took a breath, and damn-it I counted, and said, "She was, is, my wife. We've parted, for good. So... I was just closing a few loop-holes, sewing up loose ends. I'm fine. Let's see if those sandwiches really are rubbish."

It turned out to be a communion of sorts; it wasn't wafers and wine, but cheese and salad sandwiches and coffee. If there was a deity about to be appealed to, it was nature, the nature of attraction. Our bodies were taking over, as has been the way for millions of years, beyond time and culture, even personal preferences. By the time the coffee had been drained, we were in each others arms and making hasty plans for the evening.

Kate's freedom had let loose something in me. I had never been this free with Catherine, or anyone else. It was liberating; in the midst of losing myself, I remembered...

❧

...I was seventeen. I took that job, digging the garden behind the old farmhouse. I would go there weekends, dig for a while, and then the woman would come out with tea. That summer I left high school and had a job coming up in September. I thought I'd take my last long summer before heading for the grindstone. I began to go there on weekdays. It was peaceful, a piece of old English countryside right amidst the hustle of London. It was like some Alice's rabbit hole or a tale of magic. I was drawn to the place. I found myself liking the woman, especially when, at the end of a day working, she would lay her hand on my forearm and say quietly, "Thank you, James." I'd think, 'What is that?'

She began to invade my thoughts and feelings. One afternoon in early July she came into the garden, only she hadn't brought tea, but a bottle and two glasses. The heat had set up a haze, and beads of sweat were running into my eyes; I looked up, surprised to see her, shimmering in the sun by the back door. She called down the garden, "James, why don't you call it a day, come and have something cool."

I wiped my eyes and face with the loose sleeve of my shirt, rolled it back up, and shouldered the spade and fork. As I walked towards her, she sat, and from the bottle, already opened, poured what I could see was bright, clear yellow wine. As I got near her she said, "My, you look... you look as though you've earned this. Sit down, dear." She tapped the seat beside her.

I found myself staring at her as I sat. She didn't seem to mind, though she lowered her eyes from my stare and gently slid the glass over to me. I said, "Thanks, thank you, missus Baker."

"James," she said in a voice quiet yet quite clear, "isn't it about time you called me by my first name. In fact, it's about time you remembered my first name." She looked up at me, "Though I suppose I can forgive you that, after all you were only four years old."

I looked at her, a half empty glass in my hand and a mild dizziness beginning in my head. Our eyes met, and I tried to keep my breath from catching as it suddenly stopped in my chest. "I was four?" I managed to stutter, "But that would be... I must have been... around the corner, where the grocery store is now." I swallowed the rest of the wine.

"Yes," she said, "Why don't you call me 'Wendy', now you remember?" She poured a refill into my glass and topped up her own, put down the bottle, and raised her glass. "This deserves a toast, wouldn't you say."

I followed her glass with mine and we clinked. But the wine and the work combined rendered a force to my hand that broke my glass, the wine spilling and mixing with blood from somewhere out of my hand. "Oh, my dear, Oh, dear James, put that down, come on in the kitchen." She took my arm and I followed obediently, as if we were back at the nursery.

In the shade and cool of the kitchen she held my hand under a running tap. Her other hand was around my back and resting on my shoulder. I leaned back from the splashing tap and felt her body behind me down the length of my spine. She turned off the water. Her two arms were circling me. We stood very still, as if to move would break a spell. I could feel her breath on my neck, her hair against mine. I turned in her encirclement and held her waist "Wendy..."

"Ssshh," she put her finger to my lips and then laid her hand on my cheek.

I thought, 'Don't stop, don't ever stop.'

"What are you doing here?" she says. "I lost something," I says. "It's all right you know me." And then she wanted to know what I'd lost, and

I felt as if I didn't care what happened and I said, "Lost my head, I reckon." And she laughed... and said "What did you come for anyway?"

    "I came for the Lily... it's right," I says. And she just stared at me. "And you know what they do to people who steal?" she says.

    "Well?" I said to Silas. "What happened?"

He did not speak. Finally he turned and told me in a voice at once dreamy, devilish, innocent, mysterious and triumphant. "She gave me the Lily," he said.[7]

಄

On the day of the London demonstration, Kate was not with us. She said she loved us, but thought we were on a fool's errand and was glad she had to work, so it was just Paul and me on his Triumph.

    On the motorway, a great deal of communal horn blowing and banner waving told us it was going to be a big turnout. I wondered if I would see Catherine, but it was Rosalyn I saw some three hours later, while being crushed into Portland Square by a phalanx of policemen. I had to shout to be heard above the chanting and singing that at least witnessed that every one, or most, were carrying through a peaceable protest.

    "Rosalyn, Rosalyn, over here, hi!" While her head was turning to find the source of her name, Paul's curiosity had been aroused. "Who's Rosalyn, you dark horse?" he said as he was being crushed against my back. "Does Kate know about this?"

    "Kate's her own woman; I don't think she would give a tinker's cuss. Besides, Rosalyn is a friend; that's as far as it goes." Then Rosalyn was beside us. I wasn't sure if she'd heard my description of her or my talk of Kate.

    An hour later I was sitting with Rosalyn in the Queen's Head, a pub off the Euston Road. Somehow I had got separated from Paul and the others; I think it was an accident amidst the confusion, but I couldn't swear to that. I was mellowed out with three pints in me, finishing the story of the old farmhouse I had surveyed; the telling curtailed by Catherine's Easter plans that sent me up a distant hill with Rosalyn. Now here we were again. Mellow or drunk, I had enough savvy to end the story at my 'obligingly' digging the 'old' lady's garden when I was seventeen. That was sufficient to explain how she knew me. I didn't want to go into the biblical form of knowing that ended my boyhood.

---

7 My Uncle Silas by H.E. Bates.

Rosalyn was interested, even attentive, as the evening turned to dusk outside, and the pub took on that particularly relaxed feeling of an English lounge bar. When I finished, she said, "Wasn't there something, the woman, when you first got to the house, something about a death. What was that?" The soft, deep-red, felt- covered seat cushions accepted our bodies as though we were settled for the night.

I said, "A death?"

"Yes, you remember, she said something like, 'mind how you go, one death is enough' something about the top floor."

"Oh, yes, yes that. I remember." I looked up, recalling how reluctant Wendy had been to tell me.

The pub lights, low and yellow, threw their soft light on a ceiling that had grown brown with cigarette and cigar smoke exhaled in more liberal times. Wendy had told me to forget it, 'just old, past fortune.' I suppose it was impossible for her to hold such a secret when we had been drawn together in such an intimate way.

"Well?" It was Rosalyn, "James, do you always slow to a stop when you've been drinking?"

"Slow? Sorry, I was just getting the story straight. Shall we have another drink then...?"

"I don't want to preach, James, but maybe we've had enough. We do have to make our way soon, Richard will wonder."

"Oh, right, yes, you're right. Why don't we make a move and I'll tell you as we go. I'm famished; look, there's an all night café not far from here on the way to the underground." I rose and picked up my coat. I must admit I was reluctant to end the little intimacy that our corner of the pub afforded us. "Come on, Ros." She rose picking up her coat, putting it on as we left the pub.

Out on the pavement I took her hand. The night air thinned the fog in my system; I found myself feeling light and careless. "Give us a kiss, Ros, I promise I won't cry."

Smiling, she said, "James, you're drunk."

"Madam, in the morning I'll be sober but you shall still be beautiful."

"What are you talking about, James?" She linked her arm through mine and started to bounce a little in her step.

"It's an old quote from Churchill, but I improved on it, the old cynic." The crowds we weaved through, the city, the lights, and the drinks were drawing us into their magic – later to be referred to as illusion. But right now we were plain happy. The story of a death happily left in the pub.

May 30th

I think it is given to us to know this great and agreeable beauty that is life; even yet most of us have to be reminded of its beauty. For most of our kind, life is lived in a cage of our own making, the ego. On the occasion when James found himself, it was not a self of the ego, or a self we would recognize. It begins with the flowering of the Cherry Blossom tree, a connection that brings him in touch with something inside himself, beyond his known senses; his sensing of the tree reaching out to touch and remove the confining walls surrounding it echo his confines in the womb and during his sickness. He knows about confinement and life's desire to go beyond itself.

It is this reaching beyond itself that overcomes the blanket of death. It is in searching out that which is greater than Self that we find what lies beyond a single life, a single moment, the separated dislocation that fear engenders. His description of the poplar trees lifting skyward indicates that what he sees is that somewhere, in some way, there is a joy to living. He wants that joy. In our silent searching moments, free from distractions, we all seek that joy of living. Living with equanimity in the face of whatever arises, such that amidst the shadows and fog we experience the brightness that is Life itself, and beyond itself.

As we sat eating in the small café, sobered now by the activity and night air, I remarked to Rosalyn, "You seem particularly happy this evening, Ros. Anything you want to share?"

"I am happy, a bit more than that. I can't remember just being out, wandering around just for nothing, just for the doing of it. My life has always seemed to have been so ordered, reasoned, known, I suppose I'm saying."

"And this, this evening is unknown, free?" I said, "Open to anything – only, not quite, I think."

"What do you mean 'not quite', don't be a spoiler, James." She wrapped her hands around her tea mug and took a sip. "You'll not get that kiss like that."

I looked into her eyes. "I'd pretty much given up on that. I think it blew away with the walk," I said, "besides it was wrong of me to ask, I was overstepping our friendship, and Richard's."

"Maybe you should let me be the judge of that." She looked straight at me over her mug; her brown eyes, slightly hazed over with steam from the tea, were not flinching from mine.

"So, you and Richard, it's not quite as smooth..."

"It's fine, James. Richard's a good man, reliable, honest..." Rosalyn hesitated and lowered her eyes, "He's never given me any cause... I've known Richard since we were at school; he's the only man I've... Well. We're not all gadabouts, James."

"No, of course... Richard's, as you say, a good man. I like him a lot, did from first meeting. You have a wonderful family, Rosalyn; I didn't mean to imply anything. I just thought you may like to talk. After all you've taken an ear battering from my life, and..."

"Thank you, James. But, well, we Quakers don't talk a lot, gossip, if you know what I mean."

"I appreciate that, Ros, but sometimes it's healthy to talk. Heavens, I make my living listening to people talk. It's not gossip if it's urgent, pressing..." I stopped chattering on, remembering that silence is the space where truth sometimes rests.

"It's boring, I'm boring, we're boring. It feels like I'm missing something; I can't describe it but, well, when you kissed me I felt different."

"Don't confuse different with better, Ros."

"I'm not; it's just that different was exciting, something that has never happened before, like being here, out in London, just hanging around. That's different, exciting. And then there's, well, you know."

"Sex?"

"Yes. I have nothing to compare it with but it feels, it feels... Tell me, James, what is it really supposed to be like?"

"Rosalyn, I can't tell you that. There's no definitive what it is supposed to be. It's what it is, for all of us. We're animals at the level of such behavior, yet we're animals that think, judge, blame ourselves and others. All these things get in the way of just procreating the species, which, after all, is the root of this stuff."

"Put like that it sounds positively alien."

"It's only alien to our cultural sensitivities, our idea that everything should be tidy and have a place. That's why people so often only make love, or have sex, in bed, under the covers at night, usually Saturday night. We subjugate our animal desires to our cultural imperatives."

"But wouldn't the alternative be a kind of debouched chaos?"

"It doesn't have to go that far, Ros. It's just a matter of allowing a bit of room for freedom, for the animal to roam occasionally." I stood up and buttoned my coat. "Look, we'd better go; time's catching us Ros. Last trains and all that."

"Right," she said rising, "I suppose you're right. God, look at the time. We'll have to run."

"We have time. If we go now we can get to Euston in about ten minutes. We're okay. Come on." I took Rosalyn's hand and we went out onto the pavement and made our way, both of us thinking, I suspected, of something we should let go of.

When we reached the station, I realized there was no way I was going to get up to Paul's. I searched the departures board, which was sparse and contained mostly night trains to the far north, the last local north having left half an hour ago. Thankfully, there was a stop-all-the-way train to Birmingham that Rosalyn could catch, though she would have a bit of a walk the other end. I said, "Will Richard pick you up if you call?"

"I'm not sure I want to call this late." I looked at the station clock. Eleven fifteen.

I said, "I don't like the idea of you walking that late. The train won't be in till after midnight."

She faced me and said, "You're a sweet, James. I'll be alright. It's the country."

I wrapped my arms about her, "Country or not, I don't feel good about this. If we hadn't met, you'd be home tucked up in bed long ago."

"And I'd have missed a wonderful evening. Look, if you're really worried, why don't you come with me? You still have a room, you know."

"I don't know, Ros, it's..."

"The girls will be thrilled to see you. Oh, come on. What else are you going to do? Your trains are all gone." She took my hand, "I'm not taking a 'no'. Come on. It's the obvious solution for both of us." I wasn't sure what I thought of the 'both of us'. And she seemed to have suddenly become very animated and enthusiastic. But it was true, I had little choice when I thought about it.

"Okay, let's go." I sought the departures again. "Platform three, come on. We can pay at the other end." It was an old trick, of course the station at Colville would be closed.

The walk from Colville to the village was lit by a near full moon. It was bright but, as full moons will be, it was cold. We walked wrapped around each other. When we got to the house, it was, of course, in darkness. Rosalyn found her key and we entered like a couple intent on robbery, creeping around without speaking. Making signals with our hands, we settled in the kitchen. For all the tiredness in us, we were having a hard time saying goodnight and going to bed. Rosalyn's conspiratorial whisper suggested hot cocoa. I said, "Alright, but are we ever going to bed tonight?"

As she prepared the drinks, Rosalyn looked over her shoulder at me, a look whose wisdom came not from the paucity of her experience, but some deep primitive well of womanhood, the same well Kate drew from. She said, "That depends."

I was floored. Now I really didn't know what to make of Rosalyn. She was clearly more complex than just a nice Quaker wife, but I wasn't sure she knew that herself. I said, "Rosalyn, Rosalyn, I can't get to the bottom of you. One minute you're..."

"Yes, what?"

"One minute you're professing a missed out, bored life, the next you're... Will you stop looking at me like that!"

"James, your cocoa, drink." She put the mug on the table and sat opposite me, once again looking over her mug with those deep brown eyes. "It's just instinct, right? Just being the animals that we are. Isn't that what we're *supposed* to be?"

"Ros, stop it! It's not you, it's not how *we* are."

"So... all that talk of a kiss was just nothing. What is it they call it, teasing?"

"No, of course not. That's not it. I really... I really like you, Ros. I don't want to muddle what you have here with Richard and the girls. It would get complicated, messy. You'd end up hating yourself and me, and probably Richard."

"So that's it. I'm the dutiful, bored housewife who had a moment, a glimpse of city life, and now should go back into the kitchen."

"Ros, Ros, for heaven's sake, you're deliberately making it sound like a judgment, a prison sentence. It's a beautiful family we're talking about here, Amy and Joan. And Richard. Richard's a good man."

"Oh, yes, he's a good man. Well, I'd better get upstairs and be good to him." With that she rose, washed her cup hurriedly in the sink, put it on the drainer and went towards the door. "You know where your room is. Goodnight, James." And she was gone.

June 2nd

They say middle age can be a time of crisis; what crisis would that be, I wonder? A crisis of conscience perhaps, a reviewing of the forbidden question first encountered lying in the long grass? Dillon Thomas may have said we should rage at the dying of the light, but that would only be so if we had not fully lived the light. But as has been noted, we don't fully live.

What is it to fully live a life? When at its end we come to know, perhaps, there was one thing that called to us, half hidden in the whirl of distractions that sought to distract us. We fail to name it, for we have known so little of it. Half known, it has lived with us, waiting on our turning, flickering like a leaf in the breeze, trying to catch our attention. From first to last, it is the golden thread in the Tapestry. Though all else may fade, it remains visible even in distant space and time. It writes upon eternity the history of our being.

If the next morning was a little tense, it was a tenseness that would not be voiced. It was Sunday, the day when, approaching God, all other things were put aside. Maybe the cynic in me just wouldn't take a day off, maybe my search was genuine, maybe I still wanted that kiss. In any event I decided to accept Richard's invitation to go to Meeting.

Rosalyn was right about Amy and Joan; their squeals of delight at seeing me in the kitchen next morning were only subdued by a reminder from Rosalyn of the Sunday habit of quiet reverence that everyone was expected to take on. Nevertheless, I could still feel their vibrant youthfulness as each took a hand when we left to walk to the Meeting House. The girls were pleased to have me along; my presence added a kind of conspiratorial element to what I felt to be just a tolerated outing for them. Richard was pleased, perhaps he saw a conversion in sight. But Rosalyn had a look, when I caught her eye, that was full of query, doubt, and crossness. Why was I coming? I was intruding again, stirring an already disturbed pot.

June 3rd
Well, what can I say; if what I do is disturbing, I cannot help it, nor do I wish to help it. My life as a child was disturbed by man and war. It continued in the classroom and later at work. Anything 'natural and true' had to be snatched from the jaws of enforced enculturation. To disturb what is false is the only way to begin to find what is true.

As church services go, the Quakers' Meeting was quite a pleasant experience, not unlike morning meditation at Indriya. After sitting for about an hour, with occasional reflections from some of those present, we gathered for tea. As a new addition to the routine company, I was sought and questioned.

During some light discussion of religion (if there can be such a thing), an elderly gentleman asked me directly, "Do you believe in God? Or better put, do you ever have a sense of God?" The general chatter stopped. I was somewhat taken back, surprised, I suppose, that a Quaker would be so forward, confrontational it might be said. The question hung there awaiting my response. He said, "I'm sorry if I have offended. I thought, young man, you must have considered it. I've rarely met anyone who hasn't. Please forgive my impertinence. I'm just a curious old man."

"There's nothing wrong with curiosity, sir," I said, "I think it's the source of discovery. As to your question, I have a sense of life and it seems to me life has both grief and joy. It has darkness and light, growth and decay, birth and death. What I'm trying to say is that that's enough for me to consider. I cannot think outside or beyond this miracle that I am fortunate enough to be a part of."

"Ah! But you are prepared to call it a miracle," he said.

"Yes, I'm prepared to call it a miracle, an everyday miracle. My assertion is that we don't see it for what it is, and that's partly because, for some reason, we want to look beyond life to some imaginary otherness. Now I'm afraid it's my turn to apologize."

"Oh, no, no, no. That's a brave answer and an interesting one. But don't you sometimes feel when you look at nature that it is such a wonder that there must be a source to it all?"

We were interrupted by a woman of about seventy or so who spoke to the old man, "Peter, dear, if you're going to get into one of your discussions, you'd better sit at a table. I'll bring your tea over. And would you like some tea, er...?"

"James," I said, "Yes, thank you. That would be good."

I could see Richard and Rosalyn making their way over to the table. "Hi there. Is this a private conversation or can anyone join in?" It was Richard, bright eyed and keen, probably thinking of that conversion again. I wondered about the old man and his wife's remark about 'one of your discussions'. 'Well,' I thought to myself, 'you did want to come. You know what these Christians are like. They'll give you a run for your money.'

Peter said, "Hello, Richard, do join us. What about you, Rosalyn. Are you having tea?"

Rosalyn spoke with the old man and Peter, totally avoiding my presence, "I'd better stay outside. I can keep an eye on the girls, besides it's too beautiful to be indoors."

"My sentiments entirely," I said, "You see, nature calls us. We have a natural inclination to be with the way things are."

Before either of the men could speak, Rosalyn snapped, "That may be so, but it doesn't refute the existence of God!" and left us for a moment somewhat speechless.

"Well," Peter said, "Your Rosalyn's a dark horse, Richard. I rather thought she came to these Meetings as a family thing. I was never that certain of her inner beliefs, which was fine by me. But it seems she has a fiery sense of God somewhere in her."

"Mm... well, yes, maybe, but it's new to me. As you say, I don't think I've ever seen her quite so animated about religion. What do you make of it, James?" Richard had turned towards me with the cup in his hand which he brought to his lips, something I had seen Rosalyn do when feeling confronted.

"I don't know what I think right now. I'm afraid it seems my presence has stirred up your peaceful Sunday."

"Oh, nonsense," the old man said, "It's good for the soul, a good challenge now and then. Speak your mind, James is it?" He put out his hand and shook mine vigorously. It was soft to the touch with a strong grip, a bit like the man himself, I thought.

Richard was looking through the open oak doors out into the garden of the Meeting room. Unmistakable lines of thought were furrowing his brow. I thought, he may be straight but he's not stupid. The old man was rattling on, but I was only half listening and I was pretty sure Richard wasn't listening at all. Fortunately, at some point Peter's wife had seated herself with us and was feeding his 'discussion'. Quite suddenly Richard flashed me a look and stood up making his apologies and went into the garden. Now I wasn't even half listening. My mind was racing over the night before, the afternoon on the downs, connecting threads that reached back... Back where, back to what? What was there, what happened? Most of it was in my head.

If it was in my head then it was in Rosalyn's as well, and possibly Richard's. This wasn't a time for speculation. I'd better accept the consequences of my thoughts. I stood up. I'd no idea where the old man had got to but I don't think he minded. It seemed his wife knew the discussion routine. "I have to go, sir. It's been good to share time with you, Peter, but I think the Dawkins are wanting to get home."

"Lovely to talk with you, James; do come again won't you," he offered his hand, I shook it and turned for the garden.

The sun was full on the west door of the Meeting house that led into the garden. Though there were still plenty of people around, for a moment I couldn't make out anybody. As my eyes adjusted I saw Richard and Rosalyn sitting together, separated from the general milieu of folk. Before I could make a move, Amy was grabbing my hand and pleading with me to come and play with them. Then Joan was there, more silent, but just as insistent. There was little I could do but comply. As they pulled me in the opposite direction from Richard and Rosalyn, I had enough of a glimpse of them to feel the tension. While my body went with the girls, my mind stuck by the door, turning and turning over.

June 5ᵗʰ

There are a lot of natural things children love to do that are now out of bounds. Climbing trees is one of them. Most of the deep joy in a child's life derives from nature, naturally, for a child is of nature and still close to it. But we intelligent adults have measured and weighed nature and taken flight from it. Yet for all our efforts at control and comfort, it is buried deep inside our psyches along with an old fear. I feel that fear sometime, in an unguarded moment.

After lunch, a terse affair, I left for Paul's place, grateful that Amy and Joan had 'occupied' the no man's land between all three of us. I didn't expect to see the Dawkins again. There was a grey pit in my stomach, but it lay still and quiet.

On the train, I looked out over the countryside that had brought us all together, and wondered what kind of fire nature puts in us to cause such disturbance. The answer, I knew only too well.

It was a fire Kate had tamed to her own wishes. That summer I came as close to being burnt as I ever want to.

There was still much about animal passion I would learn, yet I have to record an element of it I had not known or therefore considered. It was Kate who remarked, "You don't lose yourself, do you?" We were sitting in bed, our usual place, drinking tea.

"Lose myself, what do you mean?"

"When we're making love, as you like to call it, you don't... well, you're always present, thinking, I suppose. You don't die to the moment as the French would say, you know, *petite mort*, the little death. Only, I think of it as a transcendent experience, religious in a way."

"Transcendent? Religious? Really. In the midst of all that lustful animalism?"

"Oh, James, sometimes you're such a prude. Why do you have to punish yourself for enjoying it?"

"I don't punish myself." The light from the bedroom window caught the edges of her hair, falling without a worldly care, it seemed to me, over her shoulders and down her back. "Do I?" Her body was like liquid, flowing, without tension. I think the term is languid.

She said, "Perhaps punish is the wrong word, but you hold something in, you keep something to yourself." Yes, I thought, I do; it's a darkness you have perhaps never known and hopefully never will, a close cousin to death, and not the little death from which you are resurrected.

"James?"

"What?"

"You've disappeared, where are you, dear?" She turned and put her arms around me, "Sometimes I think you're too serious, thinking all the time. Too much thinking can be bad for you, you know. Now isn't this more fun." She pressed herself to me, and the summer passed.

∽

Love, or lust, is a journey that has to go in tandem. Kate was doing all the work, not that I lacked enthusiasm, you understand, but I was clearly on another journey, and by autumn we both knew it. Catherine was ensconced with her new partner; Kate was looking for one. I knew better than to overstay my friendship with Paul, and besides, I had my journey to continue on. So, October saw me going through the gates of Indriya again.

FOUR

Most of the leaves had left the great oaks. In the evenings a few silhouettes of hands waved and fell with the setting sun. In the mornings I rose at four, splashed water on my face, wrapped a blanket around me, and made the slow purposeful walk to the sala for meditation practice. I was aware of everyone I had met that summer sleeping, missing this quiet and compelling time of peace that falls on the world. This was my journey place. Here in this silence I would find answers to the grey torment that slept in me, and I believed plagues us all.

Across the playground a breeze pushes leaves around my feet. I stoop and pick one up, wrapping my hand in its hand-like form; I remember for a brief moment the 'nature table' at my first school, and Miss Anna, the teacher. She took her place beside all those others I remembered, and I thought, 'I'll write them all down, all the people I have known and know now.' It was an instant strange thought but felt right. In the quiet darkness before dawn I was formulating a path, though I didn't know it, a path to liberation.

❧

"Is there some reason why you don't bow before meditation?" It was the abbot. We were walking around the outer field having a 'chat', the one that Kusalo had alerted me to on my last visit.

"Not really. I don't have reason not to bow, but then I don't see a reason to bow either. I've never known quite why you all bow. I know you don't revere Buddha as a deity," I said.

"You're right, it has nothing to with worship, a mistake non-Buddhists often make. It has everything to do with suffering, with us just as we are." We had reached the Buddha grove, planted in the spring. The leaves, so prolific on the saplings, had all fallen. The sky was a slate grey and the air cold. The small stupa in the center of the grove reminded me more of a gravestone than a monument to wisdom. Thoughts of Malcolm passed through my mind. I understood suffering all right.

"But how does bowing relate to suffering?" I said.

"Well, let us say there's a sense in which bowing challenges our grasping, and that is the beginning of the end of suffering." He stopped walking and turned to face me, "If you want to know how that may be, you will have to try it out. I think if you do, you will be surprised."

That evening I walked into the sala. Casting an eye on the golden statue of the Buddha, I found it hard to drop some idea of worship. But I decided to investigate, after all, that's why I was here. I placed my seating cloth and knelt down, put my hands in the now familiar position of anjali, together in front of me (like prayer!) I was somehow over conscious. Something had been triggered in my gut, or was it my head; I couldn't be sure. I stared at the Buddha, 'he' stared back, waiting. A resistance solidified in my being. What was vague became real. I stiffened. By now most of the monks and nuns were kneeling, awaiting the unified bowing that marked the start of the chanting. The abbot lit the two candles, picked up the three sticks of incense, and proceeded to hold them in the candle flame. Next, he will shake the fire off them and place the smoldering sticks in their holder, then everyone will bow...

June 7th

The ego is the only self we know. Everything we say and do constructs the conduit to and from our ego, rationalizing and formulating a self such that we feel purposeful. To feel purpose is to gain success at avoiding fear. For the mark of our success is permanence against nature's ever-changing impermanence. It is our driving need for the show of permanence in the forms and material life of our cultures that suppresses and ultimately may destroy the natural world. The city is the antithesis of natural, as is agribusiness, roads, cars, planes, and... the list is endless, representing as it does the material revelation of our fear.

We are long past the need to protect our species from danger, but we seem as yet unable to overcome the fear it once engendered in us. The irony of the current life of the species Homo sapiens is in the danger it poses to itself in its attempt to avoid an archaic danger. It is to our own minds and hearts we must turn to resolve this dilemma.

...With my head touching the floor for the third bow, the struggle commenced. As I rose to sit and join the chanting, all the sonorous inner sound couldn't drown out the shout of the ego. Accusations of capitulation, weakness, fraudulence, and cowardice bounced around and ripped into the fabric of reason. I kept on chanting, clinging to it as a refuge, a life raft in a sea of rising confusion.

The chanting came to an end, silence fell all embracing around me, while within, the rage surfaced. The gentle shuffling and settling of bodies accentuated the stillness. I wrapped the blanket around me in a vain

75

hope of protection from my own storm. I breathed. I watched. I witnessed the prisoner I was, of circumstance, of desire, of anger, aversion, hatred, lust, hope, wishes and dreams, of a 'person' of blind intent set in motion at birth. It was hopeless. I gave in to the inevitability of the ego's supremacy. With nothing else to do, I watched my breath. It had settled now to a shallow, near-death hopelessness. Yet of course it could not die, for nature has fashioned us to survive until the inevitable invitation is called in.

After what must have been an hour or so, I thought I had gone to sleep, yet I had not, for I was aware. The storm had abated, so too, the despondency. But more than that: most extraordinarily, my body felt strange, as I had never felt it before. It felt like stone, solid, firm, real. *it was perfectly still!* And then it started shaking again. But now I knew nothing would be the same again, it would not be counting I would do in future.

As days followed days, morning and evening I accepted the ego's challenge. I bowed, I chanted. I sat and watched. I became aware of the personal: a self of traits learned and passions born, and of the impersonal: a non-self that simply was a watcher.

Over time, as my body stilled itself for longer and longer periods, there arose another perception, deeper and transcendent, a dark ending, a call from out of life's shadow, not death and yet...

I had no way of identifying this experience. I sought out Silo, a senior monk who I had heard speak eloquently the Dhamma.[8]

"Bunte, what is the death of the Self, is it able to precede bodily death? What is illusional, is it Self or death?"

"That's a big question, James." We were seated on the floor as usual, in a small room off the sala; the light from a pale afternoon sun lay across Silo's shoulder and onto the carpet, a gift from a grateful layman. "What has brought this question to your mind?"

In the quiet sunlit space I tried to explain my meditation experience. Slow, faltering words inadequately put the jigsaw of thoughts before him, "...And then, quite without warning, I was flying over the countryside. Looking down, I could see the monastery and the surrounding fields. I looked to my left and right, and saw my wings." The monks shave their eyebrows (it's a long story) but I swear, if he had them, they were being raised at this last revelation.

I went on, eager for an answer, "I can't say how long I was flying, but just as suddenly as I was up, I was down."

"Down?" He said.

---

8 Dhamma is Buddhist term for the way things truly are.

"Yes, I was looking up through trees as though I were lying on the ground, trees projecting skyward, interspersed with people looking down at me. 'It's dead,' they were saying."

"Dead. Are you sure they said 'it' was dead?"

"Oh, yes. I was an it. 'It's dead,' they said."

Silo sat quietly, his eyes closed, a habit of contemplating born of many years in monastic life. I could feel our breathing falling into a kind of unison. I let go of my tense urgency for an explanation. A fly could be heard, unseen, buzzing its way around the room and against the window. The sun had warmed the small, closed room to a tropical stillness. I waited. It seemed not to matter now what answer would come, the stillness and equanimity I felt was answer enough.

It was almost a shock, an intrusion, when Silo finally spoke, "It feels as though what you have described is something like Freud's theory of Thanatos, the death wish."

I was surprised by the answer, coming as it did from western psychology.

"But, bunte," I said, "what is it seen as? I mean how does Buddhism interpret this experience?" He smiled, and spoke of illusion and its confounding of truth, and encouraged me to continue watching, suggesting that the ego would change tactics over and over as I continued to remain passive, until eventually it would succumb. I thanked him for his support, made anjali, and left. I felt no closer to a definitive answer, yet it had lost its urgency. I had, in the asking and waiting, learned something. I had also decided what I would do next.

I walked into the back field and over to the Buddha grove. The earth between certain trees had begun to show through as a narrow brown path, worn bare by the bare feet of the monks and nuns. I took off my sandals and placed them by one of the trees. I looked along the path and toward the tree at its end. A line of the Buddha's came to mind: 'Walk, O Bhikkhus, for the welfare of the many folk.' That is what I would do.

June 10th

From the moment of conception there are changes that continue without ceasing unto death, and beyond death. The notion of fixity we hold about ourselves is an illusion. For what we take as a permanent Self is the reflection in form of a process, a movement along a continuum of birth, arising, decaying, dying death, and again birth.

The extending of our consciousness, the thinking of ourselves as a separate entity in nature that has taken place over the course of evolution, endows us with reflective thought. It is this knowing of ourselves that fixes the sense of being an individual, separate and discrete. What I am separate from are other bodies, bodies going through the same continuum of change I am. Together, all the bodies, all the minds, all the living entities, construct the one state, the state of nature.

It is within nature and through the exactness of the process of nature that we come and go, while nature continues. The leaves fall, are renewed, fall, renew, in a continuum that we know as trees. In the same way, we fall and are renewed as the species Homo sapiens. This may not seem very helpful to know at the personal level. So what, you may say. What does that have to do with my dying? Everything and nothing!

The paradox in that response arises out of the paradox that is the life of a being. It has everything to do with your dying because you are a part of it. Nature does not exist separate from you. It also has nothing to do with our dying because it remains continuous in spite of our being. This paradox is reflected in our cultural, political life and is, in fact, at the root of our close demise as a species, for we have not yet solved its challenge. What we have tried to do is get rid of it by overt control: control of nature, of our bodies, control of birth and of death. A paradox, by its very nature, cannot be controlled out of existence, neither can it be resolved. It has to be lived through.

I was writing my list, you remember I mentioned a while ago, all the people I have known and still know. I was stretching my memory as far back as it would go when it halted at Susan. Well, that would be natural. It was the summer of 1951...

꩜

...It was hot. I was nine years old and playing hide'n'seek in the park. All the hiding spots were behind trees, so the trick was to find a tree with a large trunk. Of course, if you were the seeker, the first trees you looked behind were the large trunks. Sometimes it happened that two of us found ourselves squashed together behind a particular tree when the counting was up and we were being hunted down. That summer in the park I found myself behind one such tree with Susan. We had both run far from the general game area and were a bit out of breath and flushed from the excitement.

"Hey, Susan."

"James. D'you think he'll find us?"

"I hope not. Shall I take a look?"

"No! No, James," she grabbed my arms. "He'll see you."

"Right." We fell to silence. I looked up into the branches of the tree, an elm.

"What 'you looking for, James, what d'you see?"

"I'm just looking." But I was thinking, 'She hasn't let go of my arms.' I could feel her hand through my shirt sleeves. I liked it.

"James," she said, "do you like me?"

I lowered my head to look at her, and noticed her lips as she spoke.

"Do you think I'm, you know, pretty?" She bent her head, her dark black hair was close to my face. Its smell was sort of soft, like soap bubbles or something.

I said, "Yes, I... I think you're beautiful."

She lifted her head. "Oh, oh really, James, really." She put her arms around my neck. A feeling I had never known swept through me like... like when you dive into deep water. I badly wanted to touch those lips with mine. She said, "Do you know how to kiss?"

"I... Mmm, I..."

She said, "Nor do I... but maybe we... Could we?" I nodded like a dumb mute, but had the wit to put my arms about her neck.

June 11th

I suppose there's nothing quite like that first kiss with all its awkwardness and innocence, that awakening of a fire waiting to consume and consummate in the service of nature.

Well, once lit, it ran every path through my body it could find, seeking a way out. But it was blocked; I was blocked up, bricked-in with timidity, a fear of the body. A near-death experience at two years old wrapped itself around me like barbed wire. As I grew older, my parents read timidity as being thoughtful, so I learned to be so. Between my thoughtful ways and closed body, the passion of youth had little space to flame. For a long time it pretty much had to stay in my mind, where of course it created havoc.

Fortunately, my thoughtfulness inclined me to study, which I did, and brought some order to the havoc. It did nothing to douse the fire.

I met Ruth in 1961. In her bed, all thoughtfulness and fearful considerations were burnt to a cinder. Seeing it and knowing it, she ignored the barbed wire and poured gasoline on the fire. Stella was conceived in accordance with nature's plan, not mine, nor Ruth's. Our plans became nature's plan, and we went on to have four children. It was a marriage no worse than many, but we had not made it. As our own lives grew, we knew it was not going to be together. But, in marriage, we shared what most parents never have to share, Malcolm. We write occasionally.

∾

Ruth is on my list. I know what I will be doing with it. It was one of the first things I knew that begins the answer to our dilemma. But first I have to complete the list. No one must be left off because of negative feelings, no one given a special place. So I set them down in order of time, when I met them.

I'm sitting on my bed in Indriya, a time away from the dusty floor of a barrack house, writing names when I can remember, or labels that will bring persons to mind. For instance, I have one here: Unity Theater. Being a theater where I learned to act, a useful acquisition in life, I met many folk. But important to this tale is Polly, my first 'love'. What can I say, bound up as I was, my advances were more like retreats or apologies. I was kind, I was supportive; I found a home for us when she was going through difficult times. I held her, I kissed her; I wanted so much for her to be the one, as my mother had assured me was 'out there' especially for me. But it was never to be.

Parting was not sweet sorrow, it was devastating. I ended up a broken young man. Ruth found me. Polly, of course, is on the list, but I must put it aside for a while. The trees whisper. The path calls. I must walk.

∾

It is now the early afternoon of Friday, December 10th. I am working in the kitchen with John, who is now in full robes, and I should call Venerable Karuno. I'm finishing cleaning while Karuno makes a list of the kitchen equipment. There's talk of refurbishing this area and he has been assigned list-making, before everything is moved away for the work. "I'm about done here, bunte," I said, "Are you free for a walk soon?"

"I don't think so, James, I'd like to get this done today. Take yourself off. Maybe see you at tea."

"Okay, take it easy," I said and turned to leave through the back door. The shaft of light from the open door meets me. On hearing my name being called from within the kitchen, I stop. It isn't Karuno calling, it's a woman's voice. A voice I recognize. I ask myself, 'What's Rosalyn doing here?'

It's cold. A weak winter sun is struggling behind clouds and a wind is running up the field, but it's the most private place to speak and still be seen not to be misbehaving. Out in the field, I hear Rosalyn's story.

"After you left, things never seemed to get back on an even keel. Richard and I, well, bickered, nothing serious, nothing, really. We just seemed to... I don't know, we'd had our eyes opened, perhaps for the first time."

"I'm terribly sorry, Rosalyn. If I hadn't come by... You know I like you both... This is so..."

"It wasn't you, James. You were just who you are. The cracks weren't just in the house, you know. It's just that Richard and I didn't want to see them."

"Maybe so, Ros, but all marriages have cracks if you look closely. Heavens, life's full of cracks. They say here, the first Noble Truth is 'life contains suffering.' Cracks!"

"Well, cracks or not, after the wind you blew through the place, I saw how tired I was of pretending not to notice. I tried getting mad at you first, but that was just another attempt at papering over my discontentment. The truth is you may be a muddle, but you're like that because, for some reason, curse or cure, you won't hide the cracks."

A terrible thought occurred to me, "You haven't left Richard, have you?"

"No, no, I haven't left, as in split-up. I just wanted some time to... I don't know, to get a better perspective on things. No, I'm not likely to leave. I'm not the type, in the end."

We walked for a while in silence, the sky darkening and a wind building up. I suggested we head for the sala, there would be tea soon. On the way, Rosalyn told me she had come to stay for the weekend. "I'm curious about Buddhism. I thought I'd start my sorting out by satisfying my curiosity. So here I am."

"Would you mind if I came down to Colville with you Monday morning?" She shot me a sharp look. "I would like to get the girls something for Christmas." Her face relaxed. "You could take it with you; it's a bit hard to post stuff from here. Letters are okay, but I'm not sure about a parcel, and, besides, I have to go to town to buy it, so..."

"Of course, right. Are you staying here for Christmas?"

"Yes. It's so nice to be out of the chaos and greed. Sorry, Ros, but that's about all I see of it. It's about the worst time of year, isn't that ironic."

"We're not all like that, you know, James. To some it's a sacred time, a time to be thankful."

We had reached the sala, and the smell of coffee invited us in to the warmth. A few people were moving about, getting mugs and filling them from two large urns on the serving table.

Taking off our coats and putting them by the wall, I asked Rosalyn, "Tea or coffee? We just help ourselves."

"I'd love a coffee, we don't have it at home. But I should get them, your hands..."

"Sit with the coats, I'll manage. Coffee coming up. Sugar? Afraid there's no milk, only Coffee-Mate, a kind of white powder." She sat and leaned against the wall.

"Coffee with sugar and white powder, thanks, James," she said, smiling, "It'll be an adventure, being here."

"Right," I said, and went over to the table to get the drinks.

Karuno was just filling a mug from the sangha's dedicated urns at another table close by. "She looks nice," he said, "A friend of yours?"

"Now, now, Karuno, you'll be confessing that one at the end of the week, John! If you don't watch it, you'll be out of those robes before you're started." He knew I was kidding, as I was almost sure he was.

But the order is pretty strict about behavior, and speech is behavior. The fourth Noble Truth of Buddhism specifies the eight areas of practice, and it pretty much covers every aspect of thought, speech and action.

"Do you know all the monks here?" It was Rosalyn, with her hands around the hot mug, a sight that brought back familiar memories. She was looking around, her eyes unable to settle on any one thing, finally resting, as we all do, on the Buddha.

"Yes," I said, "I've worked with most of them at some time."

"They work?" she was surprised. "What do they do?"

"Repair and upkeep of the place, there's lots to be done all the time. Anyone who's good with their hands is welcome here. The mendicant's life is not all slow pondering of deep and meaningful questions, in fact, little of it is. Everything is practice: sitting, walking, working, it's all practice."

"Walking?"

"Walking meditation, we walk back and forth between two trees."

"You must like that, James. But don't you get bored, I mean, isn't it a bit confining. What about just going for a long walk on the downs, wouldn't that be better?"

"Up on the downs?" I couldn't resist it. That's how stupid I can be.

Rosalyn flashed me a look, but then broke into a smile, "I suppose it wouldn't be the same, not at all."

"No," I said, "The whole point of confining oneself, as you put it, is to increase one's concentration and awareness. Every activity here is about awareness."

"Oh," she said, sounding a bit disappointed, "I thought there'd be more to it, you know, singing, incense, candles, mandala paintings and things."

"Well, you won't find mandalas here. That's Tibetan Buddhists, but you may be pleasantly surprised at meditation time," I said. "Look, I have to go. I've got tools to put away before meditation. Meet me by the doors, just here, around six-forty-five; meditation's at seven." I rose, took my cup to the kitchen, and returned through the Sala. Rosalyn was talking to another lay woman, a visitor.

I left, not to put the imaginary tools away, but to compose myself. There was still something wholesome and peaceful about Rosalyn that stirred my senses. This was going to be a challenging weekend.

෴

The blanket I had wrapped around me for meditation happened to be an old white one. Rosalyn looked wide-eyed when we met at the sala doors. "You look so different, James. You look for all the world as though you've been here forever."

"Not quite," I said, "I've still got hair." (Though it had been cut very short.) "C'mon, we'd better get inside." I opened the doors for her and whispered, "You're over the other side behind the nuns."

"Nuns!"

I was sure there had been some sisters in for tea, but when all the heads are shaved, and bodies covered in robes, it can be hard to tell the men from the women. "Yes, nuns," I said, "I'll tell you about them after meditation."

Of course, my meditation was a disturbed affair, with images of Rosalyn superimposed on the lustful curves of Kate, remembrances of Catherine, and any other female image the ego saw fit to throw my way. I breathed my way through it and tried to catch that moment between the out and in breath, like the spaces between railway carriages as the train passes. Hold that space, for it is there life and death meet. Three dings of the bell, ending the meditation, dispersed us.

On Sunday afternoon, I'd introduced Rosalyn to the Buddha grove and walking meditation, and we were now ambling down the farmer's field, outside the monastery boundary. The clouds had left and the sun had that afternoon feeling. Have you ever had that? It was one of my favorite feelings when I was a boy, a kind of seeping of light into the bones, a peaceful, untroubled eternity. We had stopped to listen to the sounds of the countryside surrounding us.

I honestly couldn't be sure who took whose hand, but there we stood like Hansel and Gretel, a little lost and wondering how to find our way back. We walked down as far as the road and turned back up the field to the boundary fence, hand in hand, in silence. At the fence, Rosalyn voiced our solitary thought, "We'll always be on this path, won't we?"

"Of course," I said, "Wherever we go." I thought, 'The past may be just a memory for Buddhists, and the future unknown, but some moments are eternal.'

∾

When I'm reading my list of names, there are some that are very hard not to stop at. I suppose it's a good time, while I'm on the subject, to outline the first practice I want to share with you. It has the delightful name of The *Metta*[9] Tapestry.

The name-list represents the weave of the Tapestry that creates our lives. Of course, in truth, it should contain everyone on the planet, for our lives are created by all those who preceded us and those whose lives touch ours, and as every life is by degrees touched by every other life, so... you get the idea. When you have completed as much of your list as you can remember, for you will remember more as you proceed, then the practice begins.

Casting your eyes in a gentle flow down the list, each name will register the person, and your being will subtly respond. It may take many times to reach the first stage, equanimity, neither favoring nor disfavoring anyone on your list. The achievement of this stage is a big step, for to do so is to let go of preferences and opinions about your immediate life and open to the way it is.

9 Metta: Loving kindness, or supreme friendship.

*F*IVE

I left Indriya January 3rd just as the rains retreat[10] was beginning. I was invited to stay on, but a restlessness had once again gripped me. But this was to be a very different summer from last year.

I had sent an inquiry to an abbey some twenty miles north of Indriya. Edgley abbey was a small Catholic retreat for Christians and those with an interested turn of mind. The reply was encouraging.

Dear James,

We were intrigued to hear of your searches and interest in the monastic life, albeit of a Buddhist nature. Your remarks concerning the deep need for us all to find a true answer, I think you say 'way', to the dilemmas of this life tell us you are indeed a true seeker. As such, though unusual for us to admit non Christians, we are willing to let you stay for one month.

As there is a great demand for our limited space, we suggest you reply by return and let us know when you would like to come.

Your servant in Christ

Brother Dominic.

I returned the application, choosing to stay from the end of February through part of March. Easter, of course, was fully booked. But having decided to leave before the rains retreat, I called Edgley on the off-chance and was invited to stay the weekend of my move out of Indriya.

Before leaving, I phoned Richard and Rosalyn. I wanted to assure my conscience, I suppose, to find out if they had resolved the turbulence I had set in motion. Richard answered, "Hello."

I wasn't quite sure what to say, I should have rehearsed a line or something.

"Oh, hi, Richard, it's James, I..."

"James, so good to hear from you. How was Christmas? What's happening?"

I couldn't quite adjust to his almost ebullient response. I thought, 'What was going on?'

"Christmas was quiet, always is here, that's the point of staying really. But I'm about to leave again and thought I'd check in with you."

"Will you be coming by on your way again?"

---

10 Rains retreat. A time when the monks traditionally stay in one place for the three months of the (Indian) monsoon period.

85

What! Is the man a masochist? I'd have thought I was the last person he would actually want to *see*. Being phone polite was one thing, but...

"No, sorry, I'm heading up north. As a matter of fact, I'm going to be staying at a Christian retreat center, Edgley abbey."

"Really. Does that mean anything? A change of heart, or...?"

I couldn't tell if he was pleased or challenged by the news. I thought he would much prefer me outside the Christian nest now.

"No, I don't think so, just me, following the ever-winding path it looks like I'm on. Sometimes it seems an endless search."

"You've a restless mind, James. Maybe the Catholics will give you some peace. Look, I have to go, but Rosalyn's here; would you like a word?"

I thought, she may solve the puzzle in my head. Richard's politeness was disconcerting.

"Right, well," I said, "Good talking to you Richard. Okay, I'll just say Hi to Rosalyn."

"Okay, bye, take care." I waited, hearing the distant voices of Rosalyn and Richard. It went quiet, then she was there.

"Hello, James." I could almost feel her breath, see her brown eyes, and sense her peacefulness. I thought how lucky Richard was, but did he know it? "Richard says you're leaving. Going to the Catholics or something."

"In a manner of speaking. No, not really. I'm going to retreat again, just trying a different approach. But who knows. If one steps in water, one must expect to get at least a little wet."

"Oh, James, what are you doing! You know, when you first came here, I thought now there's a man who knows what's what, where he's going and so on. I still think of you like that. But you seem to have all this stuff inside, like those marbles that make that rolly- man toy stand up which-ever way you push him, only *they're* pushing you. Will you ever settle, do you think?"

"Like you and Richard, you mean." The silence punched me in the gut. "I'm sorry, Rosalyn, I didn't mean it like that. It's just that talking to Richard was like nothing had happened. Everything was, well, as we said, papered over. What I actually called for was to see how you both really are."

"James, sometimes we have to compromise, settle. We have the girls, you know, and it was never as though we had any major problem together, Richard and I. We're all right. I wish I could say the same for you."

"I'm okay, Rosalyn. I am, as you once said, who I am. And I have to be honest to that. You're right, though. There are a lot of marbles banging around in me. I just hope one day they will form into a beautiful pattern. That's probably what I'm looking for."

"Well, I wish you good luck on your journey, James. You are still welcome here. Please stay in touch."

"Thank you, Rosalyn. You're a good friend. I'll let you know how it goes. Bye for now."

"Bye, James, take care."

⁓

Edgley Abbey sits at the edge of the Edgley village in the Cotswold hills. I approached by car, coming off the M4 Motorway onto such narrow roads that I had to reduce my progress to a moderate crawl. The hedgerows lining the road had been machine cut, the torn ends of branches seeming to defy the birds to nest. There were few trees, for the land has been lived on for hundreds of years. This was a land of fortifications in Saxon through to Roman times. There were cuts into the chalk of the hills, dykes and barrows, circular and square that had seen the blood of men fighting for kingdoms, for land, and for God.

When the first Elisabeth claimed the crown, and stayed queen for longer than any before her, the land at last saw peace. Settlements grew, villages clustered around the churches or abbeys, and trade began to replace conflict.

The Edgley abbey I was about to visit was relatively new, only two hundred years old, though built on the ancient abbey's site. I drove up a driveway that curved away from the road and into a small hidden parking area. My old car looked a little incongruous, I thought, but I tucked it away under an old tree, locked it, and went to find my only contact, Brother Dominic.

"Well, James, what kind of tea would you like?" Brother Dominic asked.

We were sitting in a very small room with little in it but a metal table covered with a cloth, chairs with plastic seats, and a waist-high cupboard that held an electric kettle and a small tea pot. With daylight long gone, it was lit by a single ceiling light. Almost everything was cream colored, apart from the kettle and the metal legs of the table. Brother Dominic's kindly face (which I estimated to be about seventy-five years old) shone like a beacon above his brown habit.

I said, "Whatever's easiest. Whatever you're having will be fine."

"Okay," he said, and with his back to me, bent down and proceeded to find the box of tea bags and the cups from the cupboard. This took him some time, and I could see the tea would be a while coming.

'He's alright,' I thought, 'but what am I doing here?' I looked around. No crosses, no bits of scripture. In fact, there was nothing on the walls. It could have been a room for tea-break anywhere. I thought of the staff-rooms at schools I'd been sent to a few too many times. 'Well, I won't get "six-of-the-best" here, but I may be upbraided in a very different way."

I was right about the time, but eventually we were sitting again, across from one another with two mugs of hot tea between us.

"We do some meditation here, you know, James. Yes, it's usually on Monday and Thursday evenings. We have quite a group from the village and around who come and sit with us. I usually lead it, but you'd be most welcome to do so. I expect you are more versed in technique than I." I was very surprised when I heard his invitation, but Brother Dominic, I was to discover, was a one of a kind, tolerated on account of his age. "Oh, but then, you are only here for the weekend, aren't you. Well, not to mind."

When we finished tea, I offered to wash up. I must confess, more to hasten things than out of pure altruism, though I was also happy to help this kindly monk. Brother Dominic then offered to show me to my cell, chatting most of the way about some of the do's and don'ts of staying, most of which I had absorbed from the leaflet enclosed with my application form.

By the time he left me to myself, it was ten-thirty. The first service, Lauds, is at 8:30 in the morning. I wanted to be up and ready, to get as much out of this visit as I could. I went straight to bed. Over my head, on the wall, a crucified Jesus watched my eyes close. I lay, recalling to myself why I had come here...

ᥫᦊ

...In 1974 Catherine and I moved into an old terraced house together. Catherine was teaching school, and I had finished my initial training as a therapist and was working for an umbrella organization helping the mentally ill. The work was reasonably satisfying, and left us both time for growing some of our own food, spinning and dyeing wool, making of the house a nest, and going on demonstrations to save the world. In a word, it was idyllic.

It was on a spring Sunday, three years into our idyll, when we would usually be off to the allotment, that I informed Catherine I was going to church.

"What on earth for?" was her reasonable and expected, response. We were both atheists at heart, undeclared, perhaps, but atheists nevertheless.

"Why would you want to do a daft thing like that on a day like this?" It was a particularly clear day, fresh, as English springs can be after a little rain.

I tried to explain, "Well, here I am working as a therapist, having gone through therapy myself. But we never looked at something as profound as what one believes, or chooses not to believe. It just was never on the agenda. I just feel I should investigate a little."

"So, you're not suddenly going 'gaga' on me? Just doing a bit of research, is that it?"

"Right, yes. I... it would be unethical of me not to clear this up. So. I'm just going round the corner, you know that Methodist place. Take a look-see. I'll be back lunchtime."

"Well, if that's what you want. I'm going to the garden. Who'd want to be indoors on a day like this? If there is a God, which I very much doubt, he or she is more likely to be out on a nice day than in a dusty old church. Anyway, have fun." She kissed me, and I had the distinct feeling of being seen off to Sunday school while she had fun.

Well, while that was the essence of our conversation, the truth was more complicated. The truth was I had no real idea why I decided to go. I wasn't even that sure that *I* decided. But there it was, so I left the house in some reasonably Sunday clothes and made my way around the corner. I'll do my best to relate what happened next. Not easy for an atheist.

The church I was heading for was on the main road, no more than seven hundred yards from the corner of our street. Around the corner was a wide pavement, forecourts to the shops, most of them closed for Sunday. It was quiet, with a few people coming and going from the news agents with the fat, Sunday edition of the papers. I could see the church, and proceeded to walk towards its open doors. Other folk were crossing the street or getting out of parked cars and entering the church. I'd read the service times often enough when passing by to know it would begin in about ten minutes. I was in plenty of time, except I was never going to make it.

With sixty yards to go, my feet stopped walking.

All the urging, from within my now confused mind, did nothing to re-ambulate my legs. They were as a solid pedestal upon which my body and head stood. I watched as the last of the churchgoers entered the open doors, and they were closed.

Within my chest, a swelling arose and burst out through my eyes. I was completely confounded. I found I was quite able to turn around and walk back towards the house, which I did, tears streaming down my face.

"What's happened, James, tell me." Catherine hadn't yet gathered herself for the garden. I went past her, mumbling something about being all right, and headed for the kitchen sink, adding more water to my face as a pitiable disguise. With heavy competition from the running water, the tears subsided.

Catherine was beside me, inquiring again. I seriously thought of lying. Acting skills have their uses, but I couldn't, not given the context of the tears. So I did my best, as I have with you, dear reader. If you are an atheist, you will be well able to imagine what Catherine's reaction was. If you are a Christian, you will no doubt make much of it.

Me? Well, it set my feet on a journey that found me walking between trees some thirty years on. What I did after that Sunday, I'll relate to you as I tell Brother Dominic, for he, too, was just as curious as to my reasons for staying at Edgley as you may well be.

∾

Lauds was a simple service with all the monks and nuns present, and quite a few locals from the village. After the service Brother Dominic took my arm and suggested I may like to meet some of the other brothers. They were taking tea in the refectory. As the morning had turned cold, with a bluster blowing through the village, I decided I could postpone a walk for now. I had some questions, and I was sure they had too, so it seemed a reasonable suggestion.

"Brother John, Brother Michael, Brother Gabriel," Brother Dominic was introducing me to the monks as he served them all tea. I sat at the long wooden table.

The room was simple, somewhat like the Dawkin's and more in keeping with my imagined Catholic monastery, gleaned, I have to say, not from any experience or study, but from Hollywood films! The crucifix in this room, the only adornment, was not to be missed. Against the pale walls, its size and elevation bled into the room. It kept drawing my eye. I supposed that is exactly what it's meant to do. We chatted for a while, as folk anywhere will, just to get to know each other, finished our tea and moved out of the refectory to a sitting room.

Sitting in armchairs, with flowers on the window sills and tables here and there, we found ourselves relaxed. Another layman, Robert, also staying for the weekend, had joined us. Being relaxed in such a setting, rendered to my mind the monks as quite ordinary men, which, of course, they were. Ordinary men with a vocation, that was the unusual part.

I had finished relating my extraordinary encounter on the street, when Robert said, "That must have shaken you up a bit, I imagine."

"Yes. Well, it made me think. It forced my hand, in a way. I could have just forgotten the whole thing, and carried on as though nothing had happened, and remained an unexamined atheist." No one responded, they were all patiently waiting for me to continue. "I couldn't do that; it was an experience that cried out to be investigated."

"So, what did you do, James?" It was Brother Dominic. The other brothers made silent nods assenting to the question.

"I started to go to a Christian bookshop in town. At first I would go in and just look at the bibles and books, maybe pick up a leaflet or two. I didn't really know what I was looking for or what I expected to find, or find out. It wasn't as though I didn't know the basic stuff; when I was at school religious instruction was a regular weekly class. It was pretty orthodox Church of England stuff. I'd never heard of anyone experiencing what I had gone through."

"So, was that any help, the book shop?" It was a quiet, almost inaudible voice, Brother Gabriel.

"Not much, not at first. Then one time, the woman serving asked if she could help me. She'd noticed my regular visiting and surmised I was searching for something, she supposed an answer to a personal problem of some sort. She introduced herself, Caroline, I think, and told me she and her husband had opened the shop as part of 'their service to the Lord'."

"Really!" Brother John sounded like my old school headmaster responding to a bad excuse by one of the boys. "I suppose there's a place for it. Did they help you?"

"Yes, in a manner of speaking. They invited me to attend their church, to go with them the next Sunday. I agreed. I hadn't told them of my experience, only that I was searching, looking for some meaning to life. That seemed reasonable to me, and enough to go on with."

Brother Gabriel said, "James, brothers, we must be conscious of time. Perhaps we could meet again this afternoon." I looked at my watch. Mass wasn't for an hour yet, but I supposed the monks contemplated, or something, beforehand. In the event, at Brother Gabriel's reminder they began to rise, thanking me for sharing my story, and left. Only Robert and myself remained.

He said, "That was quite a story, James. An old expression I once heard seems to apply here, God has a finger in your brain and won't stop stirring it."

"That's only the half of it. I had more to come," I said. "As to whether it was God's finger, well, that would be a matter of interpretation."

"I assumed you must think somewhat along such lines, after all, you are here. Though, of course, Brother Dominic mentioned you were a Buddhist."

"Mm, not much of one, I'm afraid. I keep coming and going. At this point my Buddhism is about as reliable as my Christianity."

"But you're not a Christian, are you?" Robert wasn't asking. It was more of a challenge.

"I'm not a Catholic, so I won't be going to mass, but there are those who would say I am a Christian, whether I think so or not. After all, I was baptized as a baby, and again as an adult."

"You were baptized? Then why…"

"Why don't we continue this afternoon. I know you will want to attend mass, and I wouldn't want to disturb your doing so. And frankly, after these confessions, I need a walk."

"Alright. Yes, okay. This afternoon then," he said.

"I'll see you later, Robert." I put out my hand. He took it and we gently shook. I left and went into the cool air. Drizzle or not, I really did need a walk.

June 16th

Henry Ford famously said, "History is bunk." Did he mean there was nothing to be learned from reviewing our past behavior, or was he just too afraid to know who he was, what he had become in the long march of evolution? One could not blame him; we are not a pretty sight at the beginning of the twenty-first century. As far back as Genesis, Lot's wife was instructed not to look back. What is it in our past that we are trying so hard, in truth and myth, to avoid?

In spite of its rapid growth during the last century, most people do not go in for psychotherapy, for, to look at one's past in such a way is to admit to pain, mistakes, and vulnerability. We take flight from our own truth, in distraction, entertainment, drink, sex, drugs, a long list bearing witness to our habitual need for a fix. Even much of the therapy we seek out has prostituted itself to the addiction of running away. What it is we run from is seldom understood, either by the individual or society, or the species.

We didn't meet that afternoon. I didn't attend mass, but there was a midday service, I sat in on, that left me wondering about my prevarications. The reading was from James. (Maybe an omen. Am I allowed to use such a word here?) The passage that hit me was from Chapter one, verse five:

If any of you lack wisdom, let him ask of God, that giveth to all
men liberally, and upbraideth not; and it shall be given to him.
But let him ask in faith, nothing wavering. For he that wavereth
is like a wave of the sea driven with the wind and tossed.
For let not that man think he shall receive any thing of the Lord.
A double minded man is unstable in all his ways.[11]

I couldn't but acknowledge the truth of that last line. Yet, as I contemplated it in the afternoon, a different interpretation entered my thinking. What of remaining open! What about an acceptance of not knowing.
I had experienced the hard and fast bigotry of those who stood only by
their own (God's) word. I had felt anger and condemnation poured like
medieval hot oils from the battlements of rigid certainty. I had been *upbraided,* not by God but by men of God.

June 18th
*Escape into ignorance as a route to the truth will not save us, neither
can we return to the cave. The possession of knowledge has not only
saved us from many ills, it provides much enjoyment. Our minds cannot just sit, like the redundant appendix, as though no longer having
a meaningful function in our evolution. We must continue to use the
mind vigorously, we shall need it to get out of this mess. But, and
this will be difficult, it has to become a servant of the world, and not
the master it has been. For as a servant, its range of activity shall be
limited to its abilities.*

The evening found me sitting, talking with Brother Dominic. We discovered similarities in our childhood years, though he was born some twenty
years before me in Germany, and I, England. He had read Marx, as I had,
and adopted a socialist view of life through the same altruistic reasoning
I had. He confessed he read his gospels as a socialist manifesto, fashioned
long before Marx or Faber.

"Listen to this," he was saying, "about the young man in Matthew's
gospel who thought he had done everything he could that was right and
good. Then Jesus says to him, 'If you would be perfect, go sell what you
possess, and give it to the poor.' What's important is that Jesus says, 'If
you would be *perfect.'* Time and again he says: Give, share, think of others
first. An unfortunate contrast to modern life, I'm afraid."

"It is. But I fear we lost our way long before Jesus arrived," I said.

11 The Holy Bible: James 1:5.

93

"But, of course, we fell from grace long, long ago. Jesus' mission was to bring us back, and how does he say we can do that? First of all by getting rid of our avarice and greed, and relying on God. Just as the birds of the air and all nature does."

I thought, 'Brother Dominic must have read this stuff a thousand times.' Yet he was such an enthusiast for God, smiling as though each reading was a new discovery. I couldn't help but like him. I said, "Brother, could I tell you a joke?"

"A joke, eh? Well, if it's appropriate."

"It's clean, a bit of a God knock, though," I said.

"It wouldn't be the first knock He's taken, I'm sure. He's strong enough. Come on then, let's hear it." He was smiling and still full of interest.

I proceeded, "Old uncle Silas had been asked by the parish to take on the dense weed-ridden churchyard garden. Some months into it, he was working one hot afternoon when the new vicar came by. 'What a splendid garden, a beautiful show, mister...er?'

'Silas, just call me Silas, yer honor. Yes, it is indeed beautiful, all done by my own hand these past months, even if I do say so.'

'Ah yes, but with, I think, help from God, let us not forget.'
Silas took off his cap, scratched his head, and thought for a while, and then said, 'That may be so, vicar, but you should have seen it when 'e 'ad it to himself!'"

Brother Dominic's face, at once concentrated on listening, burst into a broad smile and his shoulders shook. "Splendid," he said, "That vicar met his match, eh? But he was right, don't you think, James."

"I like the joke for the question it opens up, but I have to confess I'm a Silas fan."

"That wouldn't have something to do with the rest of your tale we haven't heard yet? I do hope we get a chance to know how you fared with your church going."

"Tomorrow, perhaps."

"Oh good!" There was no repressing the man. He was a delight.

A good and devout man first arranges inwardly the works he has to perform outwardly. Nor do those works draw him to indulge the desires of his lower nature; on the contrary, he constrains them to obey the dictates of right reason.

Who has a harder struggle than the man that strives to overcome himself?

But this ought to be our chief business, namely, to over-come Self, and by daily gaining more mastery over Self to grow better and better.

All perfection in this life is attended by some imperfection, and no speculation of ours is without a certain obscurity.

The humble knowledge of oneself is a surer way to God than profound learning.[12]

Sunday, an appropriate day for relating my initiation into churchgoing. We gathered straight after midday service. In the sitting room, as yesterday, were the brothers, John, Michael and Gabriel, with Brother Dominic and Robert.

I started, "That Sunday, as I made ready to go with Caroline and her husband Roger, Catherine resigned herself to my 'madness' as she called it, and left for the allotment. I remember having a twinge of doubt about what I was getting into. I was well aware of such changes in one partner inviting a potential breakdown of the marriage, but I seemed to have no choice. Of course, I did have a choice."

"Of course," It was Brother John, the headmaster. Then, in a softer tone, he added, "But sometimes we're up against more than we know."

"Right," I said, "Anyway, I met my Christians outside their shop and they drove me to the church. I don't know why or how, but I never asked them what church they belonged to, what denomination. I suppose somewhere in me I assumed it wouldn't matter."

"It certainly does; it's the difference between clarity and muddle, learning and desire," It was Brother Michael, "Treacherous thing, desire." Brother Dominic had mentioned Michael was a stickler for correct form.

I went on, "The church was an evangelical sort of free church. I think it was called Elim." At this news all the brothers shifted a bit, but said nothing. I could imagine well enough what they were thinking.

"I was a bit taken aback. The welcoming of a new face was overwhelming, but I was allowed to remain close to the back as the service commenced. I must confess, it wasn't anything I expected; a far reach from old Church of England school Christianity. As it turned out, it was the hot-cauldron that the place was, that would draw the worm from its hole."

That raised eyebrows (unshaven in this case) and brought a quiet response from Brother Gabriel, "Oh dear, it sounds as though you were in great suffering somewhere within your soul."

12 Thomas a Kempis. Of the Imitation of Christ.

His remark, and his obvious concern, stopped me in my tracks for a moment. I found a shadow of the time visiting my being; my breathing became labored. I took a drink of water, my hand was shaking, as it will, and I didn't want *that* to divert their questions.

I went right on, "After several Sundays, in which I found myself being placed closer to the front of the church, a seminal event of my searching occurred. All around me hands were in the air, and speaking in tongues was in full throttle. There was a lot of 'Jesus, blessed Jesus, heal us, Jesus.' Well, I'm sure you know.

"Within my own being was a confusion of thoughts and feelings. I had my eyes closed, when quite suddenly there was, 'transposed' is the only way I can describe it; there was transposed within my being a dark force. It threw me up to the roof, down to the floor, banged me against the walls. I was hanging on to the seat in front of me for my life, rocking back and forth. While all this was going on, my mind was calling me stupid, imbecile, weak and gullible. It got blacker and blacker until it was pitch black and still, though I remained rocking back and forth."

I had to stop and take a breath, nobody moved an inch. The room, quiet and peaceful, with the afternoon sun picking out the fine dust in its beams of light as they settled on the carpeted floor. It seemed in sharp contrast to the chaos I just described.

I went on, "I cannot describe the feeling, yet I knew somewhere that I would come out of this. Then through the darkness, as though it were a fast approaching train with a single light at its front, the white robed figure of Jesus burst upon my being. Around me, the church was brightly lit by his presence. At the same time, the windows of the church were blown outward, and it was as though a great weight had been thrown off me.

"I collapsed into the pew and slowly opened my eyes. There were hands on me and concerned voices around me. I looked down at my clothes; I was a mess. There was a lot of blood pouring from my nose, and abundant tears from my eyes, though I wouldn't say I was crying. Whatever it was, it was over. I went to the washroom, cleaned up, and took myself home."

∽

At my second school we went swimming once a week as part of our physical training. I was eleven years old and not a tall boy. The pool was outdoors, in a public park. At a time when one could get "six-of-the-best" in school, out at the pool one got away with speech and behavior otherwise sat-on hard. So it was, that on one particular occasion we were supposed to be learning to dive. We were at the shallow end of the pool, three feet deep. Lined up, and one by one told, "Dive." Any hesitations met with, "DIVE, BOY, DIVE!" When my turn came, I protested before the word left Mister Humphrey's lips. "But sir! It's too shallow, I'll hit my head on the bottom." Which brought the retort, "Don't be stupid, boy, you couldn't reach the bottom if you tried, just get yourself in there." I dived, hit my head on the bottom, and promptly became semi- conscious.

I was in my mother's womb. I was not okay, something was wrong.

৽

Sunday's compline was my last service attendance before leaving Edgley. The reading was from Galatians (Chapter five) part of which read: 'Stand fast therefore in the liberty wherewith Christ hath made us free, and be not entangled again with the yoke of bondage.' I wondered who chose the readings. Was that a coincidence? Whatever it was, I left it in the church. I've come a long way since that encounter with Christ (if that, indeed, is what it was.) In the morning I said goodbye to everyone, got in my old BMW, and back on the road. On the motorway, I turned the radio up loud – a rock and roll station – and wound down the windows. I joined in the racket, singing.

SIX

I returned to Edgley, as planned, towards the end of February. Brother Dominic was away when I arrived. Brother Michael was on guest duty. Though he showed recognition, even a bit of interest in my returning, chatting was kept short. There was no fiddling with tea either; I was shown politely to my room, and left to it. I had the feeling, last time here, that he tolerated my story in deference to the other monks, particularly Brother Dominic, who wanted to hear it. But it was he who was to prove a staunch support when the struggle once again broke surface.

My first week was uneventful. The weather was awful, even for February; it poured most of the time, and I found myself running through puddles to and from my room. I read a great deal. I had found a copy of Thomas a Kempis's 'Of the Imitation of Christ'. Intrigued by the title of the second book therein 'Calling to the inner life', I checked it out, thinking it may give me some insight into the turmoil I seemed to be living with.

As I had to deal with Brother Michael, I mentioned my borrowing of the book and why. His response was to tell me what an unsurpassed teaching it was, but, "You'd be better guided by the first part; it will give you fortification before tackling the mess we all carry within. Let me tell you this, I know you may find it difficult to accept, but there are forces at work beyond our senses, benign and, I'm afraid, malign forces. Your experiences occurred because you dared to test those forces. Perhaps you were brave, perhaps foolish, most likely you simply didn't know what you were doing. Be careful, James, the life of the spirit is a serious matter."

Well! That set me thinking, I can tell you. My interpretation of events was grounded in good old reliable psychology, the urges of the ego fighting the unconscious restrictions of the super ego, all that stuff. And I'd done pretty well at containing the mess, as Brother Michael called it, since the events I have related. Still, I have to admit, here I am at a Christian retreat. Is the atheist wavering, you may reasonably ask, is reason dead? I'm here because, of all the places one might search out suffering, here, the deep life of these monks may yet yield answers to the dilemma. For, I am told, Christ took on suffering for our mess. Yet, too, I would be foolish to brush aside the words of a man of obvious intelligence, even given that the notion of unseen forces is completely alien to my thinking. I turn to Book one of Thomas, Chapter three: Of the Doctrine of Truth. I read...

Happy is the man whom truth teaches by itself, not by figures and passing words, but as it is in itself.

Our own way of thinking and our perception often deceive us, and they see but little.

What is the good of reasoning and disputing about dark and hidden things, when we shall not be censured at the Judgment for not knowing them?

Supreme folly! We neglect the things that are useful and necessary, and we willingly give our attention to those that are curious and mischievous.[13]

I found myself in agreement, certainly with the last thought. It seems to me, and has for a long time, that we waste life. We only half live it, if we truly live it at all, for we neglect each other in favor of things curious and mischievous – as good a way to put it as I have thus far found. As to dark and hidden things, I think it high time we admitted of them in us all, and acknowledged their influence upon us, for why else would we, at the start of the twenty-first century, accept killing as an act of freedom. We are surely slaves of fear.

June 21st

It is to the first line I now refer. I have some agreement with the notion of truth teaching us, but for it to do so, we must admit our desire to constantly run from it. It was many years ago I found myself thinking, how we love to search out truth until we come too close to it; we then decide to search elsewhere. Whatever truth is, there is clearly conflicting urges in us with regards to knowing it. It has been said, 'To know God is a comfort but not comfortable.' (For 'not comfortable' the Buddhist would say Dukkha.[14]) Is the God of the theists just, in fact, truth clothed in various forms of illusion? The challenge would be to find not just comfort but a release from suffering through knowing the truth.

To be released from suffering, one must first know suffering. The first stage of knowing is acknowledgment.

I brought this up with the monks at what had become a regular afternoon meeting. There were now several lay visitors and four nuns from

---

13 Thomas a Kempis. Of the Imitation of Christ.
14 Dukkha: Generally translated as suffering.

the nuns' house. We were arranged in a circle in the now familiar sitting room. Brother John took up the discussion.

"I know it's what our Buddhist friends use, but I'm not sure the term suffering is sound theology. It may lead one to think of cuts and bruises, losing money or failing in business, that sort of thing," he said.

"If I may, Brother," I said, "the word suffering is a translation generally understood by lay folk, but, in actual fact, in the Pali language the term, as you know, is Dukkha, which has no intrinsically direct translation. Wouldn't you say it was more like angst?"

Brother John, after a little pause, said, "The bottom line is we're talking of sin."

One of the visitors, a woman whom I had not met, said, "Why does our hardship or suffering, angst, whatever, always come down to something we did wrong. I don't recall setting out in life as a bad person, and I don't think my daughter is either. So, why sin?"

The room fell silent, the air thick with thoughts. One could almost hear the voices in each head, untangling Brother Michael's mess. It was he who spoke, turning to the woman, he said, "Sin, Veronica, is not an observation of our on-going behavior. I'm sure you and your daughter are good people. When we use the word, and you're right, it is a strong word, we are referring to something deep within, within us all, a darkness that has penetrated to the very heart of our being, our souls." As he finished speaking he looked around the room as though to spread the word. Our eyes met, and the grey creature in my being crawled up my spine.

❧

Three days into my second week, I awoke in the night. I lay in the darkness wondering why I wasn't sound asleep. I had no recollection of dreaming, neither did I feel restless; in fact, I was quite relaxed, almost still, with just the gentle twitch in the left arm. Then I felt it. You know that place on your back where you can't reach no matter what you do? The place back-scratcher makers profit from? Well, right there, something was... itching wouldn't be the right word, neither tickling or, well, anything I could describe, but it was there just the same. I turned on my side to see if it would stop, it didn't.

I managed to drift back into a restless sleep, and in the morning went down the corridor to the men's washroom as usual. The four wash basins in a row, facing a long mirror, were shared by the lay visitors. I was shaving when one of the other visitors came in and was about to walk behind me, when he stopped, quite suddenly, and was looking at my back. I could see in the mirror a question forming on his face. "What's that?" he said, looking into my reflected face for an answer.

"What?" I said.

"Those marks on your back, you've got marks on your back like..."

"Like what, marks like what?" I said, feeling as though I were being singled out, pointed at.

"They... it's like a cross. On your back. Look for yourself, down there." He was indicating the last basin, that had a twin on the opposite wall with a small mirror over it. I walked down and tried to see my back, using the two mirrors, but they were perfectly vertical and not the same height. I turned this way and that, but only got glimpses of scratch-like marks.

"I can't see the whole thing," I said.

"Wait here, I'll be back in a minute," he said, and left hurriedly. I thought he had gone for a small mirror, or perhaps he'd gone to fetch a monk. Meanwhile, I washed off my face, just in case. He returned with a camera. Digital.

"Stand by the window, er...?"

"James, I think we've met in the afternoon discussion group."

"Right, oh, you're... I remember. I'm Geoff. Look, this will show you." I got the idea and turned my back to him. I heard the low click, a few, actually. Then he came round and showed me the viewing screen on the back of the camera.

In the center of my back were two thin, not quite vertical lines. Crossing them, somewhere around my shoulder blades, were two more thin, horizontal lines. It was a cross all right; it was also, I reasoned, the source of the feeling I had trouble pinning down, when I awoke in the night.

Geoff said, "What happened, James?"

"Nothing," I said, "Nothing at all, apart from waking me up, I think. Nothing happened."

✺

It being a weekday, Lauds was at eight-thirty. At ten-thirty there was a polite knock on my door. I opened it to find Brother Michael, who said straight away, "Could you come with me, James, I'd like to have a chat." I said I would and went inside for a jacket, thinking of his use of 'chat' that obviously implied something close or closed. Not a secret, I was sure; monks aren't in the habit of keeping and sharing secrets. It's bad practice that goes with gossiping. Seeing me get my coat, he said, "Let's walk in the garden, under the trees."

"Alright," I said, and left it at that as we made our way outside.

The gardens of the Abbey were made up of flower beds and an allotment for food growing. Unlike the Buddhists, whose rules forbid self-sustaining activities, here a robust gardening life is a part of every monk and nun's day. Brother Dominic is the exception. Right now, I thought, I could do with his cheerful countenance. Brother Michael seemed seriously intent upon whatever task we were about.

We walked under the quiet trees to the fence bordering the Abbey grounds. Beyond the five-bar gate, we stopped at a field of wild grasses and, I guessed, flowers, waiting for spring to fill this meadow. The day was clear, and the sun planted patches of light where we stood. I waited, content to be outside and under the trees.

"James," Brother Michael began, "These um, marks on your back. What do you make of them?" He waited, holding his hands together as though constraining his own thoughts, "What do you think about them?"

I had no idea, really, none, but I felt I should say something. I tried to think logically, in contradiction to the state I found myself in. I said, "They, it... is symbolic. I'm not sick or injured, they are not really of the body, though they are on my body. That's about as near any observation I can make."

"Mm... You said, 'It'. What is it to you, James? Does it have a name?"

I said, "A name? You mean like a cross? It's like a cross. One can hardly miss it."

"So, it's a symbolic cross, right? I think here in these grounds, we can agree on what cross it is," he said, "Put another way, you are carrying a symbol of *the* cross on your back. Can you accept that, James?"

I nodded my assent. I couldn't trust my voice. I was beginning to feel very unsettled at this line of thought. I was pretty certain it would awaken the grey creature in my gut.

Brother Michael went on, "But it's not so symbolic, is it, James? You know James was the brother of our Lord, of Jesus. They were very close." I could see he was watching me now, observing something I hoped was hidden from view. But Brother Michael had been down this road before. He finished talking and waited.

I found myself feeling very weak; my legs were losing strength, I was losing the will to stand. Brother Michael took my hands in his and said, "Let your legs go, James. Kneel." I knelt. I began to shake. "Close your eyes, James." I did so. The shaking seemed to come from outside, as though

I had been got hold of. I had no control; it became violent, words or sounds were coming from a mouth I didn't own. Suddenly I felt strength at my back. It felt as though Brother Michael had got behind me; hard against my back, he was holding me around the chest. The noise from within me blotted out everything. And then, suddenly, I was sick; it gushed like a broken street sewer from deep in my gut, straight out with a force that sent it a few feet in front of me onto the ground. I collapsed and fainted.

When I came to, I found myself propped against the gate with a cushion behind me. Brother Michael and Brother John were seated on the ground, on a blanket, opposite me. Between us was a small tray with three cups of tea and a plate of biscuits. They were looking at me; their faces had a softness I had missed until now. Brother John silently handed me a cup. I sipped and then drank. It was sweet tea. I felt it all the way down into my stomach, which was surprisingly peaceful. When I had taken sufficient, I continued to hold the cup with what was left in it, and said, "Thank you." They both imperceptibly nodded and smiled.

Then Brother Michael asked me, "What did you see? Where did you go when you were unconscious?"

"Go?" I said, "I don't recall..." Yet there was something.

Brother Michael prompted me, "Yes, just relax a moment, it will come to you, perhaps if you close your eyes."

I did as he asked. I closed my eyes, watching the two monks fade into the line of light closing out the world. And there it was. I started to speak, "I'm in a desert. It's vast, spreading around me on all sides. The sun is extremely bright. I shade my eyes and can see what looks like a shadowy figure in the far distance. I am walking towards it. My feet are bare. The sand makes hard walking, but I am making progress towards the figure, only it's not a figure. It's too tall. Now I am standing beneath it. It's Jesus on the cross. I have to find a way to get him down, but there is nothing but rocks and sand. But I think there has to be a way.

"Then he is down and in my arms. I'm turning around to lay him on the ground, when I accidentally bang his head against a small rock. He's bleeding. It's then I notice the ring of thorns on his head. I lay him down and lift his head to try and get the thorn thing off him. He sits up and smiles at me and says, 'It's alright, look.' He removes the ring of thorns, stands up, and just throws it. It soars away and disappears into the blue of the sky. We are standing now. And he has his arm on my shoulder. He says, 'Go, go up the mountain, you'll see it all from there.'

"It's gone suddenly dark. But now I see I'm in the back of a deep cave, I can see the opening far off. There is someone standing by me, someone

I sense rather than see. A voice says, 'Come' and the figure walks before me towards the light from the cave's entrance. All I can see of it is a long, black, hooded cloak. I feel at peace, though. I trust this figure.

"The cave opens onto a ledge just wide enough to stand on. Below us, the mountain we are on falls away sharply into a ravine. In the ravine is what looks like a multicolored river. I look as closely as the height allows, and see it's a river of people, people of all different races. At one end of the ravine is the desert, and the people pour out like water all over the desert, dispersing, yet remaining dense, as they begin to cover the land.

"The figure beside me falls into the stream of color, rises up again, and the cloak is now itself multicolored. It is wrapped around my shoulders and I am told, 'Go!'

"Now I have sandals on and I'm walking, walking, walking. The ground is hard sand and rocks. I am making slow progress. All around me are the people of different colors wearing bright multicolored cloaks. We are all walking. It is very bright and getting brighter. There is nothing now. I am here." I slowly open my eyes to the real light of day. I feel the air against my cheeks, take a deep breath, and drink the cold remains in my cup.

We sit in silence as I place my cup on the small round tray. I reach to take a biscuit, and Brother Michael's hand gently covers the plate, saying as he does so, "I think it is a particular biscuit you should take today. Mass is in half an hour, you are invited, James, if you would come."

June 28th

Thus it is through many a turn and turn-about that life and death are brought together in consciousness, neither one greater than its twin. This experiential awareness changes everything, for you will have moved beyond the Tapestry's living face and begun to witness the back of the weave.

I would not keep Brother Michael's counsel from you, but our story, as life does, moves on. We will hear what the monks made of my experiences anon.

Just before I was due to leave Edgley, I had a letter from Richard Dawkin, my Quaker friend. Well, I hoped we were still friends, and the letter certainly gave me hope on that score. It was an invitation to visit and possibly house-sit for them. Having, as yet, no particular place arranged to spend the summer, I phoned and accepted his invite. I said I would arrive after Easter, I thought it best. I was due to leave Edgley, however, before Easter.

The day I left, several of the monks turned out to wish me well. I could easily have been drawn to tears as I was at Indriya, but the stoicism of Brothers John and Michael held sway. As the other monks left, I found myself with these two elders. John said, "Well, James, you're welcome here any time you feel you need a refuge, or just a rest." He put out his right hand and as we shook, he covered my hand with his, then left Brother Michael with me.

"I'll walk with you to your car, James," he said, "I know you search with sincerity, but remember, not all adversaries play a straight game." We continued until at the car, and as I was stowing my bag and preparing to go, he said, "Take care, my friend," squeezed my shoulders, and left. I spent Easter on the road, most of it lying or sleeping under trees.

∾

When my dad was a boy, he had polio. As a result, his left leg was thin and his foot, too. To keep his sock from rucking up in his shoe, he put a piece of cotton wool in the toe of his left sock. He would shake it down to the toe of the sock.

One day, when I was a small boy, while dressing to go out, my father saw me putting my hand in my left sock and shaking it. He got mad at me and demanded to know, "What do you think you're doing?" I didn't know what to say. It was a copycat action that I had picked up watching my dad.

He realized what had happened, explained his own action, and told me to think before doing anything in future. What he taught me was that there is reason in doing things, and that I should know the reason or not do it. I've learned since that some things will not succumb to reason.

SEVEN

I arrived at the Dawkin's village in late April. The gardens were beginning to show the results of winter efforts by their owners, crocus and daf-
fodils in bright patches forming neat borders to well manicured lawns.
Here and there, stray wild bluebells reminded me of the woods at Indriya,
where there would be a carpet of blue stretching deep into the trees.

That was not the Buddha grove, but an actual wooded copse, near the
monastery, given as a donation. It surprises me how often such fortune
occurs when one, or a group, sets a mind to goodness. It seems *something*
concurs, and the way is made beautiful with gifts. My reason would rather
not acknowledge such a something, yet there it is. Jung's synchronicity?
Or just plain serendipity. My mathematician friends say it's chance, just
as *someone* has to win the lottery. They're right, of course, I think.

What a thing the mind is. The mere memory of flowers in a wood has
set me to thinking. What is the seduction of unreasoned, romantic notions
over sensible conclusion. What is it they offer better than truth? These
were my thoughts as I approached Richard and Rosalyn's house, opened
the gate, and walked up the path to the oak door (Nottingham forest?)
The shiny, brass lion's-head casting that was the door knocker seemed in
stark contrast to the plain interior I was about to enter. I knocked.

I heard the girls before I saw them; I suppose they saw my outline in
the rough glass of the door. It was Amy who opened the door, came out
and gave me a hug. 'Well,' I thought, 'that's a good start.'

Then Richard was in the hallway, "James, so good to see you. You
look as though you've been on the road again."

"In a manner of speaking. I brought the car this time, so I've seen
more road and less countryside."

"Right," he looked past me at the parked car, "I wouldn't have tagged
you as a BMW type, though."

"You're right, but the price was right. It's strictly second hand," I
said.

By now Rosalyn and Joan had joined us, Joan giving me another hug,
and Rosalyn suggesting we all go into the living room. As we seated ourselves, I sensed, what? Not tension exactly, nothing entirely unpleasant,
but... change, certainly, something had changed.   The family I had
known was of a different pattern, nothing I could describe, just the way
they seated themselves. You see, before, Richard and Rosalyn would sit
together, on the sofa. The girls would sit on the floor or squash together
in one of the big armchairs. Now, Joan was on the floor at Richard's feet,

he in an armchair, and Amy was sitting next to Rosalyn on the sofa. I had a distinct (therapist's) intuition that I was witnessing allegiances.

We had tea and made light chatter. Then it was Joan who showed me to my room. That, too, had changed. It was now Joan's room. The girls, who I had known as sharing a room, now had their separate bedrooms. Well, they were growing, so that was natural enough. Still, it made me think, as I unpacked.

I went downstairs and asked if Bowser would like a walk, as I felt like stretching my legs. There was assent all round, particularly from the dog. I took the lead and set out for the fields. I thought of one of my diary entries from Indriya, something about the sun and the countryside opening up the mind. I tried not to think like a therapist. I wanted to think as a friend, to feel this family's heart, to check its beat. I wanted to be at peace with them. I suppose what I wanted was for them to be at peace with *me!*

> ## July 3rd
>
> *What can be more important than true friendship. I have discovered there is nothing in this life of joys and sufferings that endures like it. Surely to be friendless is the worst of fates. A friend knows and accepts your darkness along with your light. When you do good, they praise. When you do bad, they forgive. Friendship sets the stage for intimacy, though few of us are that lucky, for we run from real intimacy as we do from the truth. Given but one real moment of the intimate, and there will one find eternity.*

I returned home in time for dinner. The girls wanted to sit either side of me; I suspect, so that they could feel my shakes. I have come a ways since last they held my hand. They still shake, but I could now calm them to a gentle quiver. Little was said over dinner. I sensed it would be after the girls were in bed that there may be a talk.

And so it was. Rosalyn brought in a tray and, instantly, coffee was in the air. 'Well,' I thought, 'this is a change I can go with.' Rosalyn said, "We don't have any white powder, James, but there is milk. Shall I pour?" Although Amy and Joan had gone to bed, I noticed we still occupied three separate seats.

I said, "Thanks, yes, that'll be fine. They have that stuff in the monastery because milk is considered a food, and, as you know, there's no food allowed after noon. But cheese is allowed, beats me. It's a strange life however you look at it, not for everyone." I stopped myself, realizing

I was making empty chatter in avoidance of something. God knows what, I'd best wait and see. I picked up my cup, and sure enough I was shaking.

"So," Richard said, "Will you be going back, James?"

"Yes," I said, "Almost certainly, in the autumn, I expect."

"But it is a strange life, as you say. Would you enjoy giving up so much? I mean, you couldn't go on your walk-abouts or visit friends, that sort of thing. Wouldn't you miss that?"

"Well, as to the walk-abouts. I was married for a long time. It was when that ended, I took to the road, but I don't intend doing it for life," I said, "Unless, that is, it had a purpose to it." I was trying to look at Rosalyn while this mild interrogation was taking place. I knew it was leading somewhere, and I wanted to measure her part in it, silent as it was.

"Like the monks, you mean?"

"Yes, it's called Tudong. It's the practice of never staying in one place for longer than three nights, moving all the time."

"Spreading the gospel, so to speak?" Richard had a smile on him saying that.

"Yes, I suppose one could say that."

I thought, 'Where's he heading?' I decided to try and change tack. "You mentioned in your letter something about house-sitting, looking after Bowser. Are you going away? Holiday...?" I let it hang there and turned to Rosalyn, "Any more of that brew, Rosalyn?"

"Oh, er, yes, certainly," she said, caught a little off guard, waiting for Richard's denouement, no doubt. "Can you hand me your cup?"

As I did so Richard answered my query, "Er, yes, we're all going away for... a bit... a break. Yes, a holiday," he stopped short. Then Rosalyn spoke. It was so quiet I had to strain to hear her, "We're taking separate holidays, as Richard put it. I'm taking Amy, we're going to my parents, and Richard's going away with Joan. We decided it may help." The air was thick and silent when Rosalyn finished.

I said, "Look, I don't pretend to understand what you have been going through, but I considered us to be friends, and I still do. I may be a bit wayward, but I have a respect for commitment, your commitment to your beliefs, your marriage..."

"Yes, well, you might have thought of that before you..." Richard was struggling, he really was a good friend.

"Richard, Richard, dear friend, if I have shown weakness, it was never a fire strong enough to burn, and certainly not destroy what you both have together. If anyone is getting burnt, it's myself in the mess (thank you, Brother Michael) that inhabits *my* life." I shifted forward on my seat; I had their attention. "It pains me to see the division that has opened up in this family."

"We're fine. We're just contemplating taking time to reconfigure our lives," Richard said, his voice had softened, "There's nothing for you to concern yourself about, James. We're still very much together."

I didn't know what to say. I knew, well enough, facing the truth of oneself, one's behavior and its consequence upon others is a hard task. It's easier to tell ourselves small lies, we do it all the time. The truth demands an intimacy the ego craves, yet shuns, lest it is revealed in all its fear. So I succumbed to their fears. I said, "Well, a holiday would be a good idea, but I wish you were all going together. I think having some fun would be a better salve than too much thinking."

෬

I must have got something right, for they did decide to go on a real holiday together, which made my house-sitting much more pleasant. When they returned, they were in good spirits. I heaved a silent sigh of relief and pleasure at their fortune.

There was, though, some unfinished business between us, and it came up while we were washing up the dinner dishes. The girls had gone out to make the most of a long summer evening. Rosalyn said, "James, when we were away, we remembered something you promised us."

"Oh! And what was that?" I said, "Something I promised?"

"Yes," she said, "You said you would tell us what 'one death is enough' meant, and how the woman knew about your dream, don't you remember?"

"Oh, right. Didn't I ever tell you? Well, I'd better make amends, but it will have to be after the girls are in bed, okay?" I said, trying to recall the events myself. As if I would forget. It may have been long ago, but it was not something one ever forgets.

That evening we settled into our chairs, that is, me into a chair, and, I was happy to see, Richard and Rosalyn together on the sofa. I said, "I'll tell you because it wouldn't be fair to keep it from you, seeing as how I gave you some of the story. But it's not altogether a happy tale."

"Well, it's life," Richard said, "I think we're out of our cocoon, James, so, let's hear it."

"Alright," I said, and told them of my discovery that the woman was Wendy, the young girl who had worked at the nursery at the end of the war. I did say I took to going there to dig her garden, and about the planting of the strange Lily bulb, but I didn't think they needed to know of my affair with her.

I went on, "This is how Wendy explained to me my leaving the classroom and having the dream: The night before, she had dreamed of the same girl, but she knew who it was."

"She did? How... how could she...?" It was Rosalyn.

"Let me ask you something, Rosalyn," I said, "You've had babies. When you were carrying them did you ever think you..., let's see, did you ever feel you *knew* them? When they were inside you?"

"I was sure Amy was a girl. Oh yes, and I used to talk to her a lot. Yes, I suppose I sort of knew her. I expect that's why she chatters so much."

"Wendy said it was her daughter," I said.

Rosalyn almost exclaimed, "She had a daughter?"

"Darling, if we keep interrupting the poor man", Richard said.

"Yes, yes, you're right, sorry. Please go on, James."

"Wendy told me that during the war, she lived in the farmhouse with her mother. Her father had been killed early in the fighting. When Wendy was sixteen, she got pregnant by a soldier who promptly disappeared." This produced a gasp from Rosalyn, but no interruption, so I continued, "To add to her invidious position, when the baby was born, it was a Downs syndrome child. Wendy's mother said it was curse, that she'd brought it on herself. Well, one can imagine what living in the house was like."

"Oh, how awful for the girl." It was natural Rosalyn would be moved. That's why I wasn't at all sure I wanted to tell them.

"Are you sure you want me to go on?" I said, "It doesn't get much better."

"I'm afraid you can't leave us there," Richard said, putting an arm around Rosalyn.

I looked at them and thought, 'What fortunate lives some have, while others seem to get sorrows by the bucket-full. Can a God they worship (or sit peacefully in the presence of, in their case) really exist?'

I went on, "The baby was kept out of sight, upstairs on the top floor. Though everyone knew of the pregnancy, no one spoke of it or inquired of the baby. It seems Wendy's mother forbade such talk. But as it happened, another woman in the district had suffered a similar fate as Wendy's. It's all too common in war. Somehow they had connected, but whereas Wendy's baby went full term to birth, the other woman's baby miscarried before anyone was the wiser. Naturally, they stayed friends. That other woman later married my father."

"She was your...?"

I let the events sink in and sort themselves before continuing, "They were to become lifelong friends," I paused. This was harder to tell than I thought. "When Wendy's baby was just under three months old, it died quite suddenly. What we now call a cot death, or crib death. Wendy was confused and grief-stricken. She didn't say, but I'm guessing she was out of things for a while."

"Out of things, James?" It was Richard who hadn't quite grasped my meaning.

"I suspect she spent a while in hospital, mental hospital, that is. What she did tell me was that she had been advised to work with children, as a primitive sort of therapy, I imagine. That's how she came to be working at the nursery." I took a breather, I needed it, even if they didn't. I said, "Do you think we could have some tea?"

"Absolutely," was Richard's enthusiastic response. I think he was feeling the need as much as I. Rosalyn concurred and she went into the kitchen. Richard turned to me, "You look a bit shaken, James. Are you all right?"

"Yes, I'll be fine with tea. Does wonders, always said so."

I stood and stretched, hoping to hide my reaction to this telling. But as I've mentioned before, Richard's no fool. He said, "It must have been a difficult story to take on when you were seventeen," he paused, I could feel a question coming, "James, you said this Wendy had a dream of her daughter, but how did she know you had that same dream?"

I said, "I'll tell all when I get some tea in me."

To my surprise, Richard went to a cupboard and pulled out a bottle that for all the world looked like whiskey. "Perhaps a drop of this will help."

"I didn't know you..."

"Medicinal, James, but you're right, Quakers don't take hard drink. However, sometimes what is labeled as wrong can be the right thing to do." It sounded like one of Richard's little jokes with the girls. But his arm around my shoulders assured me he was serious, and serious about being out of the cocoon. I accepted his offer, suggesting it could go in the tea.

Rosalyn came in with the tray, and we drank. She made no comment about the whiskey, even when Richard joined me in a tot.

Fortified, I continued, "This is where you just have to accept stuff. Stuff I find strange, but then, life has presented me with a number of strange events.

"I've mentioned, my mother and Wendy struck up a friendship over their respective pregnancies. The other thing they had in common was both families, Wendy's and my mother's, had Gypsies in their family line. When they both found themselves pregnant, they bonded as sisters, did some ceremony or something. My mother confirmed that part, but neither would say what they did. 'It's women's business, gypsy business' was all I got in reply to questions. But what Wendy did say to me was, 'I knew you were a sensitive', she used the word as an noun, 'because,' she said, 'you had been conceived in a womb that had known death.'"

I had to stop at that part and take a drink, which by this time was more whiskey than tea.

In the break I'd taken, Rosalyn spoke, "That does explain quite a lot." Richard looked at her, and I was sure he was about to ask a question, then his face cleared of it and relaxed.

"It seems that when Wendy had the dream of her daughter, in that same dream was the baby that preceded me in my mother's womb. To her that was a sign to 'call me out' as she put it, because I was the one who could bring both deaths to a close. I don't know how she did it, but it was she that made me stand up and leave that classroom without anyone moving. Then she ensured I would lie down and dream.

"When she called me into her house to garden, it was to plant the Lily. In some way *that* was the closing act that brought those two small lives together and brought peace to both Wendy and my mother, who, by the way, knew all about it, but said nothing to me. When I told her I was going to garden for the woman in the farmhouse, she just said, 'That should be a nice job for the summer.'"

೧೦

I left the Dawkins a happier family than when I arrived to house- sit, of that I was glad. Of myself, that summer and autumn, there is little to say, save perhaps one incident that took place near the end of November.

I must tell you first that the old BMW, having seen most of the country and some of Wales and Scotland, ended its days in the scrap yard around the back end of September. I was on my feet again.   Catherine's   new relationship, it seemed, was flourishing. That was a bit hard to take, but, well, it was for the best. We had settled into a friendship, which, by the way, we still have to this day.

The incident I refer to relates to a dream I had at least five years before Catherine and I broke up. It was a long dream, in color, and when I awoke I remembered all of it. That in itself was strange, for usually I just remember snippets of dreams here and there. It was a series of scenes and events, mostly real, but sometimes twisted, as only dreams can be, into some symbolic message from the unconscious.

I decided to return to Indriya, I will tell about that decision as we go. Well, I was walking on a different route which took me through the town of Heglington, and it was as I was exiting the town, moving out towards the surrounding countryside, that I saw before me a scene that stopped me walking. It was the first scene in my old long-ago dream. 'How could that be so?' I thought, 'How was it possible to dream the distant future?' The skeptic in me said I was making adjustments in my memory, but I reasoned: to what purpose? The scene could just as well not be there, as there,; it made no difference. It was there, there was no doubt about it. As I walked that day, I thought a lot about gypsies, fortunes, and fate, about Wendy's baby and Malcolm, and *a lot* about life and death.

EIGHT

I'm standing in the Buddha grove. It's December, and the winter rains retreat is due to start in a week's time, on the third of January. My hair is short, and I have on loose fitting clothes, a white shirt and dark trousers. My feet, like my head, are bare. Well, that's not strictly true. I do have on a white woolen hat. It's cold. I also have a blanket wrapped around me. I'm standing at one of the trees, contemplating the path in front of me. I'm trying to steady my thoughts, bring them, at least, to a single thought. As I'm sure you can imagine by now, my life crowds my head, searching for resolution, peace of mind, answers to too many questions. That is why I am here. Here among the trees, confined by a set of rules, subject to simplicity, away from distraction.

I'm hoping the enclosing life that's about to descend upon me with the retreat will craft a clear way for me to follow. For it is single minded clarity that I seek right now. Not to be Buddhist or Christian, though such may come about. At this time, I seek not to join or adhere. Neither do I reject anything. I do not believe or reject belief. All such urgings I put aside, as I have put the world aside. I stand here with one purpose: to walk undisturbed to the other tree. How simple a thing is that? Yet, how fraught with distraction, even in this peaceable realm.

∽

When I was a small boy, not yet seven years old, I walked the half mile to school. One can hardly believe such things were commonplace, once upon a time. In winter, it would happen some days that a fog would come up from the city, a swirling damp specter as thick as liquid sulfur, and smelling so. It's been the setting for many a Sherlock Holmes mystery. But it's no story I'm telling, just a fact of my young life, before the clean-air act passed by parliament around nineteen-fifty.

Why am I telling this now? Well, on the way to school, making my way, I would sometimes stop. You see I had, like everyone else, to walk close to a wall or hedge, something to give me my bearings, for it was so thick, there was a greyish-yellow opaqueness two feet in front of the eyes. When I stopped, I dared to move away from the wall until I was suspended, untouched by anything or anybody. There was nothing to distract me from the feeling of a timeless everything. Even 'I' disappeared.

∽

The mind is not going to settle, so I make slow first steps hoping my need to concentrate will absorb my thinking and dissolve the thoughts.

Feel the earth against my heel and rolling beneath the sole until toes finish the step. *'What's Kate doing now? A curve of body parts, hair painted with light.'* Lift the back foot, feel the weight move, heavy, down into the ground through my standing foot. *'Rosalyn's lips floating. Eyes in a car mirror.'* Move with care and place the second step a measured distance, no stretch, not slouching. Earth and heel once again meet. *'Stella's two-year-old face, an old photo from Holland. Fields of Tulips.'* Toes, earth, lift. Stay with the movement, legs even, body relaxed. *'Remember that time you collapsed, what was that?'*

The tree is before me, how? Where have I been? Take a breath, turn, stand. Seek once again the path. *'This won't work! Why do you waste your time?'*

There! Right there is the source, the bane. The dark mischief that would take me from this path. I decide to walk faster like I was bound for somewhere, for indeed I am, though it be unseen and without name. Now the trees come quickly to me and I turn without hesitation and step straight back on the path. Time is nothing, space is nothing, only walking, walking, walking, tree to tree to tree.

I don't know how long I pushed into that walk, neither do I know where I was, for I forced perception and thought under a hard tread. Cold though it was, and darkening when the bell rang for meditation, I was perspiring. Yet, I knew it was not all from exertion, but from the struggle within. On my way to the sala I washed my face and felt ready. As I joined the gentle procession, Anando fell in beside me, silent and composed. We exchanged looks and smiled, a smile of friendship, or as the Buddhists say, Kaliamita[15].

After the chanting, as the sala fell silent, I knew I was exhausted. Though I had joined in the chanting, it was a last effort in the struggle I'd grappled with between the trees. I gave in to the mind and found myself overtaken with darkness. I knew the feeling within would seek eruption in tears. I could not decide to move or stay, the tiredness had robbed me of even that choice. I sat with eyes open in the dim candlelight, and looked into the face of the Buddha.

I breathed steadily as the tears ran silently down my face onto my shirt and trousers. The pouring reminded me of the time I stood on the pavement trying to go to church, of the time Malcolm, stiff and cold, was

---

15 Kaliamita: A Buddhist term for those who support with friendship one's efforts towards enlightenment.

thrust into my arms as his mother went screaming out of the house, of Andrew, silent and twisted in the grass beneath the poplar tree, of a small me, desperately clinging to mother in a choking cellar as bombs dropped and lights flickered, threatening a dark abyss, of a darkness beyond all these I could put no name to. And when all such thoughts had run their course, I was left alone. The tears dried, while my body leaned gently forward, my head touching the floor, I slept. Submission was complete.

When the rains retreat formally began, a silence, beyond even that of daily life here, descended. Everything became a meditation: walking between buildings, eating the daily meal, even taking care of one's person. And each evening after meditation the abbot would give a Dhamma talk. His theme was always grounded in a primary Buddhist observation that things are as they are, that whatever we want or think we want, whatever we dislike and have aversion to, whatever we wish to believe or not believe, all these are laid aside by the simple, yet profound words: 'this is the way it is.' In years to come this elementary statement of fact would come to my aid, when yet again death paid a visit in my life.

July 5th

My father was a practical man. His philosophy was based firmly on the realistic observations he made of life. He would have concurred with the abbot's statement. He once told me this old story from the Arab world, a couple of years after Andrew died. That would make me about nine years old.

There once was a merchant who lived in Bagdad, and on a particular day he sent his servant into the marketplace to buy food. Whilst mingling in the happy, jostling crowd, the man saw, walking towards him, a woman whom he recognized as Death and she had on her face a strange, threatening look. The man ran home as fast as he could and told his master. His master lent him his horse and told him to take himself away to Samarra. The master then went to the marketplace. On the way, he too saw Death, and admonished her for frightening his servant, but he said nothing of his lending him a horse and sending him away, for he was a good man. Death said, "I did not mean to frighten your servant, it was just that I was so surprised to see him here, for I have an appointment with him tonight in Samarra."

The three month's retreat is over, I am walking, slowly now, from tree to tree, back and forth. Over the winter I have gained a degree of peaceful-

July 5th

ness. The trees are pushing their bright green shoots of leaves into the air, showing once again their offspring. As birds fly across the spring sky, they carry pieces of nesting, twigs, strands of sheep's wool, leaves. They are often in pairs, weaving around one another like the newlyweds they are. And visitors have begun to come to Indriya, some for just a day, some to stay for a few days, and some to see if this life is going to be their future. One such visitor is David, a young man in his thirties who has the bed next to mine in the dormitory. He tells me an arresting story, "Yes, I'm thinking of ordaining. So is my wife, she's over with the nuns."

It took a while for me to reply, "That's a bit unusual. I don't think I've come across another couple here, at least not intent upon giving up domestic life. What... I mean, why did you decide...?"

"It just seemed to be the next step," he said, "We had both been here for short stays, sometimes together, sometimes separately. Then at home we were talking about making another visit when Grace, my wife, said, 'What are we doing?' It sort of brought us up short. We talked a little more and realized we both wanted to live here."

"And your marriage? Is it unsatisfying or..." I didn't quite know what to say to this young man, and he did seem young.

"The marriage is okay, at least as okay as any, I suppose. No, it's not that we're unhappy with each other, I can just see the same old days following days and ending our life like everyone... I don't know, it seems futile, does that make any sense?" he pleaded.

"I don't know about making sense; I know some that would feel it a criticism, a slight on the sanctity of marriage. Do you think you can just let it go, get divorced?" I said.

He said, quite confidently, "Strictly speaking, as far as I've inquired, we don't actually have to get divorced, we just have to give each other our assent to leave the marriage behind."

I thought, this sounds a little like my bowing pretense, so I put it to him, "You will get divorced though, won't you, it would secure your devotion to the mendicant life?"

"Oh, I don't think it would make that much difference." He was hedging.

For his own sake, I couldn't let him do that. "You may not wish to accept this, but it would make all the difference." I added, "It's only when one goes to the edge and jumps, that one knows one can fly." I felt a bit fraudulent uttering this last, but I know it to be true, even though I, myself, stand at the edge just admiring the view.

David said, "I'd not thought of it quite like that. Grace and I haven't spoken of divorce or anything. We just know we enjoy being here, this life. It seems to lead somewhere meaningful."

"That's true, it is a meaningful life, but it's not for everyone, David," I said.

⤴

She sat in the armchair, thinking. Not always the best thing to do in old age, but often as not, the only thing left that the body will tolerate. Gone are the days of dance. Singing, while still an option, is no fun alone. She wonders, 'How did it get so late? Where has everyone gone?'

Years ago, in the Galtimore dance hall, just after the war, they would sing like a pair of love birds, songs of love. He was handsome, that was a blessing and a curse to her. The women wouldn't stay away, he didn't need to encourage them, but he might have done a bit more discouraging.

Sod him! I wish he was here. If it hadn't been for him, my life would have been very different. I was with the Theatre, you know, Drury Lane, London. They wanted me to go abroad with them to entertain the troops. Then he turns up, bold as brass, and says, "I'm going to marry you."

My mother liked him instantly, sometimes you can't rely on anyone. Rose, Dot, Shirley, Catherine, all my sisters were besotted. "If you don't have him, I will," they said in turn. I thought I'd got the prize.

I really should get something to eat. I can't be bothered. I shouldn't have to do everything, I've had enough of making house. Where is everybody?

I suppose, as husbands go, he wasn't all that bad. I think it just wasn't what I wanted, but things move so fast when you're young, and the war pushed everything out of shape.

⤴

In the sala one evening during tea, David came up to me and said, "Would you like to sit with Grace and me? She'd be interested to meet you." I wasn't sure what the interest implied, but I was curious enough to want to see what a couple they made.

I said, "Yes, I'll be right along, just getting my coffee."

He indicated where they were sitting and went to join his wife, which gave me time to see her. She was younger than David by about five years, I'd say. Her curly blond hair made her seem girlish and quite attractive. I was surprised. I don't know why. It certainly wasn't some preformed notion that only unattractive women become nuns. It would be a lot easier here if that was so. No, I suppose it had something to do with my own presumptions about why they would break up the marriage. Anyway, I was on my way over to see them.

She stood and made anjali as I arrived. I said, "Hello, I'm James. Just James, no need to bow."

"I know," she said, "but I think it's such a nice way to greet each other, don't you?"

Those few words told me a lot. Not just what she said, but her confident composure and reasoned decision. She was her own person, for sure. It struck me that maybe this whole 'joining the monastery idea' may have come, in fact, from her.

I said, "So, you want to leave old David here and become a nun, Grace?"

"Well, *he* will be a monk, if we decide it's what we want," she said, holding on to her confidence.

"That's one way of thinking of it. But once you're in robes," I said, (adding quickly: "if you so decide") "you may never see each other again. It's not usual to think of monks in pairs, let alone a monk and a nun. You would be alone on the path to liberation. That's the whole point of monasticism."

They looked at each other, as we all took a drink from our mugs. I went on, "I met a monk here last year whose sister is a nun. She was in Thailand. The last time he saw her was three years before, in passing; he going one way and she another. They write occasionally, but letters are monitored by your sangha, so they stay pretty dry. I only tell you all this because, if you think you still have, let's say, 'sweet things' to say to each other, this is not the setting for it."

"Why are you here, James?" It was David, a little stiff (I wasn't surprised.) "You must have been married."

"Yes, I was. Still am, in fact, though no longer in a marriage. I come here to search, investigate, to know who I am, what we are," I said.

He softened a little, "Will you ordain, James, do you think?"

"I don't know. It's not a decision I can feel right now. I never discount the possibility, though. That's part of why I keep returning. But, in between, I go on other retreats, last year I was at a Catholic monastery." That raised an eyebrow.

"That must have been very different," Grace said.

"Not as much as you may think, not when you get down to the heart of practice," I said, "Of course, the theology is totally different, but, you see, we, us folk, are not; we're the same. So whilst we might like to hold different ideas, opinions, and beliefs, or no beliefs at all, we can't escape from the Tapestry."

"The Tapestry?" they asked together.

"Yes, it's my way of describing how we are all part of one process, constantly weaving each other, such that there really is no Self but the self life has made of us. We are all the same wool at bottom, just dyed a different color by events around us."

Grace said, "I've never heard it put quite like that. So poetic, it makes one feel... strange, yet beautiful." I could see David thinking exactly that of Grace. Between Grace's response and David's look, I knew then they would not be ordaining.

"Enjoy Indriya. It means the cultivation of one's spiritual faculties. It takes a while to appreciate the full import of that idea." I rose and went for a refill. Then for no reason, I suddenly remembered the strange biblical words uttered to me by a minister of the Church of England, who was a friend and confident when I was a practicing therapist: 'Others he saves, himself he cannot save'.

There's just enough light to walk in the Buddha grove for an hour. I know the trees.

July 6th

Two more names are added to my Metta list, two more to thank for my life. Does that seem odd to you, that I count David and Grace as adding to my life? It may have seemed as though I was talking to them, giving them advice, adding to their lives something of mine. Indeed I was, but the natural flow of the Tapestry is always two ways. We make a mistake in thinking only the successful, front runners in life have something to offer. There is no such discrimination in nature, for what we perceive is encircled with our own thoughts and opinions. It's a foggy appearance of truth.

There are lines in the Metta sutta one does well to remember:

> *Let none deceive another,*
> *Or despise any being in any state.*
> *So with a boundless heart*
> *Should one cherish all living beings.*

After just over a year at Indriya, during the second rains retreat, I had settled on walking as my primary meditation form. Though I sat every morning and evening, always grateful for the silence and the sheer joy of cool sunrises during particular months of the year, I found myself going to the trees more and more. It began to occur to me that the two trees represented the confines of the monastic rules, and the freedom they bestowed on one.

After the retreat, when visitors once again returned, I found myself, as a half layperson, assigned to taking them on an introduction to the monastery and its routines. I always introduced the idea of walking meditation as natural, and something they could take with them anywhere, the sort of thing one could graft onto home life. I often remarked, "If you have room in your garden, you might like to plant two trees and grow with them." Or I would suggest asking of the possibility at the local park. I think I pictured something like those scenes one sees of the Chinese doing Tai Chi *en masse* in the town parks and squares. I pictured a lot of trees, and that was a satisfying thought.

For myself, no decision was forthcoming. I seemed happy, yet there was still something I could not resolve. The something that stood in the way of the kind of resolution that would let me decide definitely and finally to stay or go. During the second rains retreat I was given a Buddhist name that means 'one who does the right thing.' Something of an irony, I think, considering how long I take to find the right thing.

೧⁀

In the summer, among the visitors, come the evangelists. Because the place is so open, they bring themselves in groups, seeking to convert, well, I don't know who, certainly not the monks and nuns, perhaps other visitors. I often find myself surrounded and having to parley with them. On one occasion, a hot afternoon in July, I found myself with three young women and a young man, all holding bibles; I supposed to keep the evil vibrations away. We were, as it happens, under the trees in the Buddha grove. A crazy thought passed through my mind, 'Maybe I could get them walking.'

They were asking me if I knew Jesus. As many times as I've heard it, I never quite know what to say to the question. It prompts the facetious in me, so I hold my tongue. (No amount of kindness practice has delivered me of those prankster thoughts.)

As it happens, I have known Jesus, as much as one can know an idea, for surely two thousand years after the event, that's about all he can be: an idea of something, a combination of our reach for perfection and admission of imperfection. For it is ourselves we seek to find a solution to. We are the complexity we know without fully knowing. We carry unseen urges from far deeper in our ancestry than two thousand years ago, remaining hidden from conscious view. Not until the nineteenth century and the advent of psychology did we even begin to grasp the depth of our being. Given such a multifaceted nature to unravel, the question 'Do you know Jesus?' with the inference that, not to leads to eternal damnation, seems, I'm sorry to say, trite. Rather, I would turn to the pages of Thomas a Kempis and heed this simple advice:

> He whose taste discerns all things as they are, and not as they are said or accounted to be, is truly a wise man, and taught rather by God than by men.
> He that knows how to walk inwardly, and to make but little account of outward things, does not look for places, or wait for seasons to perform his exercises of devotion.
> The man of inward life soon recollects himself, because he never wholly surrenders himself to outward things.[16]

For I could be accepting of the term 'God' as created thousands of years ago, encapsulating everything unknown and sought for, often feared, but also providing answers when such fear is faced. My thinking was too complicated for the bible holders. I left them, saying, "I wish to walk between trees, please excuse me."

And so it was, that for the eighteen months of my third stay at Indriya, I took all that came upon me, in thought and through others, to the trees. There, confined and yet free, a revelation of meaning began to dawn.

༄

As much as I was drawn to monastic life, when I left in the spring of nineteen-eighty-seven, I knew, just as I had of David and Grace, I would never fully ordain. I would visit many times, and still do. It's been twenty-five years now since I first encountered Indriya. A lot has happened in that time.

---

16 Thomas a Kempis. Of the Imitation of Christ.

WALK AGAIN

*He is half of a blessed man.
Left to be finished by such as she;
and she a fair divided excellence,
whose fullness of perfection lies in him.*

William Shakespeare

NINE

"Why are you walking up and down?" The question came from a small boy with blond hair that caught the July sun and almost disappeared in a halo above a high forehead. He reminded me of a photo my parents had of me when I first started school. At the same time as seeing the boy, my eye caught sight of a woman making her way over to where we both stood. I waited, as did the boy. It must have looked, from where she was, like a scene from a painting, fixed but unframed. I thought of Gainsborough's The Blue Boy; he was wearing a blue shirt and had his hands behind his back. The stillness between the boy and myself slowed the woman's steps. The anxious look left her face to be replaced with curiosity. I was about to meet my Anima.

Her name was Joan. We were sitting on the grass in the park beneath one of the trees, sharing a picnic, while I tried to explain, "It's a kind of letting-go, a surrendering to who or what we are."

"Surrendering?" she asked.

I could see I would have to measure my words, first impressions and all that, "Well, life is full of distractions, always something to pull us this way or that. I just wonder what it may be like to just be still, yet not

123

asleep or unconscious, but just being who we are. I've found it's not easy. The idea is simple, but not easy to carry through."

"But isn't sitting here kind of like that?" she said, "It's still and pleasant. Isn't that enough, to know we are here doing this?"

"Yes, this is pleasant. But it won't last." I said, "It's like everything, temporary, transient."

"More tea?" she said, "Before it's all gone." I wasn't sure if she was making fun or showing understanding. She had a flat way of speaking that I couldn't decipher.

"Thanks. Look, I feel I've taken half your picnic. Will you let me buy you and er...?"

"Robert," she said, nodding towards the boy busy eating the last of the crisps from the bag.

"Could I take you and Robert to the Café?" I asked, "Perhaps an ice cream or something?" At the mention of ice cream, Robert looked at his mother nodding his head vigorously.

"Alright," she said.

Twenty minutes later saw us walking beneath full-leafed birch trees along one of the park's avenues. The afternoon had surrounded us, and the soft crunch of our feet on the sandy path marked our gentle stroll. We could have been a small family on any leisurely summer Sunday. I looked across at Joan and found myself wishing it was so, for I had been there, yet, then, it was flawed by the ignorance of youth and the need for too much effort to make it work. Now, I knew to let events flow gently in their own way. And that is exactly what was happening on this peaceful Sunday. I let go of wishing, always a silly diversion, and took Robert's free hand, thinking it is just what it is.

July 8th
All that comes into being passes beyond being. All that comes together must eventually part. What we assume is permanent is simply taking longer in bringing about a change of state from one to another. The only true constant is change itself.

Three months had passed, following that Sunday meeting. Joan and I could count each other friends. We had shared something of our lives, and my walking between trees had been elevated from a crazy quirk to a thing of possible interest. This had happened through conversation and plain coming to know me. What I learned of Joan was that she had insight, brought about by pretty disturbing past experiences. For her, survival was an achievement, any quality of life, a bonus. (I surmised that accounted for the flat tone to her voice.) It seems she had another child, taken from her when she was fifteen. The circumstances were not that far from Wendy's. The difference, however, delivered a transforming blow to whom Joan became as an adult.

I cannot think of anything worse than being raped at fourteen.

I won't go into the details which, for reasons only friendship knows, she saw fit to share with me. Sufficient to say, there was no support from home or family. I was not surprised that her interest in something as luxurious as walking between trees, seeking answers to *man's* problem of being, wasn't going to be high on her list of to-dos. If I was ever going to bring her the insights I had thus far acquired, I was going to have to respectfully enter her world. I would be forced into a value measurement of my thoughts and actions. I would be tested.

"Have you always been a good cook?" Joan had found a baby- sitter and had come around to my place for dinner. We faced one another across a wooden table painted green, not really my style, but then I was renting the house partly furnished. The table came with the kitchen. I'd done my best with a clean window curtain for a table cloth, and distracted from that with two candles. Joan's face, softened by candle light, I was pleased to see, was relaxed as she ate.

"We just got lucky," I said, "I cook like I do most things, a bit of intelligence, a lot of intuition and, of course, feeling. It's never the same twice. But to answer your question, I started early and have managed in my time to cook for a vegetarian restaurant and seventy monks and nuns."

She asked, "What was it like, the monastery?"

"Profound. Well, that hardly describes it, does it?" I said, "It was challenging, the life style, rules, and limited sleep and food. But beautiful in a way we seldom experience. The long days, silences, and friendship." I stopped. I wasn't sure I knew how to describe the experience, for an unresolved contradiction lay between how I felt about the life and my decision to leave.

"James?" she asked, "Do you wish you had stayed, you know, become a monk?"

In the business of finding a place and some work, I had not thought too hard about my decision. Now, as it was put to me, I once again considered the question. "Umm, I don't know," I said, "I mean, no, it wasn't for me, no. I was struggling, fighting it. I think I got close, but it was too neat."

"Too neat?" She looked at me, like the first time watching me walk between trees. I had no idea what she was thinking, but I knew by now she wasn't stupid, so her question revealed something less than intelligent in my response.

I started again. "It's a system of practice that's been around for a long time," I said, "Buddhism defines this life as being confused by suffering, by a kind of angst that cannot be satisfied, and thus drives us in many directions, into thoughts and actions that are not wholesome. So, the Buddha searched and found a way out of suffering. I have to say, it works."

"But that's not enough, or is there something I'm missing?" she said.

"Two things bother me: First, how many people are going to spend years in a monastery? And it does seem to require years of practice. And, although the practice defines the dynamics of suffering, its cause and cure, what I seek is the ground of suffering. There's something deep in our psyches that we are avoiding. That's why we create suffering for ourselves and others, running from that deep something."

She took some time, quietly eating and occasionally looking at me. Then she said, "Is there something in your psyche you're running from?"

I looked at her between the candles across the table; she looked into my eyes. Her eyes were blue, deep and steady. Her stare, though, was a little withdrawn, out of compassion I could feel coming through her. She slowly put her hand across the table and touched the back of my left hand. I looked at her hand and back at her.

"Yes. But that's the point. I'm tired of having it at my back. I want to face it and have done with it," I said, "I think we all need to have done with it. It's driving us to destruction. Just take a look around."

"Some things are just too hard to look at, James," she said, looking down at her lap. I moved my left hand and placed it over hers and held her hand. "But, Joan, if the past enslaves us, how shall we live into the future?"

She looked back at me, as she turned her palm up and we clasped hands, and said, "One day at a time, James, one day at a time. Like this."

July 9th

We have our babies prematurely, half formed. In the long stride of evolution, our full grown brains have become too large for birth. So our babies need a lot of nurturing. What concerns me is what happens during that extended development. What is put in, comes out, doesn't it, like breathing? Just as we breathe this life, so we also create this life, by giving out what we have received. While this is true for the whole of our lives, isn't the pattern of our understanding of the world laid down in the growing years, the impressionable years, the years of vulnerability?

It was a few days later when Joan phoned me with an offer to reciprocate the meal. "Could you come around seven tomorrow? Robert should be in bed by then." I said that would be fine, and asked if I could bring anything. "Just bring yourself, James. Perhaps you could leave something behind, though."

"Oh," I said, "What's that?"

"Your angst, James. I'd like to see what you're like when you relax." I wasn't sure how to take that request. Then she said, "Sorry, James, that was unkind. Just come as you are." Then a bit uncertainly she said, "Will you?"

"Yes, yes I'll come, seven, right?" I said, "I'll see what I can do about… well, I'll be there."

"James? I…"

"Yes?"

"Nothing. See you tomorrow. Take care."

"Bye, Joan, see you soon, bye."

"Bye, James."

I put the phone down wondering what that was all about. I went into the kitchen and poured myself a glass of wine, returned to the living room to think it over. Just the thing Joan suggested I put aside, but it's not that easy. I sat in the armchair and thought about transference, a situation when a client will put feelings about a parent onto the therapist. That wasn't what was happening between Joan and me, but the idea nagged at me.

It then occurred to me that my angst, as she put it, was drawing her own up to the surface. I was a catalyst raising the sufferings of her childhood. Not just the conscious memories, those she had adjusted to, but the feelings that had been held in by the unconscious, safeguarding her sanity. If I cared anything for Joan, I'd better heed her suggestion.

∽

Robert was in bed but not asleep. Children and animals, I have found, always know when there's something in the wind, a change of routine. After Joan had let me in and stowed my coat, she said, "Robert wants you to go up and see him. I'm afraid he won't go to sleep until you do. Do you mind?"

"No problem," I said as I made for the stairs. "I'll find him. Be down in a jiff." I wondered if I was being a bit too obviously relaxed. Anyway, I'd taken a liking to Robert, the enthusiasm was genuine.

Joan said, "Thanks. I'll be in the kitchen."

Robert was sitting up in bed waiting for me. He heard my footsteps and called, "Hello."

I went into his room and said, "Hello, Robert, aren't you tired?" I was glad to notice it was not pristine, just tidy; the color was going from the wallpaper and the ceiling needed a coat of paint. The rug was clean but quite worn.

"Not yet," he said, "Will you read a story?" He was holding a book out to me.

"Okay," I said, "What have you got there?"

He showed me. It was Maurice Sendak's 'Where The Wild Things Are', the one with beasts and trolls or something on the cover. "Right," I said, somewhat taken aback. "Okay, let's see," I said, opening the first page. I started to read, "The night Max wore his wolf suit and made mischief of one kind and another..."

July 10th

When I was at Oxford, I had a discussion with a professor who tutored postgraduates in mythology. James will tell you about it later. She was an older woman, fiercely academic, and honest. We got into a debate about why myths have survived so long. I asked her if she was a grandmother and did she read stories to her grandchildren, to which she answered in the affirmative. And didn't they always want the same stories? "Yes," she said, wondering where this was going. I said myths and fairy stories do the same job, don't they, sorting out the demons in our unconscious, myths for grownups, fairy stories for kids. It was a bit simplified but, in essence, true. Those deep fears have to be placated. Sendak just puts them out there without the disguise usual for children's stories.

"...and into the night of his very own room where he found his supper waiting for him and it was still hot." I put down the book. Robert was fast asleep.

I crept downstairs and went into the kitchen. Joan was sitting at a small round table nursing a cup. "You've got a sweet voice when you're story-telling, James. I take it Robert's asleep after all that," she said, "I do believe he's got you around his little finger."

"He might not be the only one," I said, and sat down next to Joan.

She said, "You must be hungry after all that. Shall we eat outside? It's such a nice evening. I love these long days."

"Yes, okay," I said, a little disappointed, but realizing what she said, or rather didn't say, was more sensible than I was feeling. "Is there anything I can take out?"

She got up and went over to the stove, "It's all done, perhaps you'd like to take the pan out and I'll bring plates and stuff."

We settled ourselves near the back door within earshot of Robert, though he seldom woke once asleep, Joan told me. "Did he ask for Sendak's book?"

"Yes, is it his favorite?" I asked, "I wasn't at all sure about reading it at night, but then children are more straightforward than us. I suppose having one's fears out there in a story keeps them from some dark corner."

"If they're imagined fears, it's alright; it's the real ones that are scary." As Joan said this, a blank mask flashed over her features, just visible in the waning light, then she smiled at me, "Well, you know all about that, I think."

"I only know about mine," I said, and waited. We ate for a while in silence. The clicking of cutlery joining us together in coded language.

Quite suddenly, without looking up, she said, "Can I talk about it?"

"Yes," I said, then added, "Whenever you want to."

The cutlery code clicked on. Night came into her small garden. We made light talk as we cleared the dishes into the kitchen and closed the back door. I offered to wash up. She said, leave it, took my hand, and we went into the living room.

We sat on the sofa. She leaned her head on my shoulder. It began to twitch. I thought, 'Damn it!' Even as I knew it never seemed to bother whomever's head was resting there.

She said, "I keep thinking I'm going to die. I know I'm not, but the thought still floats around in my head all the time, stalking me."

I asked, "Is it there now?"

"It's,...I'm,... It's thinking you're going to die." She sat up and put her head in her hands, so that when she spoke again I had to strain to hear her. "It's thinking of you dead."

"And what about you, Joan? What is it thinking about you?" I said. I was facing the fireplace wall. I looked along the mantle and at the wall, its wallpaper fading like in Robert's bedroom.

Joan lifted her head and looked at me, "I'm used to it, resigned, I suppose," she said. Then asked me, "What do you think it is, James? Have you heard of it before?"

"Yes, I have," I said, "But it shows up in different forms." I hesitated, then added, "I know it, personally."

"You think you're going to die?" She asked, and put her hand on my arm. The touch of her fingers on my skin ran through all the light, women's touches that had moved me: back to Wendy, back to my mother and back into a dim feeling of indescribable... beauty. That's the only word I can find, like when a writer talks of a terrifying beauty. The touch and the conversation had thrown a switch, opened a sealed door for just a moment. I sat, unable to move, suddenly remembering when I stood on the pavement and couldn't move a foot forward to enter the church. Whatever it was, it was the same thing. "James? What's happened? You've gone somewhere."

"Oh, Joan, yes, no. No, I'm right here, Joan, I... I think I have an idea, something we could try. Maybe we can get to the bottom of this dying thing," I said, trying now to contain my impulse and await Joan's response.

"What sort of thing? What do you want to do?" she asked.

I turned to her and took her hands in mine. I was looking into her eyes, thinking this won't be easy, stay with the thinking, concentrate. "Joan," I spoke slowly, low and steady, "I think we may be able to give each other back our lives." I let her absorb my words, then continued, "We will have to trust each other."

"I trust you, James, but you sound... Perhaps if you tell me what you want to do," she said, her voice lowered to mine. I could sense her feelings already moving, feelings she perhaps wouldn't want. Did I have the right to take her there to find *my* demons?

I said, "Perhaps we'd best leave it, Joan. Like you say, you're used to it and so am I. Maybe there's nothing to be gained."

She squeezed my hands, "Please, James. It's horrible. I... If you,... if we can end it, let's try. I'll do it, just as long as you stay with me."

I was about to violate every principle I had been trained in. But this went way beyond training, whether in therapy, Buddhist practice, or just plain common sense. All my training was preceded by something in me that sent me out into the world with compassion. And it was in compassion I rooted myself now.

၆၅

When I was nine years old, I had a friend upstairs in one of the top floor apartments. Adrian was seven, an only child whose parents fought loudly and violently. Their curses and crashes could be heard down to the basement. I knew what he would do, go out onto the back landing and put his hands over his ears. It didn't matter what time of day or night it was, if he was home, the back landing stairs is where I would find him. I couldn't leave him to endure alone. I would go out of our back door, climb the two flights of iron stairs, and sit next to him. My parents never stopped me, even if it was late at night. I don't think they could have anyway. Something in me compelled me up those stairs. It wasn't as if I thought about it, or thought I knew what to do about it. It just was. It must have been a year or so before he spoke about it. I reckoned he didn't have the words before that.

∽

Joan and I went upstairs. We did not make love, neither did we have sex or anything close. We touched and were touched. We risked the pain that comes from allowing one to touch you with love and raise the demons that would keep love from you. We went to a place of dying, each one holding the other until life returned. For we had both known dying at too young an age, and it had left its calling card. We talked, we comforted, we slept. When morning came, we knew we had loved each other as friends, and that was and always would be enough.

Morning light filled the little kitchen. Joan was busy getting Robert ready for school and herself to work. I added my two pence worth; I made a pot of tea, laid out two mugs and a small cup. We all sat down for a while, I poured. "This is nice," Joan said, "Thanks."

We had found a friendship that sometimes takes a lifetime to make, and many never know it. It was deep, the kind that gets forged in common suffering and redemption. I use those words with particularity. Yes, they are religious, but believing or not believing is of no account in such experiencing. It happens far beyond our ken, and Joan knew it as well as I.

I drove Joan to work, dropping Robert off at school on the way. When we arrived at her work, I said, "It won't have all gone, you know, Joan, but it's a lot weaker."

"I'm a lot stronger," she said, "Thank you, James. I love you." Her voice, though still flat, had energy, and she was more animated than I had seen her.

TEN

It must have been one of the noisiest nights I'd heard, as I lay awake listening. The wind was up, visiting the window with force, and dropping away every few minutes. I had to go and look. Against the night sky, tinted with the light from the street, I could see masses of leaves shaking at the ends of branches. They looked like a thousand fingers wagging admonishment for our misdeeds, and the thought crossed my mind that it was just the beginning of nature's retribution. I went back to bed and covered my head.

I awoke to the phone ringing; my traveling clock read six fifteen. I was about to turn over, but something about the time, and remembrance of the storm, gave an urgency to the ring. I got out of bed and went downstairs, picked up the phone. Before I could say hello, my mother said, "Your father's dead. Come down James, come down." Inquiry, I knew, was pointless, only agreement was required.

"Right, I'll be there," I said, "It'll take about three hours, maybe four." I put down the phone. That was the assurance my mother would recognize that I was on my way. I bathed and dressed, packed a few things, got in the car and drove to Joan's.

I explained the phone call and said, "I'll be gone a few days at least, a week I expect. I'll bring my mum back, if she'll come. I'll get the train."

"Would you like me to come with you?" The question from Joan was out of the blue. I was about to grab at the company, but...

"What about Robert? I don't think it would..."

"He can stay with my brother and his wife. He likes it there, they have two other kids," she said, "I'd feel better about you going... you know."

"Alright, if you're sure it's okay with Robert," I said, hoping beyond hope it would happen. I was thinking it would be a help to my mother to have a woman around.

"We can ask him," she said. We did, and he jumped at the idea of a holiday. If Joan is anything, she's efficient. We were on the fast train to London within the hour. In London, the train change went smoothly. As we sat on the coast train, I felt I could take a breath.

"Thanks for this, Joan," I said, "My mother won't say anything, but she will appreciate your being there."

"Good, then she will feel right about you." She looked at me across the carriage. "And so she should," she added, "You're a compassionate man, James. She should know that."

"Maybe, maybe so, but I don't think she knows me, Joan. Somehow, probably since my illness as a baby, she has been separate from me," I said, "It's not at all unusual for parents to not really know their children. It doesn't take as serious a thing as illness. Parents often have preformed notions of what their children are, or should be, and that blinds them to the real qualities of their child."

"I think I know Robert pretty well and I don't have ambitions for him," she said.

"No," I said, "I'm sure you don't push him. I've watched you with him, you're a good mother. But some of what I'm talking about is cultural. It's in all of us, unavoidable, you might say."

She said, "You mean like when he goes to school, beyond my reach?"

"Something like that," I said. "When I was a boy, my father wanted to send me to Summerhill school, A. S. Neil's place. Ever heard of it?"

"No, what kind of school was it?" she asked.

"It was a free school," I said, "If a kid didn't want to go to lessons they didn't have to. But every child eventually wanted to. According to Neil, the longest a kid held out was about three months, then they would be pleading to go to classes. Interesting, don't you think?"

July 12

From infancy we are taught information, knowledge. And it is the mind that records, assimilates and remembers that information. The better our mind, the more knowledge we posses, the smarter we become. We have undoubtedly become the cleverest species on the planet because we have the most suitable brain, evolved over thousands of generations, for learning and remembering.

Acting out of our accumulated knowledge we have produced a new world out of the old, and at the same time brought ourselves to the brink of extinction. Has this perhaps occurred because we have denied awareness in favor of cleverness? When we intellectualize, calculate, and invent things, we become absorbed with our cleverness. It's fascinating, all consuming, and feeds back to us our self-absorption. Acting this way, in a closed circuit of self, blocks out awareness. For awareness requires looking outward beyond the Self towards others, beyond the immediate act towards the consequential.

Being smart is relatively easy; being kind is not.

We arrived at my mother's place around noon. My father, it seemed, had died in his sleep. His body was gone and also all his belongings. I could hardly believe what my mother was telling me, "I called the Salvation Army, after I called you." There was nothing of him, not even ash in the ashtray, nothing. While I tried to absorb the shock of such a complete eradication of my father, I remembered when I left home, making a visit two weeks after my departure to find my bedroom converted into a junk room and all my things gone. "They want someone to go and identify the body," she said, "You go, here's the address. I'll be alright."

Joan said to my mother, "Would you like me to stay with you?"

"I'll be alright, Joan," she said, "Go with James. I'll be alright now I know you're here."

"Let me make you some tea first, okay?" Joan offered, "It won't take a minute."

"If you like," my mother said, "Yes, alright, thank you, Joan." Joan went into the kitchen and my mother turned to me, "She seems a sensible girl. A bit thin. What is she?"

It was my mother's way of sounding out my personal life, the closest she could get to showing she cared. "We're just good friends, Mum. You're right, she is sensible, I like her a lot." I thought this last might hurt a bit, but I couldn't help saying it. My relationship with my mother had always been fraught, the truth always half hidden, at best.

When I was small, you quelled my fears
promoted by the size of my ears.
Telling me, "You look like Clark Gable."

You combed blond hair off a worried brow
tried to make things right somehow.

The space between us almost palpable.

I never knew you like I should
no no no, I never could.
But you were there.

In time childhood gave way,
to a stranger in son's clothing.

We never closed the spaces, just
now and again threw a line across.

Lines in a tangle
lines in a mess
lines frayed and broken
More lines saying less.

Only later, when age pinned us down
you in your chair.
Me just being around. (Sometimes)
Only then, forced by circumstance
Did we try to meet half way.

Now you are gone.
Beyond these words and pleas.
Now at last you rest, at ease.
And I remember...
...When I was small.

Outside, I said to Joan, "Let's walk, it's not too far and we can go along the sea front. I could do with the air. C'mon." I took her hand and we went down to the front. Just the feel of her hand was a comfort, having her with me kept me open. Death can be so closing, shutting down the senses and shutting out the truth. It's what my mother had to do when I left home, and now again. I imagine she had to do it when I was dying in the hospital. Death is not something we want to face head on.

I was shown into a side room at the mortuary, almost a perfect square box of a room, painted white, dark green carpet, no windows, but the low hum of a fan somewhere over my head. In the center was a table on wheels. Covering what was obviously a body was a green oilcloth. The director of the mortuary, a thin man in a dark suit, preceded me in, went over to the table and held the corner of the cloth waiting for me to come around to his side. When I did he lifted the cloth back and laid it across the chest, stepped back and waited.

It wasn't the first and it wouldn't be the last dead body in my life, but it was my father.

July 13th
Holding a large garden spade was as hard for a seven year old as
holding a big thought.

I had a piece of the allotment all to myself. I think my curiosity and constant questions about how we got food just like that from the ground had tired my dad out. One day, around the back end of summer, he took me out to the garden and pointed to an area of rough growing grasses and handed me the spade. "There you go, laddie. You may as well start at the beginning, and we'll see how far you get."

I know when he turned away there was a smile on his face as I nearly tumbled over trying to keep hold of the big spade. He walked back over to me a few minutes later and handed me what he called a lady's spade. He cleared a patch of grass and showed me how to turn and fold the sod into its neighbor. "This", he said, "is called single digging," as he continued along the line of the dig in a steady rhythm turning soil like the blade of a plough. I liked my dad, he could do lots of things.

I cried. Joan had the wit to hold my hand and say nothing. I folded the death certificate and put it in my pocket. Then I had an idea, found a phone box and called my mum's next door neighbor. Yes, she would be happy to go and sit with my mother. I came out of the box to Joan's quizzical look. "Let's go down the front, on the pier and eat. Mum's okay for a couple of hours."

"Are you sure, shouldn't we get back?" Joan had a good soul.

"It's okay, Joan," I said. "The neighbor's gone round and they'll talk a while. That'll be good for mum. She wouldn't talk with me, so I think it's best to give her the space."

We went through the pier turnstile and took the windy side, watching the seagulls swoop and cry over the waves, as our shoes clattered on the wooden planks. Down the center of the pier was a glass partition with small booths set in at intervals with fortune tellers, candy floss stalls, silly hats, buckets and spades for sale. It had hardly changed since I used to come down on holidays as a boy. It probably hadn't changed that much from its Victorian birth, a product of the industrial revolution and the coming of the train.

We were about half way along the pier when I heard my name being called.

I turned my back to the sea the better to hear, and saw a man rising from one of the deck chairs lined along the center glass partition. He came towards me, hand out, "It is you, isn't it, James?"

I put my hand in his, with only a vague sense of the man, saying, "Yes, yes I'm James, but..."

"I'm not surprised you don't recognize me, James. It's been many years," he said, then added, "Downstairs, number seven. Haven't seen you since you were about twenty, twenty-one."

"Roger!" I said, shaking his hand more vigorously now. "Of course, certainly I remember." Turning to Joan, "Roger and June were our neighbor's when I was growing up. Roger, this is Joan."

"Hello, Joan," he held out his hand and Joan shook hands with him.

"Hello," she said.

"How are you?" I said. "What brings you down here?"

"I live here now, have been for about ten years or so," Roger said. "Not June though, we broke up, must have been about three years after you left home, I think. I remarried. What about you, James? I seem to remember you were married quite young."

"Yes, too young. Shotgun," I said, "Shouldn't have happened, but that's life. I'm okay, though. Single now and that's fine."

"Look," he said, "I have to go and..." looking at Joan, "I can see you're engaged right now. Here's my address and phone number. Give me a call if you like. Stay in touch. Good to see you looking so well." He handed me a card and we shook hands and said our goodbyes.

Joan and I walked on towards the end of the pier. We didn't speak, and I don't know what Joan was thinking; I'd been taken back to remembrance of things past...

∺

...It was my nineteenth birthday. For some reason I cannot now remember, I had gone down to Roger and June's place. I knocked on the door and waited. It seemed they were out. I was about to turn and go back upstairs when the door opened and June was there. Now, although I had come-of-age so to speak in Wendy's hands, I was still very unversed in the ways of the world. But it seemed to my naive eye that June had been crying.

"I, sorry, June. I just..." I really didn't know what to say. I thought I'd best just leave.

"Oh, James, come in dear." June was about thirty-five and had always called me dear.

As she closed the door, she started to cry and leaned against me. The confusion of feelings in me moved my arm around her and drew her to me. I'd always looked at her from a distance, cows eyes I think the expression is. Now here she was in my arms and needy. "Oh, James. I'm sorry."

She placed her hands on my chest and looked at me, "Could you make some tea dear, please."

I know she told me something about her and Roger and marriage and love and loss, and I should have been listening, but I was nursing my own infantile grievance.

Yet I took away something from that time, some touch of feeling that I needed, some trust I had been given. June, of course, is on my Metta list, as is Roger.

"So who was holding the shotgun?" It was Joan. "Shotgun?" I said.

"The wedding, your first." Joan looked at me sideways, a mischievous grin on her face. That was new! "You said it was a shotgun affair."

"Oh, yes, well... it was," I said, "I had said early on it would be foolish for us to marry. Better if we just carried on in some way and I would make sure the baby was supported, cared for. At first Ruth agreed, she wasn't stupid. We could both see such stark differences between us. But her parents were of some old and long- dead school of duty, as defined by 'you marry the girl' Victorian, that sort of thing." I looked at Joan as she continued listening. "They made her life hell, I suspect, and she started putting pressure on me. To be fair, I don't think she relished the prospect of marrying me or anyone at nineteen."

"What about your parents? How did they take it?" Joan asked.

"With a kind of stoic silence," I said, "I got no criticism and no support. I was left to it." We had arrived at the end of the pier and were leaning over the rail. "If I'd run away, it would have been a *fait accompli*. They would all have had to deal with it, but..."

"You're not the running away type, James. You'd put the weight on your shoulders with the rest of the pack and carry on. Right?" Joan was certainly getting to know me. "Why do you think that is, dear friend?"

I looked across at her. The question was of genuine concern. She was indeed a dear friend. "C'mon Joan, let's eat. We can continue this foray into my foibles over lunch."

We sat by a window that overlooked the sea. Watching the timeless flow of waves and tides and the ever present seagulls' high pitched crying on the wind, I felt the life of a human is so small, so temporary, each of us a passing thread caught for a moment on a fence post. And we shall be blown off when our time comes. Yet en- masse we have contrived to be a force that is greater than nature itself, we assume. A conceit we shall have to face sooner than we think.

A few day later, when we were on the way to the cemetery, we had to make several detours. The storm that raged on the night of my father's death had taken down many old trees, blocking roads and destroying parts of buildings. The last of the devastation we witnessed on the way into the cemetery. A magnificent Victorian arch, inscribed and decorated with carved stone trees and flowers, was down on the ground beneath an old oak. We were ushered around a back entrance service gate. I thought my dad would smile at that. He was a workman all his life.

July 14th

I couldn't help thinking there was something ironic about a real tree being nature's instrument of destruction used upon imitation stone trees.

My mother didn't come back with me. I was not really surprised. She had always been fiercely independent and looked upon me as much too needy to take care of her, a legacy from my early hospitalization. It was another of life's ironies, for I had achieved a great deal over the years and would progress further, but my mother's ears had trouble hearing positive news about me. Yet any troubles I had would resound loudly and confirm her view of my fortunes.

I ran Joan home in the car, picking Robert up on the way. She invited me in, but I decided to go straight home. I had to give myself space to absorb and deal once again with death. There would be time, in a day or two, for sharing it with Joan, for I knew she would want to support and search for meaning with me as to this ever present dilemma in the midst of life.

The next evening saw me between the trees. I had designated one of the trees as my mother, the other, my father. I walked slowly, my head held up so that as I approached a tree it grew in my consciousness. Thus it was after about half an hour of walking tree to tree, between my mother and father, their presence within me was raised to awareness. It was not visions of them, neither were there words, except occasionally some would run through my head. What I experienced was essence. I can find no other description; it was the essence of my mother, her stoicism, strength, ribald humor, and a space I can only think of as a feeling of absence. The 'father tree' brought forth conviction, honesty, anger and odd feelings and smells, strong remembrance of Sundays. (I suppose that's when I saw most of my dad.)

Old songs from the war,
sung with mum
Sunday lunch making;
roast beef, Yorkshire pudding
and
greens that are good for you.

∽

The wireless plays
Forces favorites
from Koln[17]
"For all those sweethearts that are
alone."

∽

Dad's down the Fallowfield pub.
The heat's in the kitchen.
"Go and get yer father."

∽

Lemonade and crisps
taste just fine.
The smoke and talk flow
out of the swing doors
on an aroma of Guinness.

∽

Lunch is a quiet affair
between two lovers
long out of love.
I — eat two portions of everything.

∽

---

17 Pronounced Colone.

Sleeping on the sofa.
Dad's body straight,
dead to the world.
I feel him at my back as
I drift into the familiar comfort.
Dream of men, of his voice,
see hands at the machine.
Saturdays at the factory bench
making toys for boys
who are alone.

After a while longer, I experienced, just for a moment, a coming together of the two disparate elements of Mum and Dad, some core state in both of them. I surmised it had something to do with my being their offspring. I was the unifying principle of their being. The effect this had on me was a realization that dead, as my father was, or alive, as my mother, made no difference to me. I mean, not to seem hard and cold, I saw that death and life, at least the death and life of my parents, had a commonality, in me. This surely meant there had to be a universal commonality too.

The gradual effect of this discovery was an erosion of my defenses against the pain of the deaths I had endured. I stood just about half way between the two trees and looked up. The feeling of gratitude that arose in my bones and spilt out through my tears, bore witness to the release of tension I had carried too long. I wanted urgently to tell Joan, and almost in the same thought came Rosalyn and Catherine, and Kate, and my mother. Then with sad apprehension I knew I could not tell my mother, for she has never been privy to my struggle. She doesn't know who I am. It was too late for a revelation with such particulars and complexity.

I just stared into the full beauty of the leaves above me and resolved, at least, to tell my mother *something*. Something only I could do, for I was at least part way out of our joint imprisonment.

ॐ

It was a Saturday just over two weeks after my father's funeral. Joan and I were shopping. We had taken to meeting in the town market and walking around together. There had been a market place here well back into history. It's possible Cromwell's army marched through, and probably bought goods, on their way to Bosworth field, a decisive battle in the many the Crown lost. But today it's just people from many lands and parts who shop here; besides locals, there are Northerners, Scots, Welsh, Irish, Indians, Muslims, in fact, people from every part and land that was once the British Empire.

July 15th

They reflect our inheritance, the spoils of war and conquest, the singular most prolific occupation of people. And we still pursue it on an ever greater scale.

But on this sunny morning in an English market place, holding the hand of a favored friend, a deep companion, I wish to think of other things, of loving kindness, compassion, joy, and a sense of equanimity acquired between the trees. As we had our separate fare to buy, we agreed on a time to meet in the small Italian coffee house in the main street, and went each to our own way.

"So what you found was that you were your father and mother's offspring?" Joan was saying, and almost laughing, over her coffee. "Did I get that right?"

"Ha, ha, very funny, Joan. You don't make a chap's task easy, do you," I said. "What I'm trying to say is something like a unifying condition arose, a state of being for a moment where my mother and father were one. The Anima and Animus undivided."

"Right," she said, "but jokes aside, you obviously *are* your parents son, they must both be in you in some way."

"Of course, but it's more than that," I said, "It's this business of death and life. My father is dead, but Animus is a constant. Don't you see that implies that in life death is a constant. And as the Anima is still present in the union, then life is present in death."

"Do you mean like reincarnation? Do you want a doughnut?" she asked.

"Thanks, no. I mean, yes, thanks... Look, reincarnation is just something to make us feel good about dying, like going to heaven. What happened between the trees may be called mystical in some sense, but it didn't require belief in anything beyond itself. That is, it was an experience which simply demands looking into and understanding."

"And that's what we're doing over coffee on a bright Saturday morning." Joan said this with a sort of 'that's what makes men tick, I suppose' voice.

"I've integrated my dad's death and that's helped me with all the others," I said, trying to give my theory a practical face.

"Good," Joan said, "Do you want more coffee, or shall we eat?"

"Eat. But let's go out," I suggested.

"Okay, I'm done." Joan went ahead. As we walked to the car park, she said, "I'm sorry, James, I cut you off a bit. I do know it's important to you, but what's really important is that you're feeling okay about your dad dying. I'm glad. I can't pretend to understand everything that goes on in your head though, dear."

"No, I see that." I was silent, unsure of what to say. I found myself, as I was holding two bags one in each hand, thinking, left hand, right hand. Doing the same equation as between the trees. It struck me then.

July 15th
Paradox! Everything we think through long enough comes to a paradox, a condition of irresolvable contradiction, the grand archetype of which is: 'To be born is to invite death.'

"You okay, James?" Joan said. "You've gone very silent."

"I'm fine, Joan, fine. Trying not to think too much. I think a pint will help. Come on, the car's just over here."

ELEVEN

The phone rang. I looked at the clock, it was eleven thirty at night. I lifted the receiver and said, "Hello?"

"James, I can't sleep," Joan's voice sounded tense, fearful, "It's back. It's worse, James. I'm..."

"I'm coming round," I said. My heart had started jumping around in my chest. It was a case of almost instant transference, something I'd always been susceptible to. "Just go in the kitchen, put the kettle on, I'll be there before it boils."

"Thank you, James. I'm sorry..."

I hastily said, "It's alright, Joan. I love you. Just sit tight, I'll be there." I put down the phone, went through the hallway, picking my coat off the peg on the run.

As we held each other under the glare of the kitchen light we were both shaking. The kettle joined us as the water turned to steam and pushed its way through the spout, crying for attention. I moved and turned the gas off. Joan started to say something. I said, "We don't need tea. Come on." I took her hand and as we left the kitchen, switched off the light. In the dim reflections from the street lighting we climbed the stairs. In her bedroom we hardly let each other go while removing our clothes. Still shaking, we got into bed, pulled the covers over our heads and clung to each other.

Slowly, very slowly, the shaking eased. Our bodies softened against each other. Senses returned. I could smell her hair, feel the curve of her back and the roundness of her hips. We still held each other, but now with ease...

> *Two eyes meet two eyes and*
> *that meeting of two eyes with*
> *two eyes lifts the falling.*
>
> *Two arms encircle, enfold and*
> *that folding of arms encircling,*
> *unfolds a fearful keeping.*
>
> *Two minds join in knowing and*
> *that knowing clears the past to*
> *bring the present shining.*

Two lips touch two lips and
that touch of two lips on
two lips, wakes the sleeping.

A heart flows full loving and
that heart seeks to draw out
A heart that seeks its becoming.

It was clear that all the love we could give each other wasn't going to deter the demons planted by time and circumstance in our psyches. I reasoned it is the same for everyone. It is not love that casts out all fear, for love, gentle and compassionate that it is, is no match for the dark adversary guarding the gates of the subconscious of the species. But before we dare journey there, we must first seek the secret unconscious keepings that each of us holds, and that holds each of us separate from one another. Joan and I had come together in our hearts. We now had to face the deep recesses of mind. For I suspected that it would be as one mind, male and female, Anima and Animus married in each of us, that would open a peaceful pathway through life.

As morning light filtered into the small bedroom, the slender beech tree outside the window played shadows on the curtains. I got up, pulled the curtains aside and looked out onto the street. The town was waking, people here and there making their way. The world, at least this corner of it, was moving into another day. I wondered what the news would be today.

Who did not wake to see this morning? Who, in some far off place, was crying for lack of food, who was being killed, who was killing? Of course there would be laughter, joy, delight, and wonder, too. Perhaps today someone will write a beautiful letter, compose music that will make the heart soar, or bring a sadness out that seeks release. Perhaps the finish will be put on a painting that will hang in a house and give joy, wake the senses, delight the eye. Maybe today a politician will be honest for a while, a banker generous, a businessman make a fair deal. What if today a general in the army decides enough killing has been done, a man of God admits he's not sure God is there, an atheist gets down and prays? What if we were able to tell the truth, admit our fears and doubts, climb down off our self-made pedestal, and rejoice in our commonality with all things sentient.

I turned and looked at Joan, moving slowly out of sleep, thinking again what a miracle life is, reaching out to us through a curve of body, a waving leaf, a gale, rain and storm, earth, sky and, of course, trees. The trees, so like us, half seen and half hidden. Joan opened her eyes.

"Hello, morning, Joan. Cup of tea?" I said.

෧෨

There was no way Joan and I could engage in formal therapy, not now.

On a free Sunday when Robert was at her brother's place we went to the park. I found two trees about thirty paces apart. I wasn't certain as to what I had in mind, but I let my intuition have its reign. "Joan, try this," I said, "stand by this first tree, think of it as two things, young and feminine."

"Young and feminine?" she questioned, "You mean it's me, as I was?"

"You don't have to go that far, not yet," I said, thinking how fast she had picked up on my embryonic thought. "Just young and feminine will do, I think. That," I said, pointing to the second tree, "is the opposite."

"An old man?" she said.

"Older, and yes, masculine." I don't know why I was using such formal language. Perhaps I thought being in a therapist's role would make Joan feel safer. I can be bloody stupid at times. But I knew when the insight came it would get serious. I decided not to go into too much explanation, just let the trees do their work of confined freedom, safe, yet open.

Joan asked, "So what do I have to do? I mean, apart from walking from one to the other? Is that it?"

"Basically, yes," I said, "But think as you walk, to whom are you walking towards, a young woman, or over there, an older man. Just give it a try."

"Should I walk ever so slowly, or just... what! James, stop frowning," she almost shouted.

Perhaps I had miscalculated. Having done so much of this kind of practice, I'd formed expectations of how it would go this Sunday. My visions were smoother than the real thing. I said, "I'm sorry, Joan. I don't want to push you into this if you..."

"Look, I'll do it!" she burst on me. Then added quietly, "I trust you, James, but I want to get it right."

"Right, yes, okay," I said. Realizing I was being over presumptuous and ignoring her very real experience, which I knew well enough was the teacher in life. "Well, the idea is to establish a temporary paradigm reflecting the source being investigated. Walking, just normal pace at first, and imagining the two dichotomies of the paradigm, strengthens the effect, not just the remembrance, but the experience." Joan looked at me with a question in her eyes. "I'll be right here, Joan. The beauty of this work is, when it gets hard to bear, just look up. Look at the tree for its own sake for a moment. It will give you strength and peace."

"Thank you, James."

I said, "Walk, Joan, walk for your soul's sake."

July 17th

It doesn't take long. The keeper of our unconscious plays a trick on us; all therapists know it. If we don't ask questions of our fears, they knock loudly on our conscious self and convince us of their power and force, thus we turn away from them and their power becomes real. Yet if we face them, we learn all their power comes from the very act of our turning away. For faced, they become what they are, just old memories, perhaps bad memories, but dead lifeless specters without the substance to even whisper, 'boo'.

Don't think that it is easy though. If a fierce giant is at your back with a club the size of a house, turning to face him is the bravest thing you will ever do. Most of us, most of the time, just keep running. It takes courage to stop running and start walking between the trees. I knew Joan had that kind of courage.

I was there when Joan crumpled. She lay back in my arms while the sound from her lips wailed across the grass and lifted into the branches of the trees. Eventually tears washed down her face and her expression cleared like clouds moving away from the sun. She closed her eyes, breathed steadily, and went soft in my arms. Oh, how I felt for her now. I knew the pain and the coming through, the courage and the surrender.

I laid her on the grass, sat by her holding a hand, and waited for her return.

July 17th

The inner struggle lies between head and heart, intellect and feeling, and yet our feelings are confounded by the past, by unconscious fears. How may we live within this complex of paradoxical conditions such that equanimity is the outcome? For surely it is the living of a balanced life that will bring a state of peace and harmony so urgently needed.

If I die too soon.
It will not be
For the lack of joy
Of loving, but
Because I could not learn
The art of living.

147

Joan was not to journey alone; the next Sunday it was I who walked the trees while she waited. My trees were designated the present and the past, thus I walked backwards in time and returned to Sunday in the park. I wasn't sure what I searched. I tried not to think, just accept past, present moment, past, present...

My pace changed. I started moving faster towards the present, slower and hesitating on the return to the tree of the past. Something back there was rising to the surface. My protector was forcing my steps away from it and holding them back when approaching it. Though paying no attention, I heard Joan's voice, "Try not to run, James, even out your steps."

On the next turn at the past tree I waited, forcing the unconscious to release its keeping, then started walking slowly as a grey stirring moved in my gut. By the time I reached the tree of present moment, the stirrings were dark imaginings. I turned and looked at the past, started walking into an abyss of half-formed feelings. Half way between the trees I looked up, grabbing with my eyes the beauty of the leaves, dappled with sunlight, peaceful, still. Joan's gentle voice reached my hearing, "It's alright, I'm here." I continued, pace following pace. "I love you." The tenderness in those words opposed and brought screaming into consciousness the source of my fear. I reached the tree and folded to the ground.

I held James in my arms. He was soft like a baby, but he was a man, one of a gender that had forced me, hurt me, covered my mouth until I thought I was dead. Now he cries as I cried. Now he is in pain as I was. I said I loved him and it hurt him. How he wails with what pain, what past. James, James. "It's alright baby. I'm here. Here, here's my hand." She kisses the man in her arms, and it feels like kissing a part of herself. *We are brought together. You are me and I am you. What separates us?*

"James, dear," Joan says, looking into my eyes. I can feel her body, her legs, behind my head. She wipes around my eyes. Her hand is soft. Her fingers glide gently across my forehead. I try to sit up. "Don't rush, James, just look into the tree." I do as she says, and the dark and light patterns moving in the leaves remind me of the leaf that fluttered in the wind so long ago. Then into my mind comes the remembrance, the suffering so long hidden from me in unconscious custody. Now, all power gone, it is just a memory. "What are you thinking, James?"

"Thinking?" Now I did sit, and leaned half against the tree and against Joan. "I was thinking when I was just past two years old, lying in a cot, bandaged like a mummy in a tomb."

Joan asked, taking my hand as she spoke, "Is it over?"

"Yes," I said, "It's over. At least for now." Then I leaned a little further and kissed her, for love, for friendship, and for me.

Twelve

It was early December, my father had been gone for two months. I was down at my mother's place.

My mother had always been a strong woman, of London-Irish stock, with gypsy somewhere in there. A hard working, working class woman. I thought when my father died she would up and go back to London, where she had a woman friend of many years who made an invitation. But the life seemed to have gone from her, which was strange, for she and my father fought silently for as long as I remembered. It was a lesson to me. But we had unfinished business. I wanted her to know at least what I knew. I had to throw a line across the years, thread time into this present moment, and let her have peace of mind, at least on my account.

I sat on a stool in front of her, and took her hand, once so strong, now not so. "Mum, I want to tell you something." She was uncomfortable, she would have pulled her hand away, but I held it fast. I cannot remember ever having such a strong tactile connection with her. We were physical strangers. "I want you to know what I know about us, you and me. I know you love me." The space between us filled with her agitation. She looked past me into the room, I went on, "I know we were caught in the bloody mess that comes in families: aggravations, frustrated dreams, hopes, and plain arguments."

She suddenly said, "You didn't know anything about that. We kept that from you, you were just..." she tailed off as some realization arose in her. Her eyes began to water.

I went on, "Yes, I know, I know you tried. But mum, it's like a war. There was a war in the house, and if you live with a war around you, you know it, even if you don't know why or what it's about." She looked up then, looked into my eyes. I realized it was the only time forever that we saw each other. Now I could say it, now she would hear. I put my free hand over hers so her hand was now completely covered and held in my two hands. I said, "I love you, Mum." I waited, but just for a moment, then released her hand, stood up and said, "Time for a cup of tea, I think," and went into the kitchen.

I could just see between the edge of the kitchen door and its frame, my mother crying. She would not want me to know, so I clattered about making the tea while taking some deep breaths to get me back over to my side of the barrier. I heard her blowing her nose and knew she was settling back on her side, to the comfortable familiar separation that marked our lives.

July 19th

We arrive into this world under many diverse circumstances. Our parents may be rich, poor, young or old. The culture we find ourselves in may be ancient or modern, primitive or materially advanced.[18] *We may be healthy or born sickly, perhaps with congenital challenges from the word go. We may be a boy or a girl or it may be hard to know. It sometimes happens that birth and death will arrive together. The answer to the question, 'What does it mean to be born?' I learn, is that birth invites death.*

The importance of this understanding lay in the profound, yet hidden, effect this has on our thinking and behavior. On the surface we don't want to acknowledge the power of such awareness. So we try hard to remain unaware. The effort expended in avoidance becomes the source of many ills, in our bodies, our thinking, and our behavior towards each other and the world.

After making that connection with my mother, a strange thing happened. As my mother became weaker, thinner and frail over time, I began to feel unwell. At first I thought little of it. I have a good constitution, as they used to say, and usually shake off anything threatening to my general health. After some time, I realized I was not so much ill, as weak and growing weaker, as though my life was leaking out of some unseen opening in my being.

It was on a visit to my mother's the following spring that I saw the same thing in her as I was experiencing. She was slowly giving up life, would say as much, in fact, "I don't know why I wake up in the mornings, I'm done with it," and, "What is there to live for, I'm tired. I pray every night to be taken." It would have been disturbing to me, except that I was more disturbed by what seemed like my being brought into her dying, as though I would die with her. I said nothing to my mother, but when I got home I knew I had to do something, but what?

I'm not sure how it happened; I wouldn't have thought it of me, but in the end I went to a hypnotist. I don't know what I thought he could do; I may have had some vague notion that he would break a spell or something. If I'm beginning to sound a little crazy, well, it may be so, but by now I felt I was in such a bizarre trap that I might actually be dying.

The fellow seemed alright. He worked in his home, a Victorian terraced house with high ceilings, molded skirting and window frames. He showed me into a back room that looked out over a narrow well-kept

---

18 I cannot use the term *civilized*. I cannot concede that we have got to that point yet.

garden of grass and flower beds. The room was quietly decorated, cream I'd say, with little ornamentation. There were flowers in a white and blue Ming-type vase in the cast iron fire grate. The carpet, also blue, was laid on a polished wood floor. I noted these things for it gave me a measure of the man. It felt acceptable to me. The man, about my age, wore a white shirt, no tie, and light trousers. Light trousers, I thought that interesting; I surmised he wasn't particularly using his dress to impress. He spoke quietly, but quite distinctly as he ushered me into the room and bade me take a seat.

After some preliminaries he said, "Is there a particular problem you are concerned with?"

"Yes," I said, "but I'm not sure what it is, or rather how to describe it without sounding a little crazy." Now, though I felt all right about the man, I didn't feel okay myself. I began to see the whole thing as foolish, an over-reaction, and wondered just what I thought he could do.

"If it comes out sounding crazy, then perhaps that's the truth of it," he said, "Just start with a word, any word, the first that comes to mind." He waited. He had the look of a patient man.

I began to relax. I said, "Dying."

"Who's dying?" he asked, and waited again, unwavering. I began to like the man.

"My mother, I think. And I'm dying with her," I said. Now it was my turn to wait.

After a few silent moments he said, "Alright, shall we make a start? Why don't you rest your arms on the chair arms and relax into the back. I'm going to tilt it back just a little to help you." He stood and went around the chair. It tilted slightly as I sank into it and did as he asked with my arms. He went to the windows, and the daylight in the room became a muted blue-green as I heard the rolling down of shades. He came around and sat in front and to one side of me.

"Close your eyes, James," he said, "Take three deep breaths and then just relax and breathe as you will." I followed his request. "Imagine a flower, closed, and in bud. Let the color and type of flower be whatever comes." I didn't see a bud, but the bulb of the Lily. We had agreed on a silent signal I would give when I felt ready. I opened and closed my hand. "Now can you place the flower on your tummy right over the umbilical." I opened and closed my hand. "I'm going to count backwards from ten. As I do so the flower will open, you will be relaxed and able to tell me what is happening." There was a moment, then his voice, soft but clear in the peace and silence of the room, "Ten, nine..." The bulb began to

151

transform into the Lily. "Eight, seven, six..." A flaming red and purple Lily in full bloom. "Five, four..."

⁐

I was moving up through white clouds with glimpses of blue. The light became more defused, softer, turning a color I'd never known, more of a feeling or tone than a shade. It was extremely silent, so silent that I could again only detect a feeling of sound. Then before me was a great rock, split down its center. It towered above me beyond my vision like a wall with a narrow opening, dark, yet inviting my exploration. I moved toward the rock's opening. As I approached I saw it was easily wide enough for a path through. Stepping beyond the rock face into the dim light of the passageway, for that was how it seemed, there was grass now beneath my feet. I was on solid ground and realized I had not been, and had no idea how I came this far. I knew instinctively it was far, far from anywhere or anything I knew, far from thought, far from being.

I moved along the path into the heart of the rock. The soft but now faint light remained to show the way. There came a point at which I could see neither back to my original opening or forward to an exit. I was in the center of the rock.

I told the hypnotist. He just said, "Lie down where you are, on the grass on your back." I opened and closed my hand. "Place the flower once again on your umbilical." I did so.

⁐

As the Lily once again opened, the colors leaked into the light, the light became brighter and brighter, the feeling of color and of sound permeated my being and expanded to forever, around and out, it seemed. I no longer felt myself, only bliss existed...

I have no idea how long he sat and waited in the silent room with me in the chair, but as I said, the man had patience. I, or somebody, something, heard his soft voice, "Where are you, James?" and I heard an answer in my own voice.

"I am gone." Then there was silence again, save for the beauty that was within and around me. His voice came again.

"James," it said, "I'm going to bring you home now..."

"NO! No, I don't need to go anywhere." It was my voice, yet I had no part in its voicing.

152

"You will be all right. The journey will be easy and swift. Listen." Into the timelessness came music. A classical piece (one of Edvard Grieg's, I think) came into my hearing, then the man's voice, "Listen, James, listen to the music." After he said that I began to feel my attention returning. The place I had been became dimmer and dimmer. The music was beautiful; I listened and felt the chair behind my back, my arms resting on the chair arms, my legs. I knew now I was in the room. I slowly opened my eyes. "Welcome home, James," he said, then turned his head a little towards the door and raised his voice a little, "Sally, dear."

From beyond the door I heard a faint voice say something and after a few minutes, a woman, slightly older than both of us, came in with the ubiquitous tea pot and two cups and saucers, all on a tray with a white and blue linen cloth cover.

❦

I didn't make a return visit to the therapist; the need had been attended to. My apparent dying ceased, and a vibrant life returned. The funny thing was he didn't seem surprised I was well again, or even inquired as to what I thought about the experience of hypnosis, if indeed I was hypnotized. I suppose I was.

I added the man to my list of Loving-Kindness, the *Metta* list. I suspect you have forgotten that by now, but it is important, as you will see later. If you're serious about developing change and creating a better world, this may be a good time to begin your list. Reading changes us but temporarily. It is acts of awareness continually returned to that will affect change. That is why I must return to the trees.

July 20th
What we say and do makes our world, and what we say or do springs from experience, the experience of birth, childhood, culture and those around us who weave our lives through their words and actions upon us, as we do unto them. Maturity is taking responsibility for what we say and do in response to such experiences. So often our responses are in reaction to the experiences we have. They are determined by the experience itself, not by an examination of experience. We react from our ego with predetermined views and opinions to each arising situation. Thus we may rail at God when life is full of suffering, because 'he' didn't do as we expected, or we may rationalize God making him acceptable, whatever happens.

We may believe God does not exist, considering ourselves free of ungrounded belief. We think we speak and act out of clear rationality, and equally fail to examine the ego that chooses to believe there is no God. In either case, what we believe in is our own egoic picture of the world. This is a self-centered way of living.

Yet again, whatever we think we believe does not always determine what we say or do in any given eventuality. In other words, we can, and often do, act in contradiction to our beliefs. Most of our strongest held beliefs are in deference to unseen fear, but sometimes our behavior is a challenge to that fear. Something in our frustrated deep being breaks through, pushing aside the self-protecting ego, and acts heroically, often spurred by the common good.

Such actions arise in the heart.

One weekend, around the end of July, Joan and I along with Robert had driven out to some woods about ten miles out of the town. We had brought along a picnic, some reading, and a ball. The day was cloudy, but the forecast dry. By the time we arrived, however, the clouds had darkened and it poured, one of those summer storms that come fast and are over just as fast. We sat in the car and waited, not exactly glum, but bordering on disappointed. Then Joan said, "Why don't we just go out in it, there's nobody about." I didn't get what she meant by the last bit until she continued, "We could take our clothes off and just feel the rain. Oh come on, James, let's." Robert was hunkering down in the back seat with a book. There was no way he was going out there. I thought, 'what a sensible lad'. But Joan had started to remove some outer garments. I don't think I mentioned, when Joan sets her mind to a thing... well, she was going out there. I couldn't let her go alone, it began to feel churlish, so I started stripping.

"Oh, good," she said. "Right," I said, "Alright."

We were parked by a grass area that edged onto the woods and ran down like a bowl before rising to meet the trees not more than twenty yards away. The downpour was such that a pond was forming in the bottom of the bowl. Getting out of each side of the car, we quickly closed the doors and looked at each other across the bonnet. It was ridiculous, we couldn't stifle our laughter. I ran around the car ready to grab Joan out of sheer delight, but she started down the slope and splashed her way into the pond. I followed and we stood, water halfway up our legs, rain pouring down from a sky beginning to lighten. I think it was the happiest I had ever seen her. The feeling was mutual. We held our arms up to the rain and I remembered when I was a boy searching for where the rain came from, and thought, I'm still searching, but not for long this day, the rain washing thinking away in an ecstasy of feeling. My heart was happy with the simple joy of it.

Back in the car, we dried off with some outer clothes and put the rest back on. No sooner had we dressed than the rain stopped, the sky cleared, and we decided to have our picnic. This time Robert put his book down and joined us. The sun shone and dried the grass above the pond, which by now had become murky with soil and worms wriggling their way out to the edges and onto the drying grass.

"What shall we do now?" Joan asked.

"We could do *Metta* trees," I said. "It's walking, but different; I don't think I've shown you it, have I?"

Robert burst out, "Trees!" and threw up his hands. If ever I heard a boy swear without using a swear word, that was it. And his mother heard it too.

"Robert dear, don't you like trees?" she said, half smiling with a sort of cheeky smirk at me. "And I thought you loved the countryside."

"Alright, okay, so we don't do trees today," I said, "Give me that ball," and I grabbed it and started out across the grass with Robert after me. I'd had children. I knew what to do, run them until they're tired, then you get some peace. Of course, you end up tired too, but that's the price, and that's just about what happened.

After a while, we were all lying on our backs looking at soft blue sky edged with trees, their tops waving in and out of sight. "So, what are *Metta* trees?" Joan asked. "Hey, James, you asleep?" It was some time before I answered.

"No, I'm not," I said somewhat lazily, "but I might have been."

"What's *Metta* trees then?" Joan repeated, still lying on her back.

I leaned up on one elbow and looked at her. "It's all about Loving-Kindness," I said, in about as seductive a voice as I could, willing her head to turn and face me.

It worked. "Loving, kindness," she said, and leaned up on an elbow to face me. I wasn't exactly sure what to do next; I could certainly go with the loving, or... I should go for kindness, this is, after all, a precious friendship.

I said, "D'you think you can remember all the people you've ever known?"

She replied with a slice of lemon in her voice, "Would I *want to?* There are some people I'd rather forget, better still, if I had never even known."

"Yes, I know. A lot of folk have people they feel best forgotten," I said, "but they, more than those we care about, tie us up, keep us prisoners of our own pain and anger." I waited, letting this sink in. "All the killing that goes on across the world, think of it, Ireland, Israel, Korea, Vietnam, Darfur, the two great wars, as they call them, hating people for their color, their beliefs. The carnage is endless."

After a while she said, "But there are deep, sometimes personal and real reasons for anger. Justified anger, James." I knew what she was referring to, but I had also discovered how unconsciously we turn such internal pain on others, how it morphs into a general hatred, as Joan may well feel justified in hating men.

The paradox I've observed with such hating is it often pardons known individuals. When I was a boy I would hear remarks like, those bloody Irish (who had come to London seeking work) they're just a lot of drunken lazy brawlers, but old Mick next door he's alright, a nice bloke. The hatred feeds on our remaining alienated.

I looked her in the eyes and said, "But you love me, Joan, and I'm one of them." I know she was about to say, "you're different." I spoke up, "And I could do the same thing."

A look of confusion, disappointment, anger, and finally cold blankness crossed her features. She got up and walked away from me. She turned, throwing words at me, "You've spoilt it, you've spoilt it all, I hate..." she couldn't say it, but she was feeling it. I knew what she really hated was that she had such feelings still imprisoning her. I knew those feeling were the fuel that kept the fires, that burned people, that made the wars, that destroyed all the good we ever tried to do. I knew that we, all of us, have to face the demon gate-keeper that imprisons the future in the past. Only when we stop dropping black into white will we ever know the grand possibility we are born to.

There was nothing I could do. I just waited on the grass, feeling the struggle and the hurt that was Joan right now. Eventually, after walking far enough away that she nearly disappeared, her figure started to grow as she made her way back to us. Robert asked, "Is mummy mad?"

"No," I said, "Not with you and not really with me. Your mummy's just unhappy, she'll be okay in a bit. Here she comes."

As she came closer, he got up and went to her, hugging her legs and said, "I love you, mummy." She ruffled his hair and answered back, "I love you too, Bobby." Then she looked at me. I was sitting up. I waved a silly little wave and said, "Hey." She sat on the blanket, and Robert sat on her knees. Joan put her arm around him. We let the silence close the wounds.

July 20th

Cleverness simply requires brain cells and ambition to succeed within a clever culture. We are well fitted through thousands of years of evolution to gain dominance over the world. But understanding, that includes kindness towards each other and the world, is more than cleverness, the mix comes out as wisdom, and that we are in short supply of.

There have been, and are among us, a few wise people. We either put them on a pedestal as being a different manner of being from the rest of us or kill them, historically often doing both in predictable sequence.

We can no longer look to the few wise ones, not with adoration or envy, to save us from ourselves. No president, minister, king or queen, lama or guru can create the magic of change. It is our own awareness, our own collective consciousness that will, if we have the courage, bring about a humane society.

As we were driving home in the car, Joan reached across and put a hand on my shoulder, and then let it slide gently down my back. It was a signal, an ancient signal at that, the sort of things we did when we lived in trees. I knew the signal without exactly knowing, its message is woven in our bones. It meant our friendship was greater than our fears.

The message said, let's keep going, let's hope, let's face whatever we need to face to get out of prison. It meant I love you, and for the love of that love, I want done with anger.

I hadn't felt my own anger. At first I suspected it was because I didn't have any clear target to aim it at, to draw it out. Joan's anger could be drawn by my words, a reference to my gender, and what men can, and too often, do. But I came to know my own anger had been beaten down by fear, by an experience I suffered when I had no means to understand it. I had unwittingly been tortured. It was one evening while sitting with Joan, having read Robert a story and seen him off to sleep, that I made the discovery.

Joan and I were seated side by side on the sofa just chatting. Her arm was across the back of the sofa, and in an absent-minded moment, Joan started to stroke my hair. At first my senses, suddenly alerted, tried to block out the feeling, but the need, conflicted though it was with feelings of abandonment, cried out within: Don't stop, don't ever stop. I don't know why or how it happened, but the cry reached my lips.

Joan, her hand stopped still on my head, looked at me and said, "What, James? What is it? What don't you want to stop?"

"You were stroking my head, Joan," I said, and could say no more.

"That's what you didn't want to stop? Me just stroking your head?"

"Yes, that," *he said.*

I said, "But you cried out so, in such pain, dear. I thought you were hurt or something." *James was looking small, almost afraid, but not that-- vulnerable! He looks fragile as though he will break.*

"Yes," *he said. But I can hardly hear him.*

I'm not sure what to do with him. "Look, James," *I tried to get his attention,* "I'm going to stroke your head again, okay?" *He nodded, so here goes.* "I think you should tell me what you're feeling while I'm doing it, James."

He said, "I'm... it's everything, it's..., there's no borders, my body is liquid, I'm floating in myself. You mustn't stop!... I can't stand it. I'm lost. I..."

He has to find out, I have to help him. "James, I'm going to stop. Tell me what happens, James, okay?" *I stopped stroking.*

He's rolled himself into a tight ball, he's fighting it. "Stop it, James, stop fighting it, just tell me what's happening. Do it now!"

"I'm dying. It's grey, it's cold, please hold me."

This is terrible, but I stay where I am. "James," *I use as soft a voice as I can and still be heard.* "James, tell me what you see."

He almost shouts, "Nothing! Nothing. I see nothing, grey, no, white, it's completely white everywhere. I can't... I can't think. My mind, it's... there's deadness." *He uncurls and lays back against the sofa.*

~∾

I open my eyes and Joan is there with me, close by. I take a breath and turn to her, "I thought it was just that I was left alone, abandoned in the hospital. But I think it was worse than that. I'm not sure, but... What did I say, Joan?"

"You said you were dying, it's grey."

"No, just now," I said, "What did I say just now?"

"It's white, not grey, white. You said you couldn't think."

I said, "I wonder what was white?"

"What do you think? What does white mean? Does it mean anything to you?" Joan was beginning to sound like a therapist.

"No, Joan," I said, "White is just white, weddings, clouds, anagari-kas, death, paper, egg white, you know."

158

"Death?" she said.

I said, "What about it?"

"You said death, death is white, how is it white?"

"Did I? You sure?"

"Yes, James. You said death." She challenged me, "What does it mean, James, that death is white?"

"It doesn't mean bugger-all, Joan. Stop with the interrogation, will you."

"Why are you angry with me? All I'm doing is telling you what happened, what you said."

Something's coming out. I'm not sure I want to see it. I think we've opened a can of worms. I'm afraid.

"What you're doing is manipulating me. White is not dead, dead is not white, I'm not white, it's... it's... I'm not... I'm not... Fuck you!"

I say nothing. I'm keeping my fingers crossed. He's very tight. I hope he doesn't hit. I've got to say something.

"Fuck you all," *he said.*

Well that was a bit softer. Here goes, "What did we do, James? What happened?"

"You left me in the hospital to be tortured. You left me to die. I hate you."

∽

James put his hands over his face and cried into them. His shoulders shook, and the sound, muffled as it was, moaned its way through his fingers and filled the room. Joan worried that it would wake and frighten Robert. It didn't. It gradually subsided and he became still. Then he spoke again, "I love you. I've always loved you. Please don't leave me." Joan was confused, a little frightened, and yet drawn inescapably to comfort James.

She said, "I won't leave you, James," even as she knew it was not to her the plea was made. James leaned into her open arms. He was soft now, loose. He fell asleep.

∽

When I awoke it was late. I felt relaxed but weak, I said as much to Joan when she asked.

"Stay here tonight, James," she said, adding, "Come on, let's go to bed." Joan still had that flat tone to her voice, so I wasn't certain of her meaning, or perhaps I was hoping a particular invitation had been made.

I said, "Yes, you're right, I'd best stay." I got up and we moved out into the hallway, switching off lights as we went. I followed Joan upstairs and into her bedroom. I really was tired, though thoughts of love-making sat in my brain, and my body, as though under commandment to maintain the species. But it was Morpheus that had the upper hand over Eros this night.

I laid my head on Joan's breast. I could hear her heart, feel her closeness. I slept like a baby.

෴

Now we had both touched the demon at the gate. We'd forged into the unconscious and felt the flame of anger ignited by a primal fear. We had pushed against our opposite, we had opposed, dared to want synthesis, a bringing of contraries together, a dissolution of paradox. We had, just for a moment, brought a light into the darkness.

Could we do any more, I wondered.

෴

March came, 1989. Winter was slowly fading, spring not yet showing. I was feeling restless, so I made a trip north and was staying with Paul. I made a visit to Kate's, of course. She was well and enjoying another friend's company.

"You're looking different, James," she said, "Older. Oh, sorry, I didn't mean it like that, I didn't mean you *look* older, more you are older. Oh, bugger-it, it's not coming out right. Just tell me, what have you been up to? You've been up to something."

I smiled. Of course I knew better than she, what she saw and couldn't describe. I said, "It's a woman, but..."

"Of course, should have known..." she started to say.

"Not like you think, though, Kate, not at all like us," I said, "I met my nemesis, she who would curse me."

"Curse you! How bloody awful. Why did you do that to yourself?"

I said, "Because I could curse her, it gave me permission to know my anger."

"I didn't know you had any anger. You were always such a sweet man, a bit too sweet sometimes," she said, "I wondered if your fire had gone out."

"Not out, just heavily dowsed when I was too young to know it."

"So how is it now, then?" I looked at her, only half getting what she was saying. "You know,... lust, James, lust!"

"I wouldn't know," I said.

"What! You haven't?..." she began.

"No. Not yet, and maybe never," I said, "We're friends up to this point. It's as you said once, if we did get to lust, as you put it, I wouldn't be there, would I? I'd be off thinking. Well, we're both, Joan and me, in the same boat. So... we decided to try and do something about it."

It seemed to silence Kate. She looked pensive, and I wondered what demons my little speech had stirred in her. But she just said, "Well, good luck with that, James. Joan... nice name, is she nice, when she's not cursing you?"

"Yes," I said, "she is nice."

◇

Friendship has no ceremonies like births, deaths and marriage. I think it's an omission that should be put to rights. My friendship with Paul went deep; it wasn't just that we had shared events in our lives, or even the politics, it was a thing hard to name. It was as a friend that Paul was speaking one day, "You know, James, you could go to university; you've never been, right?"

"No. Done plenty of things, not that, though," I said, "I think they bummed me at school because of my dad. So I never got in the stream."

"Your father's politics, you mean?" he asked.

"Yes, that and the trade union stuff," I said, "You see, he worked just a block from home, and the school was only three blocks away. When a strike was on, it was all over the district. I remember the year I was taken down a stream, it was '52, I would have taken the grammar school exam the following year. As it was, I took the technical. I did alright."

"Yes," he said, "But now you could still pick up the grant and do university."

"Oh come on, Paul, I'm getting on for mixing with a load of youngsters," I said, "Besides, where would I go?"

"There's a place at Oxford, one of the colleges, Ruskin, that only takes mature students." He suggested I give them a call, there and then, so I did. I told them my age and a quick, rough resume in answer to their questions, and they said they would send an application. That made Paul happy, which was fine by me because I promptly put it out of my mind.

By the time I got back home, though, a thick envelope, marked Ruskin College, was on the mat. I thought, bloody-hell they're keen. I took it into the living room, and after eating, sat down to inspect its contents. There was the usual stuff, a form about personal details and previous schooling, and instructions for making a formal application. They were requesting an essay of around two thousand words. There was a list of essay subjects tied to each particular course of study. Under English Literature and Politics, they were asking for comparison and critique of two novels of one's own choosing. Two thousand words! I'd hardly written a post card in the last five years. Of course I talked to Joan about it. I think I wanted her to say, why bother or you don't need it or some such thing.

She said, "Why not give it a go, James? Think of it, university, Oxford. Oh, do go, James. Let's find a couple of really thin books, that'll help."

It seems there was no way out without seeming truculent, and I'd have to report to Paul as well. So we searched for one thin book. I decided one of the books would be Steinbeck's *Cannery Row*, a story of a bunch of homeless hang-a-bouts. I knew the book well. We found another thin book, the title of which eludes me, about Catholic monks on an island off Ireland. I'm sure you can see the connections I was about to write of, as write I did, two thousand or so words, to my own surprise. I sent off the package, thinking I had done my duty by my friends and would hear no more.

Dear Mr. Owen,
Following your application to this college, would you please attend an interview on 10th May. Please confirm your attendance as soon as possible and no later than 1st May.

"Joan, Joan, I got an interview at Oxford," I was on the phone before I read the closing remarks.

"That's great. Oh, Oxford. I can visit, it's not far," she said, "I'm so pleased for you."

"It's only an interview, Joan," I said, "I may not pass, I mean, bloody-Oxford!"

"If they've asked you, they must think your essay was good, and they'll love you, I know they will." She was a little biased there, I thought.

"Can you come round, or shall I?" I asked. "We should celebrate. Even if I don't get in, it's worth a celebration, to be called for an interview, right?"

"I can't get out, James," she said, "Come round and bring something, you know, to celebrate with."

ເ◦ອ

We sat with the wine bottle on a small table in front of us; it was the last of three that I had brought round. "I think you're the most beautiful woman I've ever seen," I said.

"And I think you've had enough wine, Romeo," Joan said, looking into my eyes like an optician.

"Your eyes are so deep," I was saying somewhere, "I wonder what's really going on back there, in the depths, miss Joan."

"I was thinking coffee, back there in the kitchen," she said. "You are beautiful in the kitchen, beautiful in here, beautiful under the trees," I replied.

"What are you thinking, James?" she asked. "There's no trees in the kitchen. I'm going to make some coffee. Come on, the walk will do you good." She got up and offered a hand, of course I took it. So soft, a woman's hand.

"I love you, Joan," I said.

"Yes, I know, James, better than you know right now." That was a funny thing for her to say, better than I know?

"Kitchen. Coffee. Come on," she said.

I got up, put an arm around Joan's shoulder, and we made it to the kitchen, where I promptly sat down at the table. Joan busied herself with the kettle and cups and what-not.

I swear it was magic, for there in front of me was a cup of coffee, and sitting opposite me was Joan; she too had a cup. I said, "Cheers, Joan." She moved her cup a little and we drank.

The heat flowed down and settled in my stomach, soothing my body. I relaxed and saw Joan, a little flushed, like the blush on a flower, a Lily perhaps. For the briefest of moments I saw the girl in a long-ago dream, that same flushed cheeks. I felt a rush of love, like going under in a great surf wave at the seaside. I was thrown. I must have suddenly tipped a little, for Joan was startled, "James! Are you all right?" She had put her hand out and grabbed my arm. I took her hand in mine. I said, "I'm fine, Joan. Never felt better."

I kept hold of her hand while I took another drink of coffee. I knew I could feel even better. I wanted to be close to her. I put the cup down and said, "Joan, I want to stay the night. I mean I want to..."

"I know what you mean, James, I know what you want," Joan's voice was still flat, for all the work we had done in plunging the depths of our demons. I wasn't sure what she was thinking behind her words. But then she added, "I want it too, James, but not through a bottle of wine."

"The wine just helps get past the fear, Joan," I said, not being quite sure what I meant.

"You're not afraid of me?" she asked, "Are you?"

"No, not exactly, I mean, no, not you. It's like holding a precious piece of china, a Ming vase or something. I'm afraid I'll break it, hurt it, you. I'll damage our friendship and..."

"But you don't *want* to hurt me," she said, "Do you, James?"

"NO! No, no. Never! I... I just think I'll do something wrong, I'll... I don't know. I'm just afraid that's how it will go. You'll think..."

"James. Stop it. Stop thinking, James." When she said that I was brought up short. Joan had almost mouthed Kate's exact words on the subject. But Joan was not Kate. She said, "I love you. I'm not measuring anything, I just love you." She reached across and put her hand over mine, "The wine's dried up now, hasn't it?"

"Yes. Sober as a judge now," I said, "thanks to the coffee and a bit of a shake up."

Joan stood up and came around to me, I stood up and our arms were around each other. She leaned into me and kissed my neck. I could smell her softness. She whispered, "Come on, James, let's go upstairs. We can face our fears together." We turned the lights off and slowly climbed the stairs to the small familiar bedroom.

In the morning we were exhausted, relaxed, and inexorably changed. Joan had lost her flat voice. I had stopped thinking, at least for a while, and been present. What had not changed was our friendship.

❦

I duly went to Oxford for the interview, and received a letter of acceptance in mid-June. I was to begin studies the first week of October. In the acceptance letter was a list of summer reading I was advised to do. I could hardly believe where my life was heading, or the peace I found with Joan that summer. At weekends we took Robert out to the park or local canal or sometimes just sat in Joan's small garden with books on chairs and tables, sometimes reading aloud, and at times alone.

Joan and I never quite returned to the passion of that celebration night; it was an unfamiliar engagement, too far from a lifetime habit of self effacement. But we were comfortable and enjoyed a more limited acceptance of shared comfort. We were friends, taking care of one another. So when the time came close for my departure to Oxford, it felt like the advent of a shared ambition; I felt Joan would be with me in my studies. For her part Joan was looking forward to making visits, Oxford being but a two hour train journey away.

> *Quietly walk into my room.*
> *While I, working at the loom*
> *weave word pictures*
> *while soft sounds seek caress.*
>
> *Lento rising as we sit.*
> *While we, with silence knit*
> *parting prints in snow*
> *while knowing,*
> *soon I shall go.*

I gave up my rented rooms and stayed the final week of September at Joan's place. On the day of my departure, as usual I had little to pack, apart from all the books, and so we took ourselves and my backpack to the park. We landed up by the two trees where we first met.

"Home and away," I said to Joan, "The two trees could be home and away. Let's walk between them together." So we held hands and walked between two trees, away to Oxford, and back to the home tree. After a few times back and forth, Joan let go of my hand when at the 'home tree' and said, "Go on, James, go on, you walk. And then fly, James, fly as high as you can."

I hugged her close to me and kissed her, "I love you, Joan."

"I know," she said.

Then I picked up my pack and walked to the 'Oxford tree', turned to look at her, turned back to the tree, and said under my breath, "Keep safe, dear friend," and walked on to the station and Oxford.

THIRTEEN

Oxford of the dreaming spires, of the river, of fields and trees, of the canal, the same one I had walked when first I journeyed away from Catherine, searching for the next turn in the road.

The college consisted of two separate buildings, one in the heart of the town, the other on the outskirts. It was north of the city where I was to spend my first year as a student. My room, just big enough for a bed and desk and a few drawers in a small chest, overlooked a group of trees that, before moving, I would find time to paint from my window. Time alone, it seemed, was now something I would have plenty of, but of course life has a way of directing us, connected as we are at its heart.

We were given our first assignment on the second day in residence, a two thousand word essay on George Orwell's writings. It was considered, by the staff, an easy breaking in. I'm not sure where they got that idea! Along with the other students in my study group, I groaned at the task ahead of me, wondering just what I had let myself in for. I'd imagined I'd spend the first week getting to know the college, the city, and its parks and surrounding countryside, but the glamor of 'going to Oxford' was replaced with hard labor. It was a month before I was broken in enough to look up from my studies and look around. Until that point, though I phoned Joan and my mother once a week, there was little to say beyond what I was writing.

It was a cold, bright Saturday in November that saw me down in the center of the city. I was taking a breather, strolling the covered market and thinking of going for a pint. It would be my first since arriving. (Walking the trees, it seemed, had been relegated to the back of my mind.)

"Hey, Rooski!" The young man beside me continued in a broad Birmingham accent, "You go to Rooskin, riaght? 'Seen you in the canteen. What you stoodying, then?"

I turned and held out my hand. I don't think he expected that, but shook it anyway. "I'm doing English literature and politics," I said, "You?"

"Trade unions and law," he said, "I'm Andy."

"James," I said. He looked at me a bit old-fashioned until I added, "I was just going for a pint, coming?"

"I'm with you. Where to?" he asked.

"King Billy, down the ally," I said, "You been?"

"No. Lead on, mate. I'll follow," he said, "What you doin' bloody-English for? Had enough of that stoof at school."

"So's I can learn to talk proper," I said, in my best cockney accent.

"Piss off, you limey prat! Where's this pub, then?"

It wasn't exactly how I had pictured being an Oxford student, but my fellows at Ruskin were all, like me, working class folk who had missed out, one way or another, on higher education. This was their chance. They were rough diamonds, but by graduation they would all be polished to varying degrees of finish. Those who survived the course and didn't leave. Andy left, with curses, after three months.

Andy had come down with his wife and small child. They lived out of the college in a house provided for families. When he left, his wife, Helen, remained, as she too was a student, but intent on staying the course. It was hard for her. Although any affection between Andy and Helen had clearly died some time back, breaking up is never easy. She was now faced with taking care of her two-year- old Jo, and a demanding study program.

Joan's words on the pier came back to me, as I began to make offers of support to Helen. 'You'd put the weight on your shoulders with the rest of the pack.' Some things are in our natures, I suppose. I was older, too old for thoughts of an encounter, though I admit it crossed my mind or, better said, passed through my bones. I let it pass, she had enough on her plate. So Helen and I became friends. You could be forgiven for thinking by now that I slide in and out of friendships with every passing body, but it is not so. The insight Joan had, marked out those who move me: I take on suffering.

I have come to know, the gift of suffering is compassion. Such compassion is not particular to others or myself, but to all, for as the Buddha noted, in some way we all suffer. When I take on suffering, I am saving myself as much as I am the other. Thus it was that being with Helen, supporting her life, proved a gift to myself. When such a coming together occurs, it is the intimation of the divine.

To an Englishman, tea is almost divine. It certainly was to Derrick. My room was on the second floor of the students' residence. Derrick lodged on the first floor and, like Andy, was studying Trade unions and law. We were about the same age and both originated from London. There wasn't a time when I would visit his room that he didn't greet me with, "Cuppa tea, mate?" It was as ritualistic as Paul's flamboyant kiss on both cheeks.

I've observed over the years, friendships, of the deepest kind, almost instant, unquestioned and lasting, have a common base. They are the natural ways and means we choose of seeking an answer to the eternal question, and the paradox it throws our way: Why are we born just to die? Derrick and I became instant friends.

One thing we both discovered as students was the illusion that intellectualism fosters, an illusion of completeness, of gaining something, and commanding the world. It has become just another form of distraction, an escape from the giant with a house-size club. That's not to say it doesn't hold certain truths worth seeking; ignorance of the world is no passport to equanimity or peace of mind.

In my chosen discipline, literature, I was to find, at its core, efforts to engage one in consideration of a fundamental paradox, a reflection of life and death through the struggle between mind and heart, thinking or feeling. There are things known by the heart that the mind seeks to deny: love, hate, fear and death. Things common enough to our daily discourse, yet only half-felt as we skim this life on a flight from truth. For with the pursuit of learning, truth is what we set ourselves to find, yet when it is too close by, we turn and seek elsewhere.

After the first month, Derrick started to go home at weekends...

> ### July 22nd
>
> *...aloneness is not a condition most people can endure. For it is when we are alone with ourselves, it is hardest to run. Fear, hammering on our consciousness, drives us to seek distraction and comfort in shared agreement that we are alright. Almost everything we do that is destroying the world has its genesis in such action.*
>
> *Generation after generation, we have managed to defy and deny the call that life makes to us, indulging our distractions, our desires and wants, and forgetting our place. In our forgetting lies suffering, for when nature accepts the invitation that is birth, we cry out and are broken by death. Yet it is only our arrogance that is broken, for she sees through us, and if we seek her, forces our hearts to see too.*

Before the Christmas break was upon us, Joan came down for the day, to check out the college, Oxford, and my life. Short of manipulating circumstances, which I had no mind for, it was inevitable Helen and Joan would meet. We three, plus Robert and Jo, were sitting in a café in the covered market for lunch. It was just this side of all right, our animal back-brains and nature's indifference to consequences, were throwing around gut feelings and unsaid thoughts in a chaos of ancient gestures and looks, while the conversation remained contained and, I thought, friendly.

"So, how's the tree walking going, James?" It was Joan inquiring and turning the conversation home, so to speak.

"Slow," I said, "I'm so busy I've hardly been walking."

Helen's interest had been piqued, "What's tree walking?"

Joan sought to answer before I could, "You pick out two trees and walk back and forth between them. It's a sort of meditation."

"Meditation?" Helen asked, "You mean like contemplating-your- navel stuff? Do you really do that, James?"

I was about to open my mouth when again Joan spoke, "He's an expert. He'll have you walking your socks off if you don't watch it." That was a bit naughty, I thought what's Joan so peeved about? It was obvious really. I just credit folk with being able to use their brains to deal with the heart, but I knew only too well it doesn't work that way.

"Is he all right, Joan? I mean, does he have any other funny habits?" Helen and Joan had now become conspiratorial. I may be slow, but I'm not stupid. I'd seen this pattern before; I was a dead duck in the water.

Joan said, "I'll give you my address, if you need to escape, you'll have a bolt-hole." They both turned to me, laughing quietly and affectionately.

Most of the rest of the day saw me showing Robert the city while Joan and Helen went shopping. It wasn't to purchase anything, but to be about women's business. However that particular mystery works is, of course, beyond my ken, a world I am quite rightly separated from.

July 23rd

Some will rail at that assertion, but though we men and women may procreate together in the service of nature's demand, and help and support each other, we are markedly different in our approach to life. The requirement made upon women, of sustained nurturing, is surely the source of social and community evolution, whereas men have over time spent their energies defending their broods, fighting each other, and dividing the world into tribes and nations. It is to the feminine we must now look for salvation. An Anima that resides in men, just as the Animus is a part of women.

I was happy for Joan and Helen; it's progress of a sort every time women get together. It's a pity if it has to be in opposition to men, but it may have to be if we are to survive as a species.

❧

My first year at Oxford finished around the end of June. I had done fairly well and managed to pass the end of year exams without disgrace. I felt

good, and I was ready for summer. It was as well I understood the unpre-
dictability of English weather, for that year saw plenty of rain, and I found
myself indoors more than I would have liked. But I did visit the park and
walk between the trees, in the rain. It provided for very different reflections. I recalled my first school, and life with Andrew...

⁕

He was a year ahead of me, but in break-times we'd meet in all weathers
out on the field. It was the year before he died falling from a tree; we were
out in the pouring rain while most of the other kids were taking break
in the school hall. We sat under a maple tree in full leaf, which held off
the heavy rain, but dripped sufficient water on us that we were able to
pretend being at sea on a battle ship. The war had been over only five
years or so; it was still the best game going.

"U boat at four-o-clock! All stations, all stations!"

"NO! Battle stations, dib 'ead. Not all stations."

"Right, Captain. Battle stations, you lot, and move it!"

"Thank you, number one. Look, there's jerry's telescope."

"Periscope. Captain, the bugger's on the hunt."

"Order depth charges, number one. And jump to it!"

"One's away! Sod this rain, can't see a bleeding thing."

"Could do with cocoa, number one, see what the mess can muster.
And tell the engine room we need more speed."

"Wilco, sir. Weee, Weee, Weee. Engine room. Put the coal on the fire
Coaky, Captain wants more speed!"

July 24th

*The fertile imaginings of the young mind built scenes out of thin air.
Using language from the radio and comics, we lived the war our
parents fought, we became part of the hero myth of victory, and the
glory of empire. In the classroom the map of the world was liberally
covered with pink: the British empire. Not a thought could enter
through the barrage of history that made natural to us what was
patently unnatural, that one group of our species had been busy for
over two hundred years killing, maiming and subduing other members of the same species. But we learned this was the way of the world
and always had been. We were taken back to Greece and Rome, and
brought forward to the Vikings, the Saxons and 1066, a date we*

> *had implanted in our 'thick sculls' as the Normans established a unified Great Britain.*

Walking between the park trees in the summer rains, having just completed a year at one of Great Britain's most auspicious centers, from which men went out to force such mayhem upon the world, I thought of the lines John Steinbeck wrote, 'How did it grow so late, have we learned anything? Are we more mature, wiser, more perceptive, kinder?' I wondered what use education was to wisdom, to kindness.

FOURTEEN

It's July 1990, the month of my birthday.

Astrologers will tell me that makes me a Cancerian. How we are indoctrinated without even knowing it, for the truth is there is no such person. Though there are those who build lifetime careers out of Astrology, that merely reflects human gullibility, for it belongs with the ancient tales and gods long ago put to disrepute. Education may not, by itself, produce wisdom, but ignorance of the real world in favor of illusion is culpable folly. I do not mean to be hard, for I know the reason escape into illusion is so prevalent lay in unfathomable fear. It can take a lifetime to resolve such demons even with a will to do so.

It is the ever-present search that sends me back and forth to Indriya during the summer. The Buddha grove is now five years old and more trees have been added, it's almost a forest. Between the trees, criss-crossing paths have been worn in the grass, marking the many hours of walking meditation. The place has a peaceful feel, it is taking on the intention of its walkers. At first I walk as I was taught, mindful of breath, mindful of feet against ground, staying aware of what surrounds me. This is known as *Samatha Vipassana*, the practice of tranquility and insight. There's much to be gained from such a walk.

In time, the steadiness of walking lulls the guardian at the gate to the unconscious, and there arises the hidden impulses that have been directing one's thoughts and feelings. They are not pleasant, if they were they would not hide. It is now that tranquility must be well practiced, strong and steady, as at each turn by each tree, the face of fear once hidden becomes clearer and clearer. How one faces up to such a demon determines who will survive the walk, the old fear or a new freedom.

❧

There is a story of an ancient god and the devas being out one day from the palace. On their return, the devas enter first and find *Mara,* the evil one, occupying the throne. The devas run back out, distraught, to tell the god, who is in no particular hurry. The angrier the devas get, the bigger *Mara* becomes, such that by the time the god reaches the palace, Mara is a giant, filling half the throne room. "Ah, Mara," the god says, "Good to see you, dear fellow, I hope the throne is amenable to your taste, perhaps you'd like some tea?" The god continues in this friendly talk, and as he does so *Mara* visibly shrinks, until with a wave farewell from the god, he disappears.

෯

The teaching makes clear that we have to make friends with our fears. The particular method of friendship is outlined in the *Metta* sutta, which we shall come to. What is central to *Metta,* and indeed all friendships, is well-developed equanimity, known as *Upekkha.*

It was a strengthening of that particular quality I sought this summer at the monastery, for I had discovered walking between the trees produced awareness and insights deeper than the unconscious, insights into the species subconscious, a primal fear driving all of us to destruction. If I were to continue I would need to develop strong *Upekkha.*

෯

It was a weekend in September and I was back for a last, short stay before returning to Oxford. I had put myself on the rota for meal preparation and duly went to the kitchen after morning gruel. There were two of us helping the anagarika. When he called us together with meal instructions, I was surprised to find my prep partner was Rosalyn. It had been quite some time since our last phone chat and even longer since seeing her, she had changed. Once we had been given our duties, we were left to it for the time being.

"Rosalyn," I said, as we peeled and chopped a large bag of carrots, "how are you, how's everything? The girls..."

"Everything's a tall order, James," she started, "The girls are fine, getting big and sassy, fourteen, you know."

"Right, yes, I suppose they must be. It goes so fast," I said. "What brings... I mean, are you just on a visit?" Her hair was very short, "Or...?"

"This is my third visit," she said, "Last time I stayed two months. I'm not sure how long I will this time, I've been here three months so far."

"That's funny, I haven't seen you, I've been coming on and off most of the summer."

"Well, it hasn't always been Indriya, I spent time in another of the monasteries, too," she said, "I went down there with the nuns."

"I have to ask, Rosalyn," I said, "Are you...?"

"Not right now, no. The girls are too young, they still need me around," she sounded matter of fact as though she had a list of things to do and a right order to do them in.

"And Richard?" There was a silence. I waited, listening for a word between the carrots plopping into the large pan of water between us.

"He's okay. Supportive," she said, "Says if I need to explore, I'd best get it out of my system. I'm afraid he blames you a bit. He doesn't say as much, but I know him well enough. Sorry, James. It wasn't really you, if it wasn't you, it would have been something else. The irony of it is Richard and I got on except for... well... sex. You know. It wasn't okay for him either, but he wouldn't admit it. Now I'm in this place, a house of celibacy." I was glad to see she could smile at that thought.

"I don't know what to say, Ros." I went silent. We peeled and chopped. Then I had to get it out. "Yes I do! Ros, this is crazy. This life is not for you. I bet somewhere in your bones you know it too. You're a warm... you... You'll meet some one else, if you give it half a chance."

"Stop it, James!" she almost shouted at me. Then after a silence added, "Don't confuse me, James, that seems to be your forte. This place gives me some peace, a chance to think things through." She returned to peeling, breathing a little too heavily, but finding calm in the work.

I judged it best to accept her request. I, too, got on with prep. For the rest of the time, we went quietly about the business of preparing and cooking with the returned anagarika for the hundred or so that would eat in a couple of hours.

When we finished our allotted tasks, I spoke quietly to her as we were leaving the kitchen, "Rosalyn, just promise me you'll think about what I said." She looked at me as we got outside into the sunlight, touched my arm, and said, "Alright. I have to go now." I guess she wasn't hungry.

We met a few times over the next few days of my stay and talked of the practice, of its value, and of the girl's ambitions. I told her I was an Oxford student. That surprised and impressed, it also shifted talk to safe ground. We spoke nothing more of her future or Richard. I'd said enough. I knew what she was going through wasn't easy and would probably get tougher until it broke one way or another. We were unconsciously particular not to be entirely alone and out of sight. Instinct told us danger lay there. Though I have generally sought to bring friendship to bear before the demands of the physical, it's not always easy. Rosalyn was still an attractive woman, short hair or not.

❧

Returning to Oxford, I had a larger room in the city-center campus. I thought Joan might be able to stay over, but life goes its own way, and in the summer, while I found Indriya again, Joan had found a steady job she didn't want to compromise. We were, and remain to this day, friends, and I count that no small thing.

Helen returned, determined to complete the course. I thus fell into helping any way I could, as a result of which, about a month into our studies, we were in London. Helen had to make contact with some trade union headquarters as part of her thesis. As London was familiar ground to me, it was natural I would accompany her. Her inquiries took up the morning, but left us free around one o'clock.

"How about you let me take you to lunch?" I asked, as we exited the building.

"You puttin' on me, you old man, you?" she said.

"No, not exactly. Take the offer, please, 'cause I'm famished."

She put her arm through mine and said, "Alright, you dirty old man, I'll risk it. Where're we goin', Romeo?" I was happy to see her relaxed and funny, she had a lot to deal with.

"Well..." I said, "there's the Grovesnor hotel, or Fortnum and Mason, I believe the palace does a great roast duck when her majesty's home, we could check for the flag, or... there's Fred Costa's flaming pastie grill."

"You, James, could do with a good smack," she said, laughing, "What's this grill place, then?"

"Many, many years ago, when I was young, even younger than you, I worked in London. It was my first job. We used to get lunch vouchers as part of our wages and..."

∽

I'd go to Costa's grill. A place that only those of us who worked in the area had any idea existed. It was in an old basement. I was seventeen and could eat a horse at a sitting. I would have two portions of everything. It was not exotic food. Two sausages, two eggs, two slices of bacon, two portions of chips, two pasties, two slices of bread and tea till it came out my ears. I'd been eating like that for as long as I could remember. At school lunches I'd be the dustbin that finished everyone's leftovers. I never put on weight.

July 25th
I didn't know it then, but the fearful fires of the unconscious consumed everything I put before them. There are more ways than one to hide from the giant with the house-size club.

...that's where I used to go. I'm pretty sure it will be closed, that was over thirty years ago. C'mon, I know a decent place, it's not far."

∽

My studies were taking a turn towards my ever-present search. From literature, written language, I adjusted my perspective towards the spoken word and thought. I started making notes for a final thesis...

∽

...We began as Homo erectus, out of the trees and onto two feet. / We were tribal, we wandered, without the protection of the trees, we were vulnerable / We had <u>cleverness</u> – and opposable thumbs. We learnt fast, a matter of survival / With learning our brains grew and directed our hands to make, to gather, to carry, and to invent / Though clever we were still a part of nature / Did we look around us and at the stars and were afraid, we must have also wondered / <u>Possibly our fear and wonderings were stored in a corner of the brain</u> / Did we begin to articulate them over and above the primitive <u>onomatopoeic</u> sounds of gathering and making tools? / <u>Complex language finalized our separation</u> from nature.

Language became how we think. Our actions were now under the direction of thought. The language of thought (born of fear and wonder) became the engine of evolution / evolution became subordinate to growing cultural imperatives. <u>We had become self directing</u> we, and not nature, would now manage the path humans would take upon this earth. / We would write all this down.

∽

Of course, trees had to come into it somewhere for a very real reason, the trees are our sustainer. We are living on a knife-edge of suffocation as we increasingly destroy acres of forest each year. I was pretty sure by now my thesis was going to lean heavily on the natural world, for it began to occur to me that it was in nature the balance between sounds and silences made a deep connection with our being, a rhythm that we still carried within us. I thought of the sound I heard beyond myself when I lay down in the ploughed field, of Joan's release as she lay in my arms, both of us giving up to nature. We were and are nature, and nature has to express her suffering. I began to ponder on the depth of suffering the human species is embroiled in, and wondered just how loudly does nature have to cry, from within us and around us, before we hear.

It seemed these thoughts were a long way from English literature, yet an examination of the classics, both for content and syntax, indicated that was not so. Our writings, and oral tales before them, contain, at their core, explorations of the paradox, of the suffering that has come upon us, deep in our evolution. They all deal with the nature of being, a being divorced from nature. The power of story, I discovered, lay in its containing the rhythms of nature, and the cry that marks nature's suffering within us.

∽

I stood at the door of professor Jane Harrison of the Oriental Institute. It was just a walk around the block from Ruskin, but clearly another world, one of searing academia. I felt the same awe and trepidation I'd had when being initiated at the famous Bodleian Library.

I knocked and entered. She was sitting behind an ancient oak desk (Sherwood, I bet) and looked at me over half-glasses, with what I thought was a trifle disdain. "Come in. Sit," she motioned to a chair my side of the desk. She must have been somewhere between sixty and seventy, white hair pulled back into a bun from a face with contours that must have once attracted attention. She sat straight, but relaxed, I thought, no hint of a matron, but a definite air of control. "So, James, what exactly did you want to see me about?" There was just enough emphasis on 'exactly' to make me nervous. She would truck no time-wasting.

While I was trying to frame my request with all the intelligence and brevity I could find, she went on, "Aren't you a bit old for university? What are you studying?" Now, I didn't know quite which question to answer. This was not going well, whatever was I thinking.

I'd had some vague idea that I needed to examine myths, old oral tales, and the manner in which they were handed down to us. I was trying to find roots. I don't know how I found out about professor Harrison, but had come to understand she possibly knew everything there was about ancient myths. I had made a phone call, got her secretary, briefly explained I was an Oxford student, and secured this appointment. Now I had better speak up.

"Do we have any idea what makes a story stick? Endure?" I corrected, "Is there any common core or essence to them?"

She didn't answer, not yet. She looked at me, the disdain replaced with curiosity. I think hearing my voice, my accent – decidedly not Oxford

English – probably sent a stream of questions running through her mind. She was in a position to ask them, "What are you writing? What's the context of your question?"

"I'm... Well, what I think I'm trying to do is determine what makes a piece of writing a classic," I said, "What does it contain that we keep going back to, what are we looking for?"

"Really!" She raised her eyebrows, removed her glasses. "That's quite a task, I would say. I'm not sure I would expect that much from my students." I had been told she had a small, elite class of M.A. students, and a couple of PhDs she was nurturing along. I wondered if I was making a fool of myself. I replied, "I know it's not strictly literature, but literature is language and language is ancient. I feel that somewhere in its beginnings it must have rested on the real world, the world of nature, its rhythms and possibly rhymes."

"Interesting, but I'm not sure I like the idea of your *feeling* it's so," she looked hard at me with these words and continued, "If you're going to write, you will have to *think*, not feel. There is so much nonsense written as a result of sloppy thinking, or no thought at all. And once in print, it's taken as viable scholarship, which it patently is not!"

Well, that was telling me. It pulled me up short, but I respected her clear integrity. I felt it was in her consideration of my efforts that she was speaking this way to me, so I said, "Thank you for that advice, professor. I know what you mean about so much nonsense being written, I'll try and heed it." After that exchange we seemed to find each other on another level.

July 25TH

I write this incident in James' life, not because I think you need the story, but of its value in proving that we can overcome barriers, differences, and find common ground. I happen to think that it is, in fact, the 'ground' we stand on, nature, that is our common bond. I came to understand from my studies that myths do, indeed, hold the story of our struggle with death, our denial of death, and consequent fear of life.

When we returned from London, Helen was tired, and seemed, in spite of my afternoon efforts, somewhat depressed. A realization of just what lay before her caught her up.

"What am I doing, James?" We had picked up Jo from the college nursery and were bathing her ready for bed. "I don't know what I was thinking, doing university with a baby. This thesis, it's a bit much." It wasn't a question that needed my opinion. I got the big bath towel and handed it to her. Jo was duly dried, put in her pajamas and put to bed. I read her a story while Helen went out to the chippy for our supper.

When she came back, it was with another part of the obstacle race that was her life. "I'm never going to meet a bloke again, am I? Not looking like me, and with a baby." I supposed what she was referring to was her size and strong Birmingham accent, which contrasted like a deafening horn with sedate Oxford English. Helen was small and slim, attractive in an elfish way. I thought, who cares about accents nowadays.

"Nice fish and chips," I said, "Eat up, you could do with a bit of flesh on your bones."

"You could do with a slap," she had taken the quip well, flung her head to one side, looking at me, and added in a long drawn out heavy accent, "Old man."

"Hold me back," I replied, "On second thought, I'll finish the chips first."

"You'll finish the chips and then go home," she was at least smiling now, "Go to your room, James." She said this last in a mock Queen's English.

"Yes, right, well, I can take a hint," I said, determined to leave her with a lifted spirit, "Will it be the green room or the blue room, marm?"

"Oh, James, I wish you were twenty years younger," she was back to sighing again.

"Twenty! I'm not that ancient," I said.

"No," she said, "I just meant, I mean, I wish you didn't have to go. This is a big space for just me and little Jo. It gets..."

"I could sleep on the sofa," I said, "That should fill the place a bit."

She smiled again and turned her head to the side, a habit she had that I imagined won interest, I was certainly interested. "But what about your work? You've got nothing here to work on if you stay."

"I'll take the night off. My brain's busting anyway," I said, "Ever since I saw professor Harris I've been struggling."

"Why, what did she say?"

"Told me to be sure not to write rubbish," I said, "To think before I put stuff down, be sure its good scholarship, that kind of thing. It was good advice but it made me revise a lot of my notes, now the bloody thing's spreading like melted jelly. I'm not sure how to contain it."

"That's soddin' hard," she said, slipping into her home accent, "What's Davis, your adviser, say?"

"I haven't told him," I said, "I want to work this out for myself." I stood up and went over to the sofa, "Anyway, that's why I'm taking a night off. So! Will it be here or...?"

"I'll get you some blankets," she said, and went out of the room with that turn of her head. I thought: I must be out of my mind. Why do I do it?

Helen returned with blankets and a pillow, "I hope you can sleep all right, the street light's a bit bright in here."

"I'll be okay," I said, "You got a book or mag I can read for a bit?"

"How about the history of trade unionism? It's pretty light reading for a man of your letters."

"Perfect. That should see me off in no time," I said. She was happy. I thought, well, that's why I do it.

She came over to me with a paperback, which I took, and said, "I'll shout you when I've finished in the bathroom, okay?"

"Right," I said, then she put her arms around my neck, "Thanks, James, thanks for staying. I'm glad."

"It's a pleasure, marm. Tea will be at seven."

"You're an old brick," she said, let go of my neck, and went into the bathroom.

∾

I lay most of that night awake, maybe it was the street light, or the feelings I was dealing with. In any event, I determined what I wanted to write about. I knew how I would frame my thesis.

What connects us? Where in the vastness of time and space can we find ourselves as a species undivided, I thought. In the rhythm that pulsates in the breast, in the tides, in the winds and the spheres that make our universe. The continuous flow of sound and words that is language, the language of the classics is in the breath. Watch the breath, I was taught at Indriya. Language is breath, even if it is written, it must be written with breath, with the beat of life, or it is dead. I felt elated, I had found my muse. I wanted to tell Joan, for it was *our* connection that weaved into my brain that night and revealed all. Friendship offered up its secret.

∾

My time at Oxford was coming to a close. I had made new friends, some I still have, others on my *Metta* list are weaving lives elsewhere. Helen will graduate and with Jo travel north to live with her sister. I success-fully defended my thesis and earned a distinction. I had one final assign-ment to complete, an offshoot of my thesis, a piece concerning language and ontology. Just who, or what, do we think we are when we speak of our Self? It was in that piece to begin an understanding that would even-tually bring synthesis out of the disparate elements of being. Elements fragmented over time by the life and history of our species. I was coming close to Truth. I would write...

> *...this search, aided by an inner dialogue, so revealing of the requirement of an 'other' for its own voracity, does not divorce itself from social reality. Truth exists in the individual as well as in nature, for we are of nature. Logos resides not simply as an objective phenomenon of life, but in each and every one of us. If Truth exists anywhere, though it comes through the mind, it must be attached to the* feeling *of being.*
>
> *If there is a chance of a communicable ontology, a shared experience of Truth, we have to have the courage to know we have gone wrong, that we may well have made, and continue to hold, incorrect assumptions and world views, and that our responsibility is total, far more extensive than we have thus far admitted.*

The Oxford years forced me to think clearly, opened me to the history of our species as we struggle with an ever more complex identity of being. It was also overshadowed by a growing awareness that we could *not* continue to recycle old views and patterns of encountering the world. My final writings and observations were to set me by turns on a path I could have no hint of when I left Ruskin. Life, and death, would come full circle, forming the helix that would heal the paradox.

FIFTEEN

When I cleaned and oiled the spades at Indriya, I was continuing something my father taught me as a boy. The Second World War that had just ended, terrible as it was, provided a lesson for those who could grasp it. After that war, rationing was in force all over Europe. Everyone was forced to live a simple existence with few possessions and enough, but only enough, food. My father voiced his observation in the phrase, 'Live simply that others may simply live.' Things, such as our gardening spades and forks, were to be maintained for as long as possible, waste was rightly deplored. Life slowed down, giving 'time to stare'. Thus it was that I 'saw' nature and experienced an essence to life that most are deprived of today. I'm not sure if a post-war world that had dropped the atomic bomb on thousands of people could be called civilized, but at least it felt to me, as a boy growing in it, to have such a possibility.

July 28th

It seems to me, that possibility was lost in the exercise of personal and cultural fear-driven egos. The result today is something like a monster out of control.

The fearful collections of egos, bowing to their own illusions, have produced a Frankenstein we call civilization. This observation, severe as it may seem, is merely a description of the sum of its parts. For whenever we 'invent', 'make', or otherwise change the material nature of existence to our own (fearful) designs, each thing we produce has an unseen and generally unwelcome side effect: what I call the Frankenstein effect. The more we try to correct such 'defects', the more persistent they show themselves to be. The car, for instance, designed to get us from one place to another, has killed more people over time than the rifle.

The very least of these Frankenstein effects is the products themselves, which eventually become 'waste' that has accumulated to such an extent upon the earth and in the oceans, that we are in danger, along with the wildlife of the planet, of being swamped by it.

What we think we are doing is making a better life for ourselves, and in one sense we are, for it suits the ego to indulge in something that feels and looks like making a fixed, secure state (civilization) out of insecure, ever-changing conditions (of nature). In fact, all we are doing is exchanging a system that has low (longer lasting) entropy for one with increasingly faster change. Put another way, we are using up all the available sources of energy in order to surround ourselves with more and more Frankenstein monsters.

The number of films made of Shelley's story, along with many more depicting out-of-control people or monsters, confirms a deep fear that our drive to control is creating an equal and opposite pressure that will one day break the surface of civilization. What such films indicate is a growing awareness of our mistakes, and an inkling of the terrified source from which they arise. That source is only terrifying so long as we turn our back to it, it is the shadow side of the ego that hides and lies about impermanence, thus driving us on to create more monsters. We are in a classic paradoxical bind: the ego protects us from our fear. Our fear, going unrecognized, drives us to make more fearful monsters.

The entropic shift we must concern ourselves with now is the shift in energy within the species. Along with our reduction of nature's store we are using up the core elements of our own kind. As much as we pride ourselves at 'conquering' disease and extending life expectancy (in some of us), what we are experiencing globally is a declining ability to put forth optimism, and an increase in various forms of mental disruption: Autism, Downs Syndrome, ADD, Alzheimer's and many lesser states. But the single outstanding condition that bears witness to entropy within the human population is the spread of nihilism, a state of hopelessness in the face of overwhelming conditions.

Living with the monsters, we have given up or given over energy to them, we are in a state of depletion. If our past actions and continuing habits produced Frankenstein conditions around us, they have reduced the psyche of our egos to that of lemmings. This, of course, is an analogy, I have no idea how a lemming thinks. The story is they run in packs towards danger, seemingly unable to turn the other way. The weakness we show, in the face of our created monsters that are destroying us, draws the analogy sufficiently well.

What such an observation tells us is that serious, and possibly devastating, change is close upon us.

But we are not lemmings, neither do we need the monsters of our fearful ego for us to survive in this world. We can, if we so choose, turn and face the dark shadow with a house-size club that stalks all of us. We can liberate a true ontology of being from the destructive grasp of an ego driven by the fear of its own death.

SIXTEEN

After university, I started teaching adults a range of classes, one of which was on philosophy. It was to a self-formed group who wanted to know what use philosophy was to us, how could it serve our everyday life. The question interested me, it was a challenge that sent me searching my own experience as much as within libraries and standard texts.

"*Cogito ergo sum*, I think therefore I am," I announced to the class, then asked them if such a statement fulfilled their perceptions of how they saw themselves. Well, to ask such a question of adults, particularly women who have born children, nurtured men, fed families, and nursed the follies of the world, is to throw down a glove. The challenge was accepted. The retorts were endless, even though I tried, in my fledgling tutoring, to point out Descartes' meaning, they insisted that the dimensions of being *must* include all aspects of what it is to be a human, thought being but one aspect of Homo sapiens.

They were right, part of our suffering lay in the split between thinking and feeling and an insistence on placing one much higher than the other. Along with thinking, we have elevated control and manipulation of nature, and conquering of the material world to serve our fearful grasping.

Joan came and sat-in on the class one evening, after which we went for a drink in the Three Swans. I mentioned that first class and the response it produced, to which she said, "You're lucky you got away with your life, James. Most women would consider it a daft idea that we are measured only by our capacity to think." She continued, "Look what you and I went through, what we experienced. It was not thinking."

"No, but without thinking, at least *about* what was happening, we'd have no idea how to solve our suffering. Thinking is what directs us."

"Maybe that's the trouble. Maybe something else should be directing us."

"Like what?" I asked.

"I'm not sure, but you're the one who says: go to the trees, walk between the trees," she said. "Why trees?"

"Well, it's trees because it started out that way in the monastery," I said, "It's a forest tradition, so... it's trees. But then, since beginning the practice, I have felt it is more than that. It's nature, an all-embracing, continuous state, bigger than us, any one of us, or even all of us. I've come to feel it's something of a miracle."

She said, "Strange to hear you talk of a miracle, James. I thought you didn't believe in all that stuff. Thought you were an atheist."

"A realist," I said, "Enough of a realist to see water, air, sunlight, and all that they nurture into life as a miracle. An ordinary miracle, if you like, not for believing in, for knowing, understanding, and fully accepting."

"Maybe that's what should be directing us, some kind of acceptance," she said.

"You know, Joan, when I was first in the monastery, I didn't bow, you know, at meditation in the evenings. I would just sit at the back and watch the others. Then the abbot gently challenged me to try it. Well, there was this tremendous resistance, a kind of defiance, and I began to wonder who was defying what and why, where was it coming from. It was the opposite of acceptance."

"Did you bow, eventually?" she asked.

"Yes," I said. "Oh yes, and more. I began to see how the ego fears true liberation, the letting go of the need to control. Because without control one really discovers one's shadow self, the side of the ego facing away from the light."

"And that led to the trees?" she asked.

"After a time," I said. "Talking of time, it'll be last orders in a minute. Do you want another, or shall we go?"

"I'd best be going," she said, "The baby sitter."

"Right," I said, " Okay, let's go." I had brought Joan with me in the car, so we made our way to the car park. She took the keys when I handed them to her. "Thanks, Joan. See us safely home."

Dying to live
I take a walk in the silent night.

Not holy this night
just silent.

Who speaks out of its blackness
no voice

No sound leaves
the safety of the silent mind.

Thoughts climb
The first
Incline
an eye on the storm.

Rising above the ridge
of conscious dawn

madness loosely held
in black clouds
threatens a deluge.

The year was 1994, life was moving along at a gentle pace, some teaching, some writing, seeing Joan from time to time, walking, and asking of myself what next.

I was making one of my occasional visits to Indriya one weekend in early August. Teaching was over for summer, I was free to respond to whatever came along, but I didn't in any way expect what was to come.

"You don't recognize me do you, James?" The question came from another layman as we worked together painting the new retreat center.

"Should I?" I asked, "I seem to recognize your voice, you're American, right?"

"Right," he said, "From California nowadays, born in the Bronx."

I stopped painting and took a closer look, "Yes, we must have met here."

"Getting warmer." He was having fun playing with me, but he seemed an amiable fellow so I played along.

"Now let's see," I pondered, "New Yorker, living in California, was... Oh, I remember. You didn't have hair in those days though, right?"

He couldn't keep up the toying with me, he put out his hand, "Kusalo. Peter Kaminsky now. How are you, James?"

"Kusalo!" Well, how are you, old friend? What brings you back, are you going to ordain again?"

"No, nothing like that, I just wanted to spend a bit of time here," he said, "and see the old man again. How about you?"

"I've been coming back and forth over the years, you know, just staying in touch," I said, "And walking between trees."

The upshot of our meeting saw Peter returning with me to my place on Sunday evening. He stayed for a week before going back to finish his holiday at Indriya. Our reconnection was to have a profound affect on my future.

You may recall in chapter two I made this remark: 'I don't really believe in time, beyond the movement of change which is ever-present and presents us with the constant flow of evolution.' That understanding derives in part from learning and in part from some interesting experiences of my own.

Towards the end of the war in Europe and for some months after, my parents sang with a band in the Galtimore dance hall. I was three years old and just out of hospital. The owner of the dance hall was my godfather who insisted they brought me along every Friday and Saturday night. I would wander about in my pajamas enjoying the fuss being made over me. The question I ask myself is: Was there an inevitability to the events about to unfold at the back end of 1994 and my being in that dance hall in 1945? You will see the reason for my questioning as the story now unfolds.

＆

As a result of my meeting up with Peter, we remained in phone contact thereafter. So it was that on a wet evening in February of the following year, he made an invitation to visit him in America, a country I had never entertained as a place to go. It happened, however, that I was taking a break from teaching, trying to figure what next. There was nothing intrinsically wrong with the way my life was, I suppose it was that old searching thing that had arisen again, urging me on with its unseen force. What happened next adds fuel to the questioning I just mentioned, for I did not really want to go. I was leading a quiet, pleasant life, and a flight to a new country that I was not the least interested in held no attraction. But somehow, by some means, lost in the depths of change and change again, I bought a ticket. But it wasn't going to be that simple.

＆

Because of the presence of American service personnel stationed in England nearly all the music and songs played at the Galtimore were American big-band dance tunes of the forties. My three-year old ears were open wide, jazz became an essential part of my perception of the world, as natural as breathing.

＆

On the day of my departure, to holiday for three month in the USA, it was overcast with dark clouds, and snowing hard. I was packed and ready early, and phoned Joan to see, given the inclement weather, if she would like a lift to work, which I duly left the house to do. On arriving back to my home, I discovered I had locked myself out. It took a great deal of inventiveness and the cooperation of two friend to get me on my way, I almost abandoned the trip. Then at Heathrow there was a delay caused by the storm that was passing. When we eventually took off, I was to have a shock of remembrance and puzzlement.

༄

The long, colorful dream I'd had many years ago, when married to Catherine, began its revelations, you may remember, when on my way to Indriya, where I saw the first episode of the dream before me, and wondered how could one dream the future. Yet all the scenes in the dream had played out before me over many years, each one becoming manifested in form and sequence as a part of my life. Now only one, the last scene, remained, and of that I will tell you...

༄

...It is a bright sunny day, the sky blue and the grass green. A long, low building with double doors is before me. As I look inside, it is filled with people from many lands. I know now the building to be the sala at Indriya. I walk around to the back of the building and as I walk, the sky begins to cloud, the grass to turn thin and muddy, and the building deteriorates. By the time I am on the opposite side of the building, it has become a dilapidated, corrugated tin structure with the double doors hanging off their hinges. The sky is now black with clouds, and the ground deep, soggy mud. I enter the place to find it is a charnel house with skeletons on racks all around the walls.

I begin sinking into the mud, and reach up automatically. Down from out of the blackness of the roof, a white rope falls, and I grab it and begin to haul myself up. As I do so, the rope pulls me upwards. I pass through the roof, through the black clouds into white clouds. Continuing up beyond all clouds, I emerge into the bright sunlight.

༄

As the 747 gathered speed along the runway, the snow falling appeared as one continuous flow. Up we rose into the darkness of the clouds and the whiteness of high clouds and out into the bright sunlight.

After the plane took off, I had nearly twelve hours to consider the questions arising from this coincidence. What is the truth behind my dreaming the future? How is it that when I was three years old, it seems I was being made ready to fit into American culture? The coincidences continued to mount up.

My father, on taking me to see cowboy and Indian films, would point out to me the Indians were the good guys. So it was that when I grew up, I studied Native American peoples and culture. That in itself would not be too coincidental, but when I returned home after three months, I went to a shop that imported books, language tapes, and almost everything concerned with such a study, to visit with the owner. He'd missed my visits to his store and asked me where I had been.

I said, "To America, to a very small, out-of-the-way town in California." He inquired as to its name, and when I told him, he said, "Oh, I know it well. My daughter goes to school there, my ex wife lives there."

The rational skeptic in me was beginning to have trouble with this ever-growing line of coincidence, but I decided to remain open. It was just as well, for the line would grow ever longer

July 31st

Carl Jung, the psychoanalyst, was of the opinion that coincidences – which he called synchronicity – in a person's life, indicate a positive path being journeyed by the soul, a lack of synchronicity indicating the reverse. What we now know is that any conscious application of the mind to a question, be it of physics or the physical or mental, that is, psychological, will alter the substance of the inquiry. Put another way, if I seek to acknowledge the string of coincidences in my life as meaningful, they are likely to become so. My awareness seems to change mere fate into destiny, perhaps! The skeptic in me asks: Do I, or any of us, truly have that choice?

I have been to a part of the world where abject poverty exists. Can I simply say to the poor: All you have to do is consider your lives, apply some examination to the path you weave, and it will reveal a destiny laid out for you, rather than this wretched fate you are a slave to. I think not, yet books are sold by the millions telling us to do just that and all will come our way. As Professor Harris remarked to me, there is much nonsense written, and once in print it's taken as true, which it patently is not.

So I return once again to the questions, and somewhere over the Atlantic Ocean remember another piece of current thought on the workings of the mind.

We may abhor a vacuum, but chaos we fear. Our egoic mind will always seek patterns in life, that is, look to make sense of it. The idea that randomness drives nature, and us along with it, is unacceptable to a mind that wants control at every turn. The one task (our) ego excels at is creative manipulation of the sufferings experienced as we grow from babyhood to maturation. That's not to say it resolves the suffering, but we become experts at exiling unwanted feelings to the unconscious.

What remains in the conscious mind is then free to form patterns of convenience, remembrances that fit with our views and opinions. Such views and opinions, the correct name of which should be preju-dices, develop from unexamined experience, for they are not upheld by rational considerations, but forced to fit a preformed pattern of think-ing. The patterns laid down in childhood.

This information as to our pattern-seeking habit reminded me of how we try making this (lost) life meaningful.

Before we touched down in America, I reminded myself of the abbot's constant advice: Whatever we want, whatever we think, whatever we choose to believe, however we frame circumstance to fit a pattern to suit our personal dictates, the way things are is just that. This is the way it is.

I am about to land in a country new to me, to the extent that I can leave behind views and opinions, patterns and expectations. I shall re-main open to *experience* this life. That's how I chose to step out into the California sunlight on March 7th 1995.

SEVENTEEN

Her name is Shanti, a name given to her in India, I learn, as we share dinner one evening at the home of an elderly lady, Beatrice. Shanti is her care-giver, a term new to me that catches my ear. I like it, I like Shanti, too. She's the reason I returned to California and is the reason I stay.

We had a delight in gardening in common, and, it seemed, not much else. Yet that firm ground held the love beyond love that finds me living here, fifteen years on from that first meeting. Many times I've searched and asked questions of myself, how did it happen this way? My new circumstances sent me back through my life searching yet again.

The discovery was profound. On the journey here, Catherine colored in my childhood dreams, Kate brought me into my body, and Joan revealed in me what was hidden. Paul, a friend among many, believed in me, the monks and nuns, who had given their lives to peaceful searching, made possible a space and place where I, too, could learn how to search. The many threads that had woven my life to this point coalesced in the home of Beatrice in the meeting of Shanti, though I did not know it then. But it was known and stands revealed in my actions and writings at the time.

I had known Shanti but two weeks, when I found myself tackling a long walk on a hot, Southern California day from my lodgings to where I knew she would be, in the house of Beatrice, some five miles away. The road was a steep climb, returning thoughts of my long ago sabbatical. There was something connecting my feet on both continents, and something stirring in the depths of my being that moved me to walk to her, and write this poem for her.

> As the breeze runs the canyon,
> the sun warms the rocks,
> the river cools the dusty air,
> birds call from their unseen nests.
> So LOVE echoes down time,
> And rests with the heart
> That beats in one with yours and mine.

I was to discover the love that encircled Shanti and me denied leaving as I had left all and everyone up until now. For I had entered the vortex of the paradox, our being together was born in the first star-burst in the timeless, integral field of the unconditioned. There was no other place my soul could go.

∽

I did not know when my mother died. I had been with Shanti just eight months, and was preparing to make another trip back to England when I received a letter, via a circuitous route. It said she would be buried on November tenth. The letter arrived November 12th.

I should have known and been present at her dying. I'd arranged everything, or so I thought, to ensure I would be informed should accident or illness occur. I was six thousand miles away, in another country, on another continent. The hole it left was ragged around the edges, full of strange, uncomfortable feelings, dark with pain, loss, and guilt. Could I have done a better job of communication arrangements? Should I never have left in the first place? Why did it have to happen this way? Yet, the event of her dying and my absence were just what they were, a set of conditions conflicting with our manipulations of nature. Thinking I could *arrange* dying to my convenience.

> **August 4th**
> *How often do you hear: 'I don't mind dying, I just want it to be quick and painless.' We quite naturally seek comfort, and freedom from suffering. In our efforts to create as safe and wholesome a world as we can for our bodies, we have kidded ourselves that we are in some degree controlling death. Thus it was that I thought I had a handle on my mother's eventual dying. But nature was, and is, more than our wishes. Nature will prevail beyond our desires, be they organizational as in my case, theological, or brutish.*
>
> *It is to nature, the embracing whole, that we must turn for support when facing death. For nature is the reality of our living and dying. Whilst we may be able to alleviate the worst of suffering, and rightly try to do so, the genesis of suffering, along with the joy of living, both arrive with our birth into this world, and are strictly of this world. What then happens at death? Does nature take a hand, can nature do what we try in vain to do, that is, carry us into that end peaceably? I would have to face this question again all too soon.*

After the finality of my mother's death, I naturally found myself between the trees. I sought, as I so often had, answers to what seemed the unanswerable. My ego was finding its defense mechanisms challenged, and the fear it keeps secret, being drawn up at each turn. Death, it seemed, was stalking my life and always had been.

EIGHTEEN

August 5th

What is the true nature of life and death that we miss by living in denial?

There is a wild field near where I live that I walk some mornings, observing the plants, ground creatures, and birds that inhabit this oasis of naturalness. At certain times of the year, to stand at its border and survey the field is to see its color drained to a dark grey, painted by the apparent dead twigs, stems, and foliage that give no reflection of the light day brings. But the light is, nevertheless, penetrating the plants' life, is piercing death. It is not many weeks before death cannot resist such penetration, and succumbs to life, then as I look, I begin to see a pale green gossamer over the field.

August 6th

We have a habit of saying 'life has returned to the field'. It is a misnomer. It never left, as neither does death leave when the field is green. Our language use betrays our fear, for we live with a split between life and death. The field is integrated, unfragmented by consideration of its parts, undifferentiated between life and death. This is the true field of being we could inhabit were we to stop running, driven by the fear of annihilation, the fear of non-being. Because we insist our being exists only in time, we look to time's hand to measure us and pronounce us alive or dead.

At Indriya, a constant refrain ran: die before you die, such that when you die, you won't die. It seems like a conundrum or a Zen koan, yet it is just a statement of encouragement to overcome the egoic insistence fragmenting us from each other and nature which is constant and complete.

August 7th

There is much written about being in the now, comparing the immediate moment of being, with an ethereal, eternal state. It's popular, for grasping at the idea of the eternal, momentarily alleviates the fear of death. But what one finds is staying in this transitory moment is not possible, thoughts and actions move us along, life being a constant movement of change. Even if we remove all distractions, clocks, and calendars, our very bodies are movement.

I have been in the most ideal conditions for practicing this exercise, and I have been in that singular state, a stopped moment, an end to movement, the Now. But it's not where we live, it's not nature's field. Where we live is in the flow of existence, an ever changing state. We are aware of that change as history, personal, cultural, and of the species.

"I know Ricky, he used to visit next door when I was small." It was Shanti's daughter, Rowan, threading yet another coincidence on the string that reached back into my past. Ricky was an old friend of mine who died some four years previously. For some unaccountable reason, I had told his story to Shanti, and in conversation with her daughter, his name had come up. Rowan used to visit England to see her grandparents who lived some two hundred miles from the town where Ricky and I lived. But his parents lived next door to Rowan's grandparents, thus it was that when Ricky and Rowan's visits coincided, as often happened in summertime, he would see her and play with her through the summers.

Should I take any account of this ever growing synchronicity? Does its history hold any significance, a lesson perhaps, surely not meaning – as in the meaning of life. Yet it seems to confirm what I wrote when I first met Shanti: I did not know it, but it was known. Does the History of man offer any answers to our being here?

August 8th

What does this mean, History, what do we do when we study history, or better, what are we trying to do? I would suggest we are trying to understand where we go wrong. An early aim of historians was to understand mankind, to know our mistakes such that we do not repeat them, yet repeat them we do. Thus we extended our search into what drives us, what causes us to repeat mistakes.

We are so familiar with our mistakes and their causes, they have become myths and tales passed down from ancient times to the present. In my discussions with Professor Harris, it became clear that the repetition of myths gave comfort by virtue of their accurate picturing of our mistakes. As we read them, something within says, Oh yes, I know that. The modern novel does the same thing. In both myths and novels, there stands the hero, the adventurer, striving to overcome his or someone else's mistake.

We, of course, are the hero in the tale, for if this life has any purpose to its false path, it lay in our striving to overcome, to reach the apogee of existence. Yet the very fact of it being a false existence renders success empty of any true satisfaction, thus, in the frustration of unacknowledged disappointment we strive even harder. The result of our striving has brought us to the precarious position we now find ourselves in.

If we are to halt our lemming-like run towards extinction, we must deal with our attachment to the hero myth. The hero is a product of ego, a narcissistic drive of impelling self verification. Yet without some level of narcissism we become destroyed, overcome with a feeling of worthlessness.

In the integrated field of reality, there is no measurement by comparison, thus there is no position that identifies success or failure, for they do not intrinsically exist. One may as well ask: Is birth a success and death a failure? In such a state one's worth is not drawn by lines and degrees, measurements and approval, worth is inherent. It is our inheritance.

When I was a boy we were taught about the heroes of the Empire, I'm happy to report I have forgotten most of them.

August 9th

Understand, I have no ill feelings towards those individuals who went out and sought to live brave, meaningful lives on behalf of King, Queen, and Empire. It is the cultural assent that produces such ambitions that disturbs me, for I know it is a reflection of fear that produces such bravery, and this inquiry seeks to undo such fear, rather than become its slave, in whatever form that takes. We are so easily drawn into defense of empire, through our inner need to satisfy a narcissism the ego creates, such that we feel some worth in this life. But too often in the exercise of self-worth, we seek to beat down on others or nature.

I remember as a boy, one of the empire's heroes being knighted by the queen of England for 'conquering' the highest mountain on earth. Of course, the mountain was not the least subdued by the man, but rather man looked foolish in such attempts to place himself above nature. Though it should be said, the local people who lived at the foot of the mountain wondered at the foolishness of even thinking of such an idea as conquering it. Many years later, another mountain decided to shrug, and upwards of two thousand of our kind died in the turmoil.

August 9th

So our task is to undo the fearful drive towards heroism with its often destructive force, and replace it with a self-worth that does not seek control out of the fear of annihilation.

I should like us to turn to the *Metta* list, the list of Loving-Kindness. If you remember, I describe this as a remembrance of everybody you have known. If you consider such a list for a moment, you will realize that those you have known are known by others, and they, in turn, have an extended circle of known people. In truth, if it were possible to assemble all the known connections, you would discover there isn't *anybody* on earth you are not, or have not been, throughout human history, connected to.

Just this realization has implications far beyond our limited cultural and national identity. Its awareness begins the process of disengaging from the separation and stratification that has so marked our history as a species. By implication, it should, if fully understood, put an end to war.

The second understanding of the *Metta* list I want to share has even greater significance for change. All those on your list are now and have been, the weavers of your life. From the very beginning, with your parents who created your physical form, through *everyone* who is and has been in your life, you exist as a creation of their being, just as you have contributed to creating them. The making of what you know as your Self has occurred because of the existence of all the 'others' that weave you.

Right about now you are thinking this is unrealistic, untrue. Perhaps out of kindness you think it's a nice story but cannot be so, because you are so sure that *you* are yourself and the maker of decisions and actions that you determine. Well, I'm a pretty skeptical person and so is he, so we don't expect you to easily accept this view without some supporting evidence. So, I'll let him try and offer some.

August 11th

Here is a true story.

One day, out along the edges of the Sahara desert, where the land is rocky and sparse of vegetation, a herdsman spotted, among the wild gazelles, what he thought was a boy. Thinking the boy to be lost, he followed the group of gazelles in an effort to rescue the boy. In the end, the animals were too fast for him and kicked up such dust that he wasn't at all sure that he had, in fact, seen a boy. He forgot all about the incident until, some months later, another herdsman happened to mention he thought he had seen a boy 'out there'. After some months had passed, there came by that way a Frenchman by the name of Jean-Claude Armen, an anthropologist and linguist. Armen had heard the story of the boy and wanted to see if it was true.

What Armen discovered was not only that there was, indeed, a boy out there with the gazelles, but that he lived with the gazelles and was in all but birth-form a gazelle himself, having acquired the ability to run as fast as them, eat the same food as them, and, as Armen was to discover, communicate with them. While those 'others' that were the makers of the boy began with humans, gazelles had a major part in creating him. The boy could not be unmade, unthreaded, as it were, from the weave that had taken place. In order to bring the boy into human society, further intensive making by humans would have to occur.

This story is an extreme case, but such instances are a stark illustration of something we can miss in the examination of a more ordinary life such as our own. Like the Gazelle Boy, we have been made by the culture and species we run with. The work of anthropologists, sociologists, psychologists and others studying man, urges upon us the responsibility of acknowledgment of this fact about ourselves and our workings. In the past, an unexamined life may have been a wasted life, in the present crisis it must be considered negligence.

August 12th

A first, understanding of Self arises with the acceptance that everything 'I' am, the bright and the dark, has been put in place by others as I have moved through this life, particularly when the first threads were woven after birth and before becoming an adult. Only by such an acceptance can one begin a change that frees one from that old bondage. Further, only by digging deep into evolution can the primitive fear that binds us be dislodged.

To begin the journey to the integrated field state is an acceptance that the Self we hold to so tightly must be unbound by our looking outward, by understanding that those who made us are, just like us, also bound. The list is thus used for two purposes: the realization of one's own freedom, and the contemplation of freedom for, and gratitude towards, all those who create our life.

NINETEEN

About a year after I returned to California and made a commitment to be with Shanti, I received an e-mail in my junk folder I nearly deleted. Its tag line was, 'Amy, looking for you'. The name Amy rang a bell. I opened it.

> Dear James, I hope you get this and can write me back. I got your e-mail address from Indriya (not easy, they took a lot of persuading, but in the end they remembered Mum.) I'm sure you remember my parents Rosalyn and Richard. Do you remember me? I was the noisy one and my sister Joan was the quiet one. I wonder where you are and how you are these days. I have some news I thought you would appreciate. Mum and Dad separated about a year ago, I think they are getting a divorce. I don't know the latest as I'm at Uni now in York, studying architecture. Please do write I'd love to hear from you.   Love, Amy

I didn't know whether I expected this news or not. As much as I persuaded Richard and Rosalyn to remain together, I always had an uncomfortable gut-feeling it was not okay. I wrote Amy a note thanking her and promising a visit to see how she was, but meaning how and where was Rosalyn, of course.

I was in America on a three month visa that I kept renewing through returning to the UK or, once, going down to Mexico for a holiday. I was running out of money for these trips. I needed to apply for a residency card. Shanti and I had to come to a decision to get married. There really was no reason why we shouldn't, apart from past experiences which had laid a deal of caution on us. Before we overcame our hesitations, I made one last visit to England, I knew, once I applied for a green card, I could not leave the US until it was granted.

It was autumn when I landed at Heathrow, cold and bright, a blue sky that took hold of my memory and swirled around thoughts of England and all that it meant to me. I missed it. I missed its weather and seasons in a way Californians couldn't understand. 'How can you miss cold and so much rain and those bleak winters?'

What I began to understand was how places make us, just as much as people. If we are a pattern woven by our parents and all those we meet, we are also woven out of the geography and climate that nurtures our early life. I was a product of this land, this soil I had so often dug, and the wind and rains that cross this place beneath the sun.

A few years on, I would read *The Music of Failure* by Bill Holm and *Pilgrim at Tinker Creek* by Annie Dillard, and the writings of Garrison Keillor and poems by Wendell Berry, later still would come *Plainsong* by Kent Haruf, so that, by turns, I would come to know what it is to grow up in the land of America. I would better know the land and the people. But right now, I was a bird who had come back to my old nest and I sought to make the most of it.

My first stop was Indriya, and there, after much greeting and recollection, I walked alone among the trees once again in the Buddha grove I had helped plant. I found acorns now, and decided to collect a few to bring with me to the new land that was my home.

I discovered that Rosalyn had spent a lot of time in the monastery and, in fact, had become an anagarika for about six months after she and Richard parted, but had not stayed on. My old friend, John, who was now a monk, told me he thought she had returned to her home, and suggested that one of the nuns may know if that was so. I sought out sister Khema, she who had made such a pointed inquiry of my intentions to ordain or not. She was now the senior nun with a growing reputation as a Dhamma teacher.

"Anagarika Rosalyn? Oh yes, I remember her. She was very intense, determined, but I think she was trying to shake off something, perhaps her unhappy marriage. I don't think she was ready for this life. As far as I know, she returned to her home. That's the only address we have on file for her." I thanked the sister and left, thinking of Rosalyn's struggle, wondering what she was doing now. Of course I was going to phone her home.

"James, is that really you?" Rosalyn's voice sounded singular, perhaps it was my imagination, but it seemed her voice was echoing inside a large space.

"Yes, it's me. Hello, Rosalyn, how are you?" My imaginings, or her voice, were causing me to falter. I could feel myself about to say something inane, meaningless, "Is Bowser still around?"

"Bowser? Oh no, he died a while ago. He was getting on." I was not helping her with this call. I racked my brain for something supportive but all I could think of were a list of stupid questions. I decided it was because I was avoiding the obvious.

"I'm leaving here tomorrow, Ros. Shall I come by? Maybe we could have a bite of lunch in the village or something?" Well, that was better, I thought

"Yes, alright, that would be nice. Will you come here or..."

"Perhaps best if we meet in the village, the Kings Head, say two o'clock. It should be quiet by then. What d'you think?"

"Oh, yes. Two, alright, I'll see you there. D'you think I'll recognize you?" Well that was at least a little joke. Good.

"Ooh, I should think so. Look for the sun tan. I've been a long way away. Tell you all about it tomorrow."

"Really, tomorrow then, bye, James."

"Bye, Ros. See you soon."

This was not going to be easy. I went to the Buddha grove and stood by a tree looking at the path before me. I wasn't quite sure how I should designate the trees for this particular walk, there were several possibilities.

> *I stand resting a while...*
> *While columbine and celandine*
> *flower in the mind.*
> *Mindfulness complete, gives blossom*
> *To the old broken blooming tree.*
>
> *I stand resting a while...*
> *While I understand*
> *the resting that is life.*
> *Now I know as a friend the great*
> *and agreeable beauty that is death.*
>
> *Now I understand...*
> *It must be longer than life,*
> *this task of the spirit, hidden,*
> *unseen, incognito.*
>
> *Reaching the last place*
> *of my leaving,*
> *leaving at last this spirituous task,*
> *for a place of going.*
>
> *No more distracted*
> *by distractions...*
> *which would seek*
> *to distract me.*

Life and death are reflected in our joys and sorrows. Yet there is a third experience that I was beginning to recognize, that of integration. In the days of my youth I studied Marx, he spoke of conditions as ever changing.

The dynamic of change, he said, was the conflict between the existing state and an opposing uprising force, a process the east calls yin and yang, the one always containing the seed of the other. For Marx, the inevitable resolution was brought about by struggle, it was a change of conditions, a new form.

What I began to find, walking between the trees, was not 'new' as in a change of state, but an ever present 'integration of existing conditions'. The walk put an end to linear time, replacing it with perpetual reality. Perpetual reality contains a change of material form but not of value. Just as in the integrated field of my morning walks, the conditions I see on any given day may exhibit a change of material state, whilst retaining its constant, nature.

So it was that however I designated the trees, the walk between them would take me beyond separated, conflicting conditions to an integration of those conditions. What the walk removes is conflict, by recognizing value in *both* conditions and *allowing* such value to retain its integrity.

I thought I could see a way beyond Marx's historically correct analysis, but an analysis limited by the lie we are living, to an actual future *practice* that had the potential for peaceful change, one not requiring the power struggles, conflicts, exploitation, and wars that have thus far marked human history. A practice, marking life for its whole duration, one of no longer knowing death as the inevitable enemy, but as: *'a friend, that great and agreeable beauty'*.

∾

Well, I did meet Rosalyn as planned and we talked and walked, and as friends do, we caught up on news. Rosalyn was surprised at my move to America, and a little disappointed. I wasn't sure if that was simply because we would not be able to meet up very often or whether there was more to it. I did not want to speculate on that point.

August 13th
There is something awkward and disturbing that arises out of our having divided and dislocated ourselves from each other and nature. James is beginning to recognize it.

This episode with Rosalyn was fraught with awkwardness. We all carry an unsatisfying ache for each other that bears witness to our having 'lost' ourselves, we have lost the completeness of integration. We witness integration now only fleetingly between the newborn child and mother, when the mother, by force of nature, succumbs to a deep maternalism, and an ego has not yet arisen in the child.

It used to be observed in so-called primitive cultures that the tribe and tribal (or collective) thought was greater than the individual. In such tribes death (of individuals) was still an integral part of life, as it is in the field of my morning walks. Thus, a personal fear of death was not driving the development of its members. At such a stage of development there exists within the tribe a strong collective ego, what Jung refers to as the collective unconscious in current society, but only weak personal egos. The advantage the tribe has over us lay in a natural cohesive functioning we lack.

෨෨

I am reminded here of a story John Holt[19] tells of a class of children he gave an exercise to. Having given out the papers, he instructed them to begin, whereupon a group gathered in one corner of the classroom. When he inquired as to what was happening, they told him: we are working on the problems. They were all children of Native Americans.

But, however attractive the idea of tribal life may seem to us in retrospect, it cannot be reproduced in current society.

෨෨

The evolution of ego appearance in individuals has overridden collective awareness. If we gather in groups now, it is *always* on the basis of an agreed view or prejudice that will most often have an opposing counter group.

Thus it is that we come into conflict each with the other at various levels of society, nations, and across the world. Our task now is to understand the ego, lay bare its fear, and evolve out from under the dominance of the egoic state.

෨෨

Put another way, we have to take responsibility for the evolution of conscious-ness beyond the time-trap of our fearful individualism

---

19 John Holt. How Children Learn.

TWENTY

In California I maintained some contact with Joan. Over the years we would write occasionally to each other, so by the time I received the latest letter, I knew Joan had made changes in her life. But the news in the letter was not about a planned change. Joan had sold the house with the garden we'd sat out in while I poured over books during Oxford summer breaks, and bought a new apartment. Good for you, I wrote, that old house needed too much work. After my adventure to Oxford, Joan got the idea to go to the local college, which led by a roundabout route to her acquiring a degree. Now she had a pretty nice job teaching in junior school. But she'd stayed single. Then I received this letter.

> Dear James,
> I wonder if you are coming over this year. It would be so nice to see you. I'm afraid I have some unpleasant news. I've been getting headaches for some time now, so I went to the doc. The upshot is I've got a tumor on the brain. The good news is it's not malignant, but it will involve quite an operation to remove it, and they say that it may have some side effects. I won't go into them now. But there appears to be no hurry for the Op except I have to keep taking lots of pain pills.
> I'd like you to be around if possible after the operation. Is there any chance? I know you have your life over there now and I would understand if it wasn't on. Just letting you know. I'll wait to hear before booking into the hospital. Hope that's okay.

The letter went on a little further with news of Robert and work and left me with very mixed feelings. I'm inclined to go when called to a friend's side, but being six thousand miles away has forced changes on my life that that old habit has to contend with. As I folded the letter, I wasn't sure I could meet this request, and walking between trees would not solve this one. But there was that old coincidence in the making, I couldn't yet know of, that would make the decision for me.

It must have been somewhere early in the second chapter of this account that I mentioned wool spinning and dyeing. The friend, Molly, who had taught Catherine and me the old craft and use of wild plants for making dyes, rarely contacted me, though we would visit together any time I was in England, and I occasionally stayed at her home. So I was surprised to open my e-mail one morning to find she had sent a message.

It simply said, 'Give me a call soon, Molly.' I kept my eye on the clock most of the morning, waiting for some synchronicity of hours, and called her when evening was over England.

"James, good to hear your voice, how are you?"

"I'm fine, Molly, you sounded as if you had something you wanted to tell me. What's the news?"

"Not great, dear. You know I went to Spain to live and then seemed to change my mind and came back?"

"Yes, I know. Wondered what that was all about, but then you've never been exactly conventional, eh?"

"Yes, well, I had, I don't know, an intuition I suppose. I just knew I needed to get back here, unfortunately I was right."

"Unfortunately?"

"I have cancer, James."

Well, that stopped me short. The tears just swelled at the sound of the words, "So...? I mean, is it treatable? Or...?"

"Well, I'm going to try, do what I can. But it doesn't look good just now. I'm sorry it's not the best news, but I wanted to tell you. It didn't seem the kind of thing I wanted to write down."

"No. Right, yes, I can see that." I was thinking. "Look, would you mind if I called you, say on Friday or something, just to keep in touch. It may help both of us."

"That would be so good, yes. You can call anytime but I don't always answer, but I'll get your message. I'll be by the phone on Friday next, though."

"Good, okay. What about your Buddhist group, are they...?"

"We're meeting here now, every Wednesday, it's a great help. Will you meditate for me?"

"I'll walk the trees. Walking meditation. I'll make Wednesdays your day. Take care, dear."

"Bye, James, stay in touch."

"Bye."

I put down the phone and immediately thought of Joan. Now I had two reasons to make a trip to England. I put aside the old adage that entered my mind from my mother's mouth: 'Bad luck always comes in threes' and started to think.

Shanti and I had been hesitating over a planned trip to India. We'd been a few times, but always balked at having to make arrangements so far ahead. On this occasion, though, I urged us on, thinking we could go via England and make a stopover. We would stay with an old friend of mine. After the usual search for a decent fare, a date was set. It was early

October when we landed at Heathrow and took the bus north. Our arrival was about three months following my call to Molly and five months after Joan's letter. I'd written Joan as soon as we had a date, and she had booked her operation to coincide with our stay.

Joan's tumor was removed without the feared side effects. She seemed bright and alert when I made a visit to the hospital the day after the operation. She left the hospital three days later to go home and rest. It was going to be all right, she felt a new lease on life. I could hear her delight and gratitude for what was a close call of death. I think it changed her, infused a sense of the miracle that being born offers, beyond the fear of death, for she had gone through that fear and survived.

But Molly's news was of death's pressing invitation. I phoned Molly after we had settled at my friend's house, to hear that things had worsened. The cancer, it seemed, would not respond to treatment, but insisted on spreading beyond its original place of entry.

The next day I made a visit to her home, to find her thin and weak, lying on her couch with a blanket over her. The image of Silas's dying came to me, for Molly was my female Silas: robust, full of craft – in the best sense, tied to the earth, and dedicated to Life with a capital ell. She didn't want to die, not out of fear, but because she so enjoyed every moment of her living and wanted to squeeze more out of time's weave. It was not to be.

"How long?" I asked.

"I may not see Christmas," she said, "I've made all the arrangements. I'm having an ecological burial, in a field."

"The integral field," I said.

"What's that?" she asked. And I explained the discoveries and philosophy of integration, of ever-present life with death, of the continuum cycle without beginning and without end.

"That's beautiful. I can hold that. I'll tell the group," she said, referring to her Buddhists' Wednesday meetings.

"Yes," I said, "That's how I will think of you, not here, not gone, never here but always present, life and death, one state of nature."

We chatted on for a couple of hours until she was too tired and had to rest. I left with a promise to come again before going on to India. I, indeed, made a few more visits, and we said our goodbyes. I was never to see Molly again. I stayed in phone contact, until, early one morning the following March, when the Californian valley I lived in was thick with orange-blossom aroma, the ringing phone got me out of bed. Her close friend, John, called with the briefest of messages, and a field received her body, just as it does of plants or trees or animals, as naturally as only nature knows how.

Twenty-One

The large envelope had printed across it BRITISH EMBASSY. It was from Los Angeles. Its contents were going to send me back to England on a strange mission that would bring to a close yet another part of my life that reached into the distant past of my childhood.

The covering letter was from a firm of London solicitors, Greenhern and Selby. They had, it said, made a search for me following instructions from their client's Last Will and Testimony. It appeared they had gone to a great deal of trouble, beginning with my birth address, and had followed a trail that they hoped had finally found me. As I read, I wanted to glance down the page looking for clues, but the discipline of Oxford kept my eyes moving along the line of gradual revelation. The letter went on to request my presence at their office, at a date and time of my convenience, to pick up some keys and a letter giving me permission of entry to Fallowfield farmhouse.

❦

As much and as fascinating as it was that threads from the past were surfacing in the present, it was irrational to consider it some design of fate.

❦

I had come far enough in my searches to know how we love to grasp to illusions of meaning and eternity in our lives. But the late evolution of the Self precludes such wishful thinking. The state of nature has been around for millions of years, and Homo sapiens for a few thousand, but the self view is but a late page in the book of evolution. If there is any design, it is in the cycle, the spiral of nature that constantly repeats its effort, changing and adjusting at each turn to the forces within and upon it, maintaining equilibrium.

We are within that cycle, yet our huge population and errant behavior are over-weighing its constancy. The fearful collections of egos, bowing to their own illusions, producing a Frankenstein we call civilization.

I use Shelley's creation deliberately, for at the time of her writing and in the decades since, we have become fascinated with our mistakes, yet we avoid the terrifying spring from which they arise. Just as we search for the truth, subconsciously wishing never to find it. We prefer to indulge the distractions of wishful thinking, of comforting patterns, and imagined realms of foreverland.

❧

Greenhern and Selby's letter informed me of Wendy's recent death. Her request, which, given their efforts to find me, must have read like a commandment, was that I was to be given an unopened letter, addressed to me, and the keys to the house. As the level of my excitement rose, I noticed an addendum that George Selby had handwritten: 'I have no idea what the letter contains, but it is not the Deed to the house. The house, it appears, has been left to the National Trust.'

I didn't really expect the house was being left to me, beyond a momentary and entirely involuntary thought. But the idea of a letter from Wendy did excite old feelings. I checked on forthcoming flights to London, and wrote back to the solicitors within the week. For all that my practice was moving forward, I could still be caught up, it seemed, in the story. But a final, devastating lesson was to come, after which my ego, which could still be caught in the remnants of illusion, would be dethroned by the absolute truth nature impels upon us.

❧

As I walked down Old Street in the City area of London, I thought of the last time I was here with Paul, and the fortuitous meeting with Rosalyn. But the thought was fleeting, overridden with speculation about Wendy's letter, the contents of which I couldn't have imagined, particularly as it touched on a world I had left far behind in my searches and practice.

George Selby must have been close to eighty, his skin was the color of the buff folder he had open in front of him on the desk between us, his thick hair like snow. The offices of Greenhern and Selby, solicitors, were on the second floor of a building that rightly was situated in Old Street. I wouldn't put a guess as to its age, but it could well have seen Dickens in his time. I felt a bit like Oliver Twist, I'd been through much and had grown into my inheritance via the good graces of Wendy.

"Well, I understand you have come a long way, mister Owen."

"James. Please call me James, mister Selby."

"Yes. Right. James. Well, it seems I am to hand you this." He slowly removed from the folder a square envelope, and with a shaky but deliberate movement handed it across the desk to me. Of course I wanted to open it there and then, but places have an affect upon us, and Selby's office breathed propriety and good manners from the walls. I said thank you and put it in my jacket pocket.

"And it seems you will need these." He opened a drawer his side of the desk and I heard a rattling of keys which eventually he also handed over the desk, saying, "These are on loan, you understand, James, they must be returned to us when you have been to the house. You can post them if you really need to, though we'd rather you brought them in yourself."

"Thank you," I said, as I took the keys, "I shall try and pass by and drop them in to you." I didn't relish the thought of having to make this detour again, but the old man seemed to have gone to some lengths for me, or Wendy, and it seemed I should. "I'll phone you, if I may, and let you know what I'm doing. I expect to go over to the house within a day or two, if that's all right."

He stood up and offered his hand, saying, "That will be fine, young man, you do what you have to. Do take care of those keys, though."

"I will, sir, thank you. And thank you for finding me. I'll be in touch." With that, I shook his hand and left, determined to head for the nearest pub and read Wendy's letter.

Sitting in the corner of the lounge bar of a pub I entered in sufficient haste that I know not its name nor the street it's on, I took one draft of the pint of beer in front of me, and opened the letter.

> Dear James,
>
> I hope you are well and able to carry out my last wish and complete something of your own life. (*That was an intriguing sentence.*) I want you to come and get the Lily. Dig it up and take it with you. I trust you will know where to plant it, James. (*So it's all about the Lily. I took another drink.*) When you plant it remember us, all of us, your mother, your lost sister, and my baby you saw in your dream. And think of me. Its resting place will bring a final peace to us all, you too. (*I could feel tears in my eyes. Through them I read.*)
>
> I love you, James. Wendy.

208

I folded the letter, left the drink and the pub, and went out onto the busy street. I took some deep breaths and walked, and continued walking for some time. I knew I would reread the letter several times, but right now I walked on to Euston Station and caught the train.

❦

There it was again, that unsettling ache that we have to live with in our separate ego states of selfhood. It shows up as being expressed through feelings, but its root lay in something beyond, something that caused the Buddha to observe the first realization: life has an unsatisfactory core to it, an angst that we suffer. So often, in our attempts to ease the suffering, we let the feelings lead us, mistaking them for a substantial expression of being, instead of recognizing their distracting ephemeral flight through the ego.

Is it not that we should live without feeling, or know that such feelings will inevitably flow from high to low and back, but we have inhabited this earth long enough and searched ourselves deeply enough that we now recognize them as the sensing place of our biology, and they should not be the determiner of our actions. When my baby son, Malcolm, died, I cried. I had feelings of great sorrow. If I had believed in God and interpreted feelings as a legitimate litmus of action, I would not have been alone in raging at the injustice, possibly turning that rage against the church, even an actual person, thinking I was justified in doing so by an event monitored through feelings alone.

❦

When planes crashed into the towers of New York, we all experienced feelings of pain and sorrow. Taking action from the core of that pain, America, as a culture, simply created greater pain and sorrow over a wider area. The irony of such action lay in its impotence to change the original suffering within our feeling ground. We do not feel better by making others feel worse.

❦

Feelings of sensitivity are part of our biological inheritance, necessary in the matter of taking care of the body, *but they cannot liberate our lost being from the fear of death.* The ego exploits them for its own ends to ward off such fear, shaking an angry fist, in whatever form, being safer than knowing the thread that runs between life and death. Sickness, disease, accidents, and the death of those around us all vibrate that thread. *Such conditions call upon our higher faculties to know and gain understanding of the deep and permanent constant that is nature. All that comes into being will pass beyond being.* Birth invites death. The Buddha's first realization rests upon this knowing. His second realization was an understanding that what we do about such knowledge determines our entrapment, or freedom from such entrapment.

∞

Two days after my attendance at the solicitor's offices found me standing at the front door of Fallowfield farmhouse. The place seemed unchanged, timeless. Of course, remembrances of Wendy flooded my mind: the young, gentle girl who smoothed my brow in the nursery so long ago, the woman who opened the door as I passed one summer, and her making a man of the boy ending school and starting work, and the day I returned to survey the house to find her still there, holding her secret in the garden. Now I was to be the guardian of that secret, the maker of its final resting place where it would find completion and peace.

I slipped the large, iron key into the old lock, having first unlocked the brass Yale added much later. I pushed on the door against pamphlets and other junk mail on the floor, and entered, closing the door behind me. I stood still, hearing the soft echo of the shutting door die out in the upper reaches of the house.

The silence was Wendy. I was hesitant to break it with my footsteps on the bare floor of the hallway, so I stood mute and let time and place coalesce in my being. I meditated upon nothing, breathing in and out the odor of past and present, until I heard what sounded like a whisper, constant, moving, coming from the back of the house.

I walked through the passage into the back room and on into the scullery kitchen. There before me was the sink where Wendy had washed my bleeding hand, and attached to the tap was a thin hose which ran out through the old leaning shed into the garden. There was a note attached to the tap in Wendy's handwriting: 'Please Leave On. Very Important.' The old plumbing, running who knows where through the house, had set the water to whispering its secret task, which I guessed upon as I followed its lead down into the overgrown garden.

Deep among the weeds beneath the now big oak tree, it offered, drip by drip, life to the hidden Lily. The water was met once again by tears from my eyes, a recollection of Wendy's gentle compassion. For even in her dying, she thought of the constancy of life and offered herself to it.

Though I had arrived at the house around the middle of the day, I decided to leave the digging up of the Lily until the cool of evening. I walked the house and garden, taking in a last abiding sense of the extraordinary events it had seen.

Sitting on the same old chair, out back of the house, where I had so often sat for tea with Wendy, I recalled the likeness of its setting to Silas's cottage. It was then I remembered where the book *Tales of Uncle Silas*[20] had come from. It arrived on my ninth birthday along with the other presents I opened. Post-war Rationing had just ended, one consequence of which was a sudden increase in books. The edition I received had just come out in a reprint with crusty drawings of Silas's life by Edward Ardizzone. I was so enthralled to receive a new book, I neglected to read the card that came with it for a couple of days, and then only when my mother told me I had to send a thank you note for it. She usually let such things go, but this time she was insistent. I opened the card and read it. It was from the lady next door in the farmhouse...

Dear James, you always liked the pictures of Silas I showed you in the nursery many years ago, so I thought you may like the stories too. Your mother says you like to read so you shouldn't have any trouble with Silas's adventures.

Happy Birthday.
Wendy Baker(next door)

---

20 Tales of Uncle Silas by H. E. Bates.

It was then I got to thinking about the whole Lily story. Was it some Silas fantasy Wendy had, living as she had in this pocket of countryside all her life. I wondered how much of it was true, and what did I really know of Wendy's life and her connection with my mother. The business of her baby and my mother's lost pregnancy was going through my mind when I thought of Malcolm, my son, who died at about the same age as Wendy's daughter. So there I was back again with coincidences pushing against my rationality.

❧

As I was digging up the Lily, I couldn't decide if I was offering assent to all these mysteries or just doing what had been asked of me. I retrieved the bulb, wrapped it, turned off the kitchen tap with a last fond glance at the sink, whilst holding the ghost of Wendy with my arms around the package. How could I be anything else but a part of the mystery, I thought.

I went out onto the pavement in the evening light and locked the door behind me. I looked up at the now ancient oak that I had walked under so many times and took my leave of it, too. I made my way to my son Allen's house for the night's rest. Tomorrow I will settle the Lily, and all that it holds within the secret of its bloom, in its new home.

EPILOGUE

People are sentimentalists. We love stories because life is a story. Who writes it? We all write each other's stories. All those people beginning with… in fact, having no beginning but a continuum through those gone before and who shall come after, if indeed there is a before and after. The story-shaped world is, of course, one of illusion, a play on the senses and feelings that coalesce into forms we call ourselves and others, an apparent separating state of being that we accept as real. In attempting to control and manipulate such a false reality, we are in great danger of missing the deep process, and rupturing nature at its core.

If it's the denial of death, brought on by fear, that has driven the story so far, then we should seek the antidote to fear. Perhaps it's love.

But love came late in the history of peoples, attaching itself to the biology of feelings and fears. Such feelings are, of themselves, ancient and can be seen in our ancestor cousins, apes and monkeys. The condition is old, only the label is new.

What then will overcome fear and end the illusion, such that we will close the story on our distractions and destructions and live with true harmony and peace?

∽

The following day I arose early intent upon my task. I left my son Allen's house around seven. I had called ahead to ensure my coming would not inconvenience, and to verify my deed would be acceptable. I put a spade in the trunk of Allen's car, along with the box containing the Lily and a bag of compost. I headed out of the town into the country.

I was happy to see the day was opening with a clear sky, that meant it would be cold and bright. The leaves were on the turn, beginning to show autumn color, a perfect time for moving the bulb. I drove slowly. I was enjoying this task in a way hard to explain. I suppose I was caught in the weave that bound us all together and felt a certain privilege, almost, to be the one closing a chapter.   My arrival was expected. I parked the car, removed the box, and made my way straight to the trees. Having seen me drive up, two of the monks were waiting for me. I showed them the Lily bulb and told them a simple version of its story. They were touched by Wendy's unusual request, but delighted I had chosen the monastery for the Lily's resting place. One of the monks asked if I intended some form of ceremony, to which I replied that I thought just planting it in such an ideal place, beneath an oak it was used to, would be sufficient. They then left me to it, inviting me to take some tea with them when done.

I thought, come springtime the grass area between the trees would show the Lily's bloom to full effect. I lifted the top turf layer with a spade, and kneeled down. Using the spade, I dug into the dark earth, recalling times past when I made dens, or dug for potatoes, parsnips, and turnips.

I recalled the summer in Wendy's garden, thinking myself a young Silas, of sitting by the back of the house, and, of course, of the original planting of the Lily. I got so lost in thought that when I came to, I found I had dug deep, deeper than I intended. But, I thought, how deep all this history goes, and I filled the bottom of the hole with the compost I had brought with me. Laying the bulb in the ground felt like a burial, but a burial that would give life. An idea formed in my mind, of *integration*. The weaving together of life and death as one, like the field I walk in California. I became moved by the thought that it may just answer the questions suffering engenders.

I gently filled in over the bulb and sought water to ease it into its new home. That done I looked to accept the invitation to take that tea with the monks.

THE PRACTICE

Empty yourself of everything.
Let the mind rest at peace.
All things rise and fall
while the self watches.
They grow and flourish and then
return to the source.
Returning to the source is stillness,
which is the way of nature.

Tao Te Ching

REFLECTION

We're all living somewhere between birth and death, closer to one than the other, but not knowing which it is. When my son, Malcolm, was seven weeks old, he had lived over half his life, while my friend Molly was fifty-seven when she died. The elderly woman Shanti cared for lived past ninety, and her close neighbor was alive for one hundred and five years upon this earth. When the Buddha was approached by a woman holding her dead baby, asking why this innocent baby, he sent her to find a household that had never known death. It is reported she returned calmer and wiser, for she had not found a household that had escaped such a knowing.

One of the most practical and open realizations walking between trees brings about is a deep resolution of the birth-death paradox. If one tree is designated the tree of one's birth, and the other one's oncoming death, then walking between them with awareness and sensitivity will begin the process of cutting the threads of grasping. For the inevitability that confronts us in a material way like this, the unknowing of just *where* on the continuum of birth and death we are, opens us to the realization of

215

the futility of grasping to things that are not in any way a part of that continuum. It's only the fear of dying that drives one to hang on as if to stop the inevitable movement that carries us. By replicating that movement between the trees, the fear of it leaves us. We begin to relax on the continuum of being, be it revealing life or death.

> *I walk between the trees,*
> *all my attachments fall away*
> *like leaves in autumn.*
> *All that I would do remains undone,*
> *resting and still.*
>
> *Then, what is afraid of me comes*
> *And lives a while in my sight.*
> *And what it fears in me leaves me,*
> *And the fear of me leaves it.*
> *It sings and I hear its song.*
>
> *Then, what I am afraid of comes*
> *I live a while in its shadow,*
> *What I fear in it leaves it*
> *And the fear of it leaves me.*
> *It sings and I hear its song.*
>
> *After days of labor,*
> *the day of Love*
> *and letting go at last*
> *brings the light of conscious dawn,*
> *And I sing.*
> *As we sing the trees shake*
> *The year turns.*

FIRST PRACTICE
THE LIFE TAPESTRY

But for your being here, I have no being. I am the sum of nature's hand and of all the beings I have known and know now. Beginning, it seems, with you, my mother and father, yet who were you made of? And where is the beginning and end to the weave, for I can see no loose ends. All is but one continuous Tapestry, *everyone*, strong or weak, tall or short, known and unknown, liked or disliked, hated even. My desires or aversions, my hopes or wishes, cannot alter the unassailable bond that is the integrated field of being. *All life,* sentient and non-sentient, from the smallest unseen atom to the vastness of the cosmos, and *all death* shapes this moment of truth.

I shall, therefore, holding this truth as clearly evident and beyond illusion, name the names of those who have woven my life by their own lives.

Prompted by memory, reflection, understanding, I write down each day, without stress or favor: family, friends, acquaintances and enemies, making of my list, a mantra of the world that weaves this being into existence.

Each day, holding that mantra, I shall breath gratitude for the miracle that is being, for all that have brought me into being, seeking only to loosen and finally untie the knot that binds being to the ego of Self.

SECOND PRACTICE
WHERE INTENTION ABIDES

In pursuit of freedom from fear, of that very same *Self* I shall make a servant, taking away from the mind the supreme crown of being, I shall place it in the heart. For the heart can have consciousness just as strong, yet of a quiet (non-discursive) form. From there I begin:

First I shall determine upon *EQUANIMITY* (*Upekkha*)[21], to make steady all that comes and goes from this being. To accept all that happens upon this being, be it light or dark. In steadiness I will sit, a solid foundation upon which to build.

On that foundation I shall place *JOYFULNESS* (*Mudita*), a delight in the integrated field, be it showing life or death, growth or decay, be it of this being or others, embracing all without fear or favor.

The third intention is *COMPASSION* (*Karuna*), for it is in the nature of things that there will be suffering unto the end of Self. Thus toward this being, and all other sentient beings that know and feel suffering, shall I be compassionate.

---

21 I've placed the Pali terms in brackets: Pali is the canonical language of Buddhism.

All of these intentions bring me to the supreme state in the heart, that of *LOVING-KINDNESS* (*Metta*), for that is what I wish to carry forward with me from this time on. That this being, give and receive, not in the grasping and aversion of the egoic mind, but in the free-flowing of the field through the heart; the final binding of all intention into an integrated, non-judgmental state of complete acceptance and concern for the well-being of all sentient and non-sentient life.

Commentary on the
First and Second Practice

Making acquaintance with the four intentions opens a pathway for the consciousness to follow. This confounds the ego's urge to distract. It places it in the position of servant rather than master of your being.

It is useful to learn the Pali terms at this stage, such that they become familiar to your ear and tongue, as later they are voiced in making a path beyond the Self.

Set aside a quiet time. Working with any person in your Tapestry, bring them to mind and move gradually through the intentions in the heart towards that person. Notice how well, poorly, long, short etc. you manage to hold the intention. Move to the next intention and on finally to *Metta*. Try the intentions first on someone you like, move to someone neutral, then on to an adversary. The more often this practice is carried out the steadier the heart becomes.

THE THIRD PRACTICE
SITTING MEDITATION

Sitting still, undisturbed by outer circumstances, we notice the urgency of the mind seeking to engage us, the rapid crowding of thoughts, like passengers on a rush-hour train. Determine then to let the train go its own way, for it runs on rails of fear that cannot or will not turn. Reside in the heart, sit on a foundation of Upekkha, remain steady, and the train will slow.

Watch your breath, for it, undisturbed, will carry the steadiness of your sitting. Feel it on the in-breath at the edge of your nose, as light as the breeze that set the leaf turning in my childhood. Feel it on the out-breath, as once again it passes to return to the air.

Sitting thus, the chain of urgency in the mind will loosen. Stillness will separate thoughts. The rush-hour crowd will thin to a trickle. In the still spaces *gratitude* arises.

For as long and as many times you sit thus, so will the fear in the mind be challenged to give up its secrets. The immutable Self will shrink like the fearful Mara at the kindness of the princely god. So be kind to your Self, for it is to remain, and become a servant after generations as master. It is the place of much useful learning that we shall have to deploy in a changing world.

THE FOURTH PRACTICE
WALKING MEDITATION

Walking meditation is cousin to sitting, and asks of us the same steady foundation within the heart. It offers movement, in place of the breath, as the site of our concentration and awareness. Placing our feet with purpose, feeling the earth roll under each foot as it supports our effort to overcome the same fearful ego that seeks to distract us, this time with boredom. In place of crowding thoughts intent upon getting us up from sitting, the ego throws out sharp critical judgments of meaninglessness time-wasting in walking for its own sake.

Remaining steady as we walk, concentrated in the action, aware of all that is around us, letting go of *any and all* intention, we begin by staying with the simple act of walking, slowly and deliberately. Thus it is that the emptiness and fullness of nature, the integral field, unites our being and denies the grasping ego its demands.

Commentary on the
Third and Fourth Practice

Taking a longer period of time, (two hours and longer) we alternate sitting and walking meditation, giving ourselves to each in turn from half-hour to one hour. Thus we bring to the heart a teaching of Loving-Kindness, and to our being, release into the integrated field.

THE FIFTH PRACTICE
INTEGRATION

We're all living within the field of integration, that is the constant. What we seek now is an insight and awareness that makes actual the field, in contrast to our ignorant perception of its division into life and death, desire and fear, grasping and aversion.

Bringing together what we perceive as separate, makes whole that which is fragmented, unveils the hidden from the seen, and places what is known beside what is not known, without fear. Integration is a state of internal completion, a returning to the source.

What you will do that gives you the strength to face the giant with a house-size club, I cannot determine. But do it, you must, if the chains of fear, forged in your childhood and in the long history of our species, are to be broken. We have knowledge now, we cannot claim ignorance anymore concerning the mind and its egoic guardian.

Connect with what is real, and abandon false refuges of illusion, look for one who is trained, seek a companion. Touch the earth and begin to know your birth. Go back, look, and accept whatever fears still seek control over your being. Bring what is in the past into the present, for it is not past or present, but ever existent. Integration is full acceptance without fear or favor of the journey you have taken and are on.

WALKING BETWEEN TREES

REFLECTION

Walking from one tree to its opposite neighbor and back again, a path of about forty meters, the mind stills itself in the service of bare awareness. This practice invites us to come to terms with death. It is in overcoming of this hurdle that we find the key to conscious evolution.

So I am going to ask you to walk with me into the face of death, to forever embrace the inevitable mortality that subtends your life. If we are to continue on this earth, it shall be with clarity towards life. A clarity that lives each moment, and each moment sees and acknowledges death as an intrinsic part of all life. Come with me, back to the trees, and back in time to your birth. We shall not climb back into our ancient home, but we feel gratitude for all that the trees have given us. We return once again to their overarching protection, this time to learn, at last, the lesson of life.

PRACTICE ONE

When we first approach the trees with consciousness, submitting ourselves to their being, even in this act of reverence we begin to break the blind right we have sought, to do whatever we want with them and ourselves. For now we see them quite differently. Now they are a part of our *Metta* list, intrinsically woven into the weave that creates our life. Their steadiness contrasts with our urgent strivings. Their constancy reveals our infidelities and lies. They, by gentle means, urge faithfulness and truth upon our being.

Begin by taking, to the trees, the concerns and conflicts that afflict your being, the contradictions you live, between your heart and mind. Begin with a small thing, in fact, begin as you practiced walking meditation, but now, confined between two trees, you will notice the ego's objections become stronger, the comments harsher. You must counter this critical, fearful mind with the heart. Fill the heart with gratitude, an easy thing to do when being with the trees, and let the mind struggle with its own resistance.

When you can go willingly into the trees and walk, the heart has found its strength against the entraining of the ego. Then you can bring the contradictions into the open, placing the champion of the heart with one tree and the mind's overbearing at the other. As you walk towards the 'heart' tree, place your awareness with the mind, as you walk towards the 'mind' tree, place your awareness in the heart.

You are not seeking a victor. It is not competing but integrating that is sought. Like the history of the Self that must be integrated, so too, must the contradictions of your life passage be held as one within that integrated field.

PRACTICE TWO

We are standing in a wood or a grove of trees. The ground is flat and grassed – I use the local park. We have removed our shoes and are looking for two trees that are about thirty-five to forty meters apart. There! There's a pair. Standing with my back to one, I can see straight ahead the second tree. How magnificent and beautiful it looks, the sun streams through its branches, flashes on the leaves and rests on the grass between us, dappling the ground with a pattern of light and shade. I shall call that one the tree of my birth. At each turn there, I shall be born.

But what of the tree at my back? I look up along its trunk, high into its branches. Light and dark catch my eye, the limbs are dark against the day. This is the tree of death my death. Standing here, I am, as it were, dead to the world. I close my eyes and *feel* the nothingness, the end of all, the no of every yes I want to say.

With my eyes closed I turn once again toward the tree of my being born. I wait. Opening my eyes, I realize I have a ways to travel that I may be born. I have to walk this path, to maintain awareness of my anticipation, my hopes and dreams, my life!

I begin to walk, each step raising up in me feelings and thoughts. I stay as detached as I can and take note. There! My feet are aching to rush forward. Hold back. There! I'm anticipating what has not yet been born. Again! My senses are churning to the delightful possibilities of birth. Each step brings the womb of time closer, for here, the time I ache for is not. Here, nothing is everything, a moment is eternity.

Then I arrive at the other tree, where I shall be born into this world. I look up at the beauty of it all, turn slowly, and know I am born. I hear the birds, see the movement of leaves, and *feel* the breeze touching my skin. My senses are alive. Yet here I stand at the beginning of my life, looking down time towards my death, for I see it before me, unavoidable, as solid as life, and I have no choice but to move towards it, for that is the agreement of birth. I take slow steps, taking in everything, all the sights and sounds around me. I live to the full, yet knowing, feeling, anticipating my eventually reaching death.

Even as I walk, the shadow of the tree's branches in front of me falls a few yards before the trunk, as though making a preparation for what is to come, an overarching of life with death, the conditioned being held within the unconditioned. The sharpness of the shadow emphasizes the bright patches that escape and fall onto the path at my feet. As I step into one, I am reminded of the constant rebirth, out of each dying moment, that is the inevitable continuum of the integrated field.

When my last step brings me to the foot of the death tree, I close my eyes, for life is ended. I stand in the stillness of nothing that is everything. My ears soften their straining to hear, my eyes see nothing, this body is so still, its borders are losing definition. I let my mind sing into my heart, and my heart release itself into death.

Only after some immeasurable non-time do I turn once again and face the tree of birth. I open my eyes and begin to move towards yet another beginning, another experience of birth.

What! Can so simple a thing as walking back and forth with intention, awareness, determination, and steadiness, from tree to tree, change so much that has been bound by a destructive half-life of fear? Yes, if it's done with courage.

It is important to understand that we are not attempting to replicate rebirth in our repetitions of walking back and forth. There should be no thoughts of reincarnation, past or future lives. The repetitions are carried out as practice *to bring about change here and now.*

It is not the world that you will change, but the root of being that has thus far, driven by fear, divided, exploited, fragmented, and almost destroyed what was once whole: a state of being in nature, with nature in your being, of one unified condition, of harmony.

BEYOND SELF

REFLECTIONS ON DIVINE METTA

If you have sought to write your Tapestry, determined upon cultivation of the four Intentions, sat and walked in peaceful acceptance of the field, and taken the courage to integrate your life, you will walk between the trees towards a final understanding of yourself and the species to which you belong. You will know the peace that comes from living from the heart, you will return to the center.

> *At each turn*
> *The way is to be found*
> *Beyond the self.*
>
> *All nature*
> *Points out the path*
> *To the center of being.*
>
> *The center of being*
> *Is the nature of a heart*
> *At peace.*

The center is also the outer reaches, just as the moment is timeless. Just as the created (material) continuum is not without the uncreated (non-material) continuum, so you will eventually embrace the unseen with the seen, the unknown with the known, the transient with the integrity of all states.

To travel from the Self to the non-Self, the vehicle is *Metta* – Loving-Kindness, a *Metta* infused with equanimity, joy, and compassion for all that is. *Such a state is defined as Divine, not to implant an imaginary heaven or super being, but to bear witness to the miracle of existence, from the unseen atom to the vastness of the universe.* To live with gratitude for the billions of small connections that had to occur throughout the continuum of the integrated field to bring you here.

To have such an experience is, finally, to know freedom from death. It can hold no sway, neither can the fear of it command our behavior. Now, the universe, as far as deep space that defies time, calls you to witness the deathless realm that is undivided.

Draw into your own heart of *Metta* Bhavana[22] *everything* by name: people, animals, creatures of sea and air, planets, suns, stars and galaxies. Expand that heart to embrace *everything,* an unfragmented whole that is the deathless.

---

22 Bhavana: Meditation.

POST SCRIPT

The phone call from my daughter began with a suggestion, "Dad, I think you may want to sit down for this news."

It was a bright fall day in California when the call came, the leaves on the maples turning yellow, a gold that flashed the mid-day sunlight through our window. The air had cooled at last after a summer of dry heat and wildfires. The deep crimson leaves of the   plum trees were darkening, ready to drop.

As Stella gave me the news, I wondered at how she must have watched the clock, holding the devastation on her breath until England's clocks and our clocks spoke a suitable time to call. Why she was the carrier of the news, I didn't question at the time. I supposed my son Allen to be too self-effacing to talk about himself in such a deep way or perhaps he was afraid he wouldn't get the words out. Or perhaps he was just plain afraid. Who wouldn't be?

"Allen's got a brain tumor, Dad. He collapsed at work last week and they did a scan at the hospital." I could hear Stella's breath, it sounded hard to come by. I waited. "It's a malignant cancer, Dad. They said it's like a net spread all through his brain."

Allen was two weeks past his thirty-fifth birthday. He lived for another eighteen months. When he died, I was fifty-nine. Past seven weeks, twenty-nine years, forty-six years, fifty-two...

Yes, somewhere between birth and death, somewhere past half way.

Change can come as fast as the turn of a leaf in the wind
Old Buddhist saying

APPENDIX

THE METTA SUTTA
[Adapted Short Form]

The path of Loving Kindness
Is honest and upright,
Is straightforward and gentle in speech,
Is contented and easily satisfied,
Is tranquil and simple in living,
Is peaceful and calm.

Wishing in gladness and joy
May you be well.
May you be happy.
May you be peaceful.
May you abide in Metta.

Whoever you are
Be you weak or strong, great or mighty,
medium, short or small, seen or unseen,
known or unknown,
Living near or far away,
Omitting none.

Cultivating an all-embracing heart
Spreading upwards to the skies,
And downward to the depths,

Outward and unbounded,
Complete in the Divine.

Standing, walking, seated or lying down
I shall sustain this recollection.
May you know the Divine Abiding.

5942970R0

Made in the USA
Charleston, SC
24 August 2010